long
lost girl

BOOKS BY JILL CHILDS

long
lost girl

JILL CHILDS

bookouture

Published by Bookouture in 2022

An imprint of Storyfire Ltd.
Carmelite House
50 Victoria Embankment
London EC4Y 0DZ

www.bookouture.com

ISBN: 978-1-80314-380-4
eBook ISBN: 978-1-80314-379-8

For Emily

PROLOGUE

There isn't a day I don't think of you, my poor lost girl. A day—? Barely a moment.

I thought the pain would numb as the years passed. It hasn't. I carry it with me, day and night, a silent demon, hands at my throat, slowly strangling me.

Some nights I wake with a start, face slick with sweat, breath short, panicked. I stare wide-eyed at the fringes of street-light edging the curtain. What if you're lost forever? What if it's too late and you've left this world before me, left it hollow, empty and cold?

No. I can't believe that. I won't. I will see you again. I must.

I force myself to steady my breathing and reach out to snap on the bedside lamp, blinking at once in the brightness. There it all is, solid and real. Dressing table and wardrobe and chest of drawers. The chair with my clothes draped, ready for the morning. The glass of water beside me, its surface trembling with shards of light.

I sense you. You are still alive, I feel you. Wherever you are, my love, you exist.

Something slackens and loosens in me, and I sigh.

The years fall away, drawing me in a moment right back to the beginning. To the sweet, milky smell of your skin, the tufts of moist hair plastered to your scalp, the shape of your lips. You're perfect, lying there in my arms, as tiny as a bird and just as weightless. Your face is red, your papery skin creased, your eyes screwed shut against the light.

Oh, my love, come back to me, please. Find me. Come, before it's too late.

PAULA

2

I remembered the lock later, when I finally saw them out and came back to help Gran clear the table, do the washing-up and put the oven on. Will was at a dinner that evening, something to do with a drugs rep, and Hannah was having a sleepover with her on-again, off-again best friend, Lizzie. She usually came over with me to eat at Gran's, once or twice a week.

I thought I was looking after Gran, giving her some company and making sure she had a decent meal. She probably thought she was doing the same for us.

'Gran, the lock's different. Did you get someone round?'

Gran smiled. 'That man fixed it. Tomas. Clever, isn't he? He sprayed something on it.'

'Sprayed something?'

She shrugged. 'Something he found in the cellar. There's all sorts of rubbish down there. Grandad's old stuff, mostly. He said he'd help me clear it out.'

I imagined him rummaging through Grandad's tools and DIY supplies. They were probably worth something.

'I can go through it if you want it sorted. You don't know this guy, Gran. Not really.'

Gran raised her eyebrows at me. 'You said yourself he did a good job.'

I didn't, actually. I went back to grating cheese. It was my turn to cook. Lasagne. I'd told Gran to put her feet up and leave me to it, but she was hovering. She couldn't help herself.

As I stirred the cheese into the sauce on the hob, ready to start layering the pasta, mince and sauce, her face appeared at my shoulder, and she gave a soft tut.

'What?'

'Nothing, lovely.' She paused, watching.

I took a deep breath. 'What am I doing wrong now?'

'Nothing!' she said again. A silence. She wanted to say more, I could tell. Finally: 'You might want to turn the heat down a bit, that's all. It's quite fierce, that stove.'

I smiled to myself as I did as she asked, then turned and kissed the end of her nose. She stood quietly as I started doing the layering: mince, pasta, sauce; mince, pasta, sauce – slopping a little on the sides. The rising steam was thick with the smell of meat and tomato.

Once it was in the oven, she stood beside me with a tea towel in her hands, waiting for me to scrub clean the pans and set them to drain.

'Where did you meet them?'

She looked innocent for a moment, as if she didn't know who I meant, then shrugged. 'Where you meet anyone. Just around, that's all.' She paused, polished the saucepan. 'Maria sits outside Sainsbury's sometimes, when it's dry. It's no life.'

I considered. I'd seen people sitting there too, just down from the entrance, crouching on sheets of cardboard, battered old tins on the pavement beside them and a sign asking for spare change.

Gran had always talked to us about being kind to other people. When I was a child, she fished coins from the depths of her handbag and told me to go and drop them in a collecting tin or a beggar's empty cup. I hated it. I didn't like getting that close to those who were begging. They were generally smelly people and when they smiled at me, their teeth were rotten. I gave to charity now and then, but cleanly, online. Keeping those people and their problems at arm's length.

I imagined Gran crouching over Maria, her knees creaking with the effort of bending, and having a chat; not just once, but often enough to invite her home for a cup of tea. Maybe Maria wasn't the only one, either.

I turned from the sink to face her. 'Are you lonely, Gran?'

'Stop worrying.' She sighed at me. 'Maria's an interesting person. She was a musician once. In an orchestra. She's just had bad luck, that's all.'

'I do worry.' I hesitated. 'I know you always see the best in people, Gran. I love that about you. But—' I thought about all the scams nowadays. 'I just want you to stay safe.'

She snorted. 'I can look after myself.'

'What if that man had stolen something when he was upstairs?' I thought how rough he looked. 'What if he'd threatened you?'

'Well, he didn't, did he?' She hung the tea towel back on its metal hook, then leaned heavily on the table for support as she passed. I watched her as she lowered herself into a kitchen chair. Her face was flushed, her breathing heavy.

'Are you alright?'

She didn't answer, still catching her breath; just waved me away with her fingers, telling me wordlessly not to fuss.

I ran the tap and poured her a glass of cool water, then set it in front of her on the table and stood beside her, stroking her between the shoulder blades. She had the bones of a bird, flesh-less. It frightened me, seeing her sitting there, hunched forward. I hadn't noticed before how thin her hair had become across the top of her scalp. Her ankles had thickened, as if the weight she'd lost recently from her hips had slowly descended and gathered there.

For decades, she'd hardly changed at all. I'd watched her turn sixty, then seventy, then eighty. I was already thinking ahead to her ninetieth in two years' time. Hannah would be ten that year, in the same month. We should celebrate with a proper family party. All these years, she was just Gran, brisk and indomitable, looking out for us all once Mum died, staying eternally young. Now, looking at her, my stomach fluttered with sudden panic as I saw how frail she'd become.

I crouched down and kissed her cheek. 'I love you.'

'I love you too.' She still sounded wheezy. 'We're very lucky, both of us. Doesn't hurt to share it, now and then, does it?'

I hesitated. 'Promise me one thing, will you? Just don't invite them inside the house – not when you're on your own. Please? It's not safe, Gran. If something happened, I'd never forgive myself.'

She scrunched up her nose, turned her head obstinately and wouldn't answer.

3

After we'd eaten, I cleared the table and carried our coffee into the lounge so Gran could settle there in comfort. It was already nearly eight thirty. I was trying to check my phone surreptitiously, wondering if Hannah was okay. Lizzie's mum, Moira, had promised to text me if Hannah changed her mind and needed collecting.

I never knew how it was going to go when she and Lizzie got together. Only two nights ago, she'd cried herself to sleep, saying Lizzie had been mean to her, ganging up on her in the playground and declaring that Hannah couldn't join in. The next day they'd been best buddies again, as if nothing had happened. I struggled to keep up. I wished Hannah would find another girl to pair up with, but she seemed in thrall to Lizzie, with her blonde plaits and crop tops and sassiness.

Now, taking advantage of this time alone with Gran, I took my courage in both hands and raised the topic that had been on my mind all evening. 'I'm wondering about applying for a job, Gran. At the art school.'

Gran looked up at once. 'A job?'

I swallowed. 'Assistant manager. I help out a lot there

anyway, you know, in the café and everything. They need someone well-organised to oversee the paperwork. Maybe come up with some new ideas. They're a bit stuck in a rut.' I hesitated, trying to read her expression. 'I think they'd be flexible too, as long as I got the work done. Around Hannah, I mean.'

She looked thoughtful. 'You've always loved art. You're good too, Paula. Don't pull that face. It's true. You've got talent. I always thought you'd make a career of it.'

'Well, this is more admin, really.'

She hesitated. 'What does Will say?'

I looked away. 'Well, I haven't really—'

'What was that?' Gran looked across at the door to the hall, suddenly agitated.

'What?'

'Didn't you hear it?' She was scrambling out of her chair as hastily as she could, hands pressed down hard on the arms to propel herself to her feet. 'The door.'

'Really?' I hadn't heard anything. 'Are you expecting someone?'

She smoothed down her dress as she crossed the room. There was a slight flush on her cheeks.

I got up too and followed her out into the hall. If someone was selling door to door or collecting for charity, I didn't trust her to say no. They'd be inside with a cup of tea and a biscuit, hearing Gran's life story, before they knew it.

By the time I reached her, she'd wrenched open the front door and was standing on the threshold, clutching the frame and staring out into the dark, empty street.

I said, 'Is anyone there?' It didn't look like it.

Gran was wheezing again, her free hand pawing at the front of her cardigan.

I pushed forward and took her arm. 'Come on, Gran. Let's sit back down.' I prised Gran's other hand from the door and let her lean into me, turning her slowly round. She was trembling.

I kicked the door closed and supported her weight as we shuffled back through the hall together into the lounge.

She dropped, panting, into the chair. Her hands were unnaturally cold, and I crouched down beside her, rubbing life into them. The skin was papery, the raised veins tracing the contours of a familiar map. On her cheeks, two bright spots slowly faded, little by little.

'You feeling okay?'

She just nodded.

'You don't look it.' I hesitated, watching her breathing deepen and settle. 'How about I call the doctor tomorrow? You haven't had a check-up for a while, have you? I'll take you.'

She shook her head, frowning. 'It's just old age, that's all. I'm on enough pills already.'

I managed to hold my tongue. She hated being fussed about, but she worried me.

'We couldn't do without you – you know that, don't you?'

'You'll have to, one day.' She managed a wry smile, still short of breath. 'None of us lives forever.'

'Don't say that.'

She seemed exhausted, her eyes fixed sightlessly on the old patterned carpet.

After a while, I said, 'Anyway, don't answer the door in the evening, Gran. It could be anyone.'

I thought about Tomas with his tattoos and Maria, sitting at the kitchen table, sipping tea.

I wasn't always there. I couldn't always keep an eye on who came round. She was so good-natured, but she was vulnerable. Anyone might take advantage of her.

'Just ignore it next time, will you, if you think someone's knocked?'

Her eyes lifted to mine and her gaze was so intense, it seemed to go right into my soul. 'I can't,' she said quietly. 'What if—?'

I blinked, not understanding. Her face held such sadness that it stopped my breath.

'What do you mean?'

She paused, her eyes still on mine. Slowly, they filled with tears.

'Gran?' I squeezed her hands. 'What do you mean? What if what?'

Her lips trembled. 'What if it's her?' Her voice was so soft I had to lean in close to hear. 'What if it's her, come back to find me? What if it's her and I didn't let her in?'

4

I wasn't used to going home to an empty house.

I closed the front door hastily behind me and put all the downstairs lights on, flushing out the shadows. In the kitchen, still in my coat, I poured myself a glass of white wine, finishing off the open bottle in the fridge door. Tidying. That's what mothers were for, wasn't it? Hoovering up leftovers.

The kitchen was pristine, all gleaming silver and chrome, dirty plates and bowls stacked inside the dishwasher, surfaces wiped clean that morning. I stood for a moment at the sink, breathing steadily, glass in hand. Soft shafts of light spilled out across the patio, slowly blurring into the darkness of the garden beyond.

It was too early to go to bed. I knew I had a long day ahead tomorrow – shoe-shopping for Gran was never easy – but I wasn't tired. I went through to the lounge and flicked through the television channels, but I couldn't settle to anything. I checked my phone. No messages from Will to tell me what time he'd be home. Nothing from Lizzie's mum. It was getting late. Hannah would be asleep.

My eye ran over the photos of her along the mantelpiece:

Hannah as a chubby newborn; then, in her highchair, food smeared round her chops, laughing; a school portrait of her in bunches. She was only four. Her uniform was still pristine, her tiny hands half-swallowed by the blazer sleeves. She was six years old in the last one, nearly seven. She was standing on a sandy beach, her feet planted firmly, her hair tousled and encrusted with sand, eating an ice cream.

She'd been the centre of my world for so long, it was hard to be without her. I blew out my cheeks. She was growing up quickly. I'd need to get used to it. I didn't want to be one of those clingy mums who interfered in their daughters' lives because they'd nothing in their own.

I reached for my laptop and sipped the wine as it powered up. Maybe I needed to do this. I could have a look at the application form and have a go at it. I could always pull out later.

I brought up the art school website, steadied myself with another slug of wine and began to type.

5

All the time we'd been shopping, Hannah, Gran and I, I couldn't shake the feeling that someone was watching us.

I couldn't put my finger on it. Just now and then, when I looked up from easing Gran's broad foot into a pair of lace-ups, helping her to her feet to walk to the mirror on my arm and have a look, the hairs on the back of my neck prickled and I had a quick glance around, trying to catch someone staring. What was the matter with me?

'You like these?' Hannah brandished a pair of stiletto sandals in my face. Bright red and strappy. 'Not for school,' she added quickly, seeing my face.

'Maybe when you're a bit older,' I said, trying to be conciliatory. 'Anyway, we're not buying for you today, remember? Just Gran.'

'Alright!' She blew out her cheeks. 'I know that.' She flounced off, muttering to herself.

I rolled my eyes and turned my attention back to Gran's feet. 'How are they feeling?'

'They pinch a bit, around the toes.' She looked despondent. 'I'm not sure, Paula.'

I looked at Hannah, now trailing her hand along the stands, fed up, then checked my watch.

'Why don't we leave it for now and get some lunch? I bet you're ready for a cup of tea.'

The department store's café was already heaving. Once we'd chosen sandwiches and drinks, I sent Gran and Hannah off ahead of me to scout for an empty table while I lined up at the till. It was partly a ruse to stop Gran seeing how much it all cost, a shock which would then lead to the inevitable argument as she tried to get her purse out to pay.

I shuffled forwards in the line, trying to keep an eye on the two of them as they threaded their way between crowded tables, scanning for anyone about to leave. Gran's movements were slow and careful, as if she felt unsteady on her feet. I felt a surge of love for the two of them, old and young, both vulnerable in their own way, each trying to look out for the other.

I finally got near enough to the till to be able to rest the heavy tray on the metal runners at the front of it, and lifted my eyes again to see how they were getting on. They'd timed it well, spotting a good table right by the windows, looking out over the high street.

As I watched, a young waitress scurried over to clear off the dirty dishes from the previous customers and wipe it over with her cloth. Gran was settling on her chair, unbuttoning her jacket, her face turned to the window, looking as Hannah pointed something out.

Then I saw her: a tall young woman, in her twenties, was bearing down on them from the other side of the café. My breath stuck in my chest. She stood out in the noisy, drifting crowd because her focus on Gran was so intense, the path she was cutting so direct and determined. I could see, even from this distance, how tightly her jaw was set. She was wearing narrow jeans and a hip-length jacket, her hair cut in a long, straight bob.

I was alarmed without knowing why. I wanted to cry out, to

I lay in bed later trying to imagine the noise and excitement of the party, kissing the back of my own hand to practise kissing boys and closing my eyes dreamily, imagining him with his true love.

I wasn't far wrong. From then on, the name Jackie started cropping up, a bomblet dropped casually but regularly into family conversations.

Jackie likes this film.

This book? [Blush] Well, Jackie said it was good.

I'm out on Sunday. Yeah, actually, with Jackie.

He never told us many details. He was secretive. But that was what made it so intriguing. We'd never seen him like this before.

Dad started asking, 'So, when are we going to meet this Jackie, then?'

And Mum, who'd obviously made a few social enquiries and drawn a blank asked, 'Where's Jackie from, love? Is she at school with you?'

And eventually, from Dad, 'Are you sure she's real, this girl-friend of yours, Alan? You're not having us on?'

After months of this, he bowed to pressure and invited her round one Saturday for a barbecue. He made it sound as if having barbecues was just something we did at the weekend, which it wasn't. Then he supervised preparations as if our guest were royalty. Dad had to dig the old charcoal barbecue out of the back of the garage and clean it off. Mum spent all morning making fancy salads, preparing fish and marinating chops.

When the doorbell finally rang, I came haring down the stairs, two at a time. Alan was there first, protective, leaning out and whispering as soon as he opened the door. It gave me a strange, sickening feeling seeing that, as if the world had just tilted on its axis. We'd always been such a close-knit family, the four of us shoulder to shoulder against the world. Yet, here he was, breaking ranks, conspiratorial, his loyalty transferred from us to this unknown someone else.

Mum appeared from the kitchen, wiping her hands on a towel, ready with a welcoming smile. Alan moved aside and there she was. Jackie.

After all the mystery about this new girlfriend, I'd expected a model. A pop star with sprayed-on clothes and a crazy hairdo. A princess with long tresses and high heels. A Goth, maybe, with white cheeks and black lips. But the girl standing there, clutching a bunch of flowers, looked terribly normal. She had fashionable, short-cropped hair and gold ear studs, frayed jeans and a tailored, pressed blue shirt.

She smiled around from one face to the next, lighting up the dingy hall.

'Is that her?' I gawped, forgetting my manners.

Alan spun around and glared.

Mum saved me, hurrying forward to greet her, exclaiming as if she'd been waiting all her life to meet her. Perhaps she had. Jackie handed Mum the flowers, and Mum's voice gushed and flowed, filling the awkward ruts and troughs. 'How kind! You shouldn't have! Do come through to the garden. Isn't it a lovely day? We're so lucky.'

'Is she here?' Dad came in from the patio, his hair sticking up in clumps where he'd raked it through with his fingers, a smear of black on his face from the charcoal and one of Mum's aprons tied roughly round his middle.

We all looked and whatever tension had lingered was broken by the sight of Dad, trying so hard and yet looking so endearingly hopeless, and we laughed.

I don't remember much more of the day, just that from then on, Jackie felt like part of the family. She fit right in; even better, we joked, than Alan ever had.

For a few years after that, I was preoccupied with my own

achievements: learning to do cartwheels and to play the recorder, mastering long division and spelling, finding a best friend forever and being betrayed by her, then, finally, finding a more dependable replacement.

Alan finished school and started training at the local college to be a mechanic. He'd always been good with bikes and cars. Jackie got a place at nursing college, less than an hour away. They met up every weekend, at our house or hers. So, no one was surprised when they announced that they were getting married. Of course, they were! Mum and Dad did mutter about whether they were old enough, but they hadn't been much older themselves and to me, Alan had always been grown-up. Besides, I got to be a bridesmaid at the grand old age of nine, along with Jackie's younger sister.

Alan and Jackie didn't have much money, but they started renting an apartment and, the following year, a baby girl came along. Sara. Everyone helped out. Mum and Dad got a second-hand cot and baby buggy from someone at church, and Dad went around on Sundays to help Alan paint the box room and turn it into a nursery. Jackie's parents bought baby toys and tiny, doll-sized clothes.

I went round to see Sara when she was just home from hospital. I sat on the sofa and Jackie placed her in my arms. She was wrapped round in muslins and a pink knitted blanket. I'd brought her a stuffed bunny, a really cute one in a red dress, and I waved it in her face and tried to get her to take an interest, but she didn't care.

She had tiny, scrunched-up features, all red and wrinkly, and she kept her eyes tightly closed as if she hadn't quite decided yet whether to accept us as her family. Then she sneezed, a small explosion that made her open her eyes in surprise, and I laughed.

Everyone was besotted, and I knew I was supposed to be

too. I did pretend, but it was hard. I was ten when she arrived, and I'd been the baby in the family all that time, and suddenly, Sara was the only person Gran and Mum wanted to talk about. For hours. I'd imagined acting as a big sister to Sara, being as cool in her eyes as Alan had always been in mine, but for the longest time she seemed indifferent. She just slept and cried and fed and expected every adult in her life to pay homage to her, which they did.

Once Sara turned one, Jackie went back to work at the hospital and left her with Mum or, on the days Mum was working, with Gran. She forced so many changes. All Gran's ornaments were packed away in the attic, and suddenly, there were stairgates blocking the way and wedges under Gran's doors and rounded plastic sleeves on the corners of the tables.

I always used to go round to Gran's after school when Mum was working, and I still did but, with Sara there, it was all different. In the old days, Gran and I had baked cakes or cookies together and, even though I could read well myself, we sat together for ages while she read children's classics to me, books she'd read Mum as a child.

Sara spoiled everything. She was so demanding, soon tottering around on her plump legs, pulling at my skirt, clamouring to climb onto Gran's knee the minute she started reading with me. I tried to get along with her, I really did. But she sucked up all the oxygen, and there was nothing left for me.

I tried explaining it to Mum, but she had no sympathy.

'Come on, love. You're a bit old to be jealous of a toddler.'

'I'm not jealous. She just—'

'Your gran's not getting any younger, you know. Try and help out instead of sulking. It's not easy running around after a little one.'

As the months passed, I saw it grow stronger – that light in Gran's eyes when Sara was there. The way she opened her arms to her and swept her up for cuddles, the way she made little dens for her with cushions and set out teddy bears' picnics on the carpet, with bits of broken biscuit and orange squash and her best china saucers. Gran's whole world revolved round that little girl.

But it wasn't long before the sky fell in.

'What are you talking about?'

I'd hesitated at the lounge door on my way in. Now I stopped completely, arrested.

Mum's tone was sharp, so unlike her.

A catch of breath, then the unmistakeable sound of gulping sobs.

I'd just turned thirteen. I considered myself old enough to know what was going on.

'Mum?' I pushed the door open and hurried in. 'You okay?' But she wasn't the one crying.

It was Alan, hunched over on the sofa, his head sunk low in his large, workman's hands. I stopped and stared, aghast. Alan was grown up. He never cried.

'Well, go on then, spit it out.' Mum's face was stony as she interrogated him. 'What've you done?'

Alan lifted his blotchy face from the sieve of his hands. 'Nothing!' He sounded anguished.

It broke my heart, just looking at him. I wanted to go and sit by him, to put my arm round him, but I was rooted to the spot, staring.

He blurted out, 'Why do you always blame me?'

Mum shrugged. 'Well, tell me then.'

'I don't make her happy. That's all she says. That it's her, not me.' He looked utterly bewildered. 'Mum! She's going. She's given in her notice. Another month and she'll be off.'

Mum narrowed her eyes. 'Going? Where?'

'I don't know. She doesn't want me to know. She says she never wants to see me again. That I'll never see Sara.'

Mum shook her head. 'She can't do that. You're her dad. You've got rights, you know.' She paced over to the window and looked out through the thin net curtains at the street. Her shoulders were tight, arms crossed at her chest.

I managed to move at last, slinking to a chair and sitting there, my legs trembling.

Alan shifted his weight to pull a large grubby handkerchief from his pocket and blew his nose.

Mum turned back, frowning. 'You haven't got someone else, have you?'

'Don't be stupid.' Alan shook his head. 'Why would you even say that?'

'Has she?'

'No!'

'Why's she leaving then?'

He shook his head as if it were all beyond him. 'She says this isn't what she wants. *I'm* not what she wants.' He sank his head in his hands again and crumpled back into sobs. 'What am I going to do? And Sara! I can't! I can't lose them both!'

Mum seemed to focus on me for the first time. She flicked me away with her hand, gesturing for me to make myself scarce. I crept out and fled up the stairs to my bedroom.

I sat on the edge of my bed, shivering, staring at the squares of posters and postcards tacked on the opposite wall, the cute kittens and puppies, the rainbows and love hearts.

Not Jackie and Alan, surely? It was impossible. I blinked

and the colours blurred and swam. They'd had arguments before, small ones. They'd always worked it out, eventually. They would this time. Wouldn't they?

8

In the weeks that followed, as Jackie worked out her notice and prepared to leave, the house was dark with adult misery. I crept to my bedroom after meals and pretended I was doing home-work, putting my headphones on to block out the stamping feet and slammed doors and raised voices. No one bothered with me, and I kept out of their way.

Almost at once, Alan had driven himself round to our place, the car packed full of boxes and bursting holdalls and carrier bags and armfuls of clothes. He moved back into his old bedroom, next to mine. No one spelled it out for me. One day his room was empty, and the next, he was back.

The wall connecting us pulsed again with the bass of his stupidly loud music, but I didn't dare complain. He ignored me. He ignored us all, slouching around the house as if whatever had happened was our fault.

When I managed to get a good look at him without being seen, he looked pitiful. His cheeks were hollowed and his eyes red and sunken. I started to wonder if he'd ever be himself again.

Mum turned into a robot. She came home from work and

moved around the kitchen, cooking the meal, as if she were on automatic. Before, I used to pop in to chat to her while she cooked. Not any more. I tracked the sounds from the lounge instead: the banging cupboard doors, the rattle of frozen veg into a bowl, the sudden flare of the gas hob, the hum and ping of the microwave.

When she called us all to eat, I came flying, first time, frightened of crossing her. We sat at the table in silence, jaws tight, eyes on our plates. No one asked me how school had been, what I'd got in the spelling or maths test, what I'd had for lunch. All those adult questions had irritated me in the past, but I missed them now. I hated the feeling that none of them cared. It felt as if we'd all become invisible to each other, each sealed in a separate, impenetrable bubble. As soon as the last person set down their knife and fork, meals half-eaten, I mumbled permission to leave and dashed upstairs again, escaping the unbearable weight of the silence.

The only person who talked to me about it all was Gran.

She put on a brave face when little Sara visited. It broke my heart to see the effort it cost her. Her eyes were red-rimmed, and the fleshy sides of her nose looked sore. I could tell, just from watching, that she was crying a lot in secret at the thought they'd soon be gone. In front of three-year-old Sara, her smile was artificially broad. Strained and forced.

Gran made more of a fuss of her than ever, exclaiming over the slightest thing she did or said as if she were a genius, smothering her in hugs and kisses until she protested and wriggled away, buying her more treats than she'd ever bought me: white chocolate mice and sherbet dips and flying saucers, all those sweets from the corner shop she used to dismiss in the old days as sugary rubbish.

Fresh Play-Doh and brand-new crayons appeared, and she baked Sara's favourite cupcakes with rainbow sprinkles and even let her lick the bowl and smear the batter all over her face.

It was only on Mondays, when I was there without Sara, that Gran sagged. She looked like a punctured balloon, slowly collapsing. While I did my homework, she sat in her chair with a cup of tea and stared at the photographs lined up along the mantelpiece: Gran and Grandpa on their wedding day, shy, side by side, framed by the church door as they stepped from the gloomy interior into the sunshine, out into married life. I hardly remembered Grandad; I was only four when he died. When I tried to think of him, I felt the rough rasp of his jacket and his stubbly chin, caught a lingering smell of stale tobacco.

Beside them, there was a picture of me, beaming, taken long ago, before I'd even started school. Then a baby picture of Sara, bald and wide-eyed, with a tiny, knitted bootie tucked in behind the frame, already yellowing with age. Recently, a new picture of Sara had appeared, taken the previous summer, forcing the rest of us to budge up. Her pudgy hand was grasping an ice cream cone, her face scrunched into a grin, trails of melting vanilla painting her lips and the tip of her nose. This was the picture Gran stared at now, her eyes brimming.

I said, 'They won't go far, will they?'

Gran sighed. One of her lace-edged handkerchiefs was bunched in her fist. She raised it to her face and dabbed at her eyes. 'I don't know, lovely.' She managed a wan smile. 'She won't say. She just says she's leaving.'

'She can't, though, can she?' I remembered what Mum had said. 'She can't stop Alan from seeing Sara.'

'It's not that simple.' Gran blinked. 'She can make it hard for him. Very hard. What's he going to do if she up sticks and disappears? What if she settles at the other end of the country? Abroad, even? He'll be hard pushed stopping her.'

I looked back at my schoolbook, but my eyes couldn't focus on the page. I took a deep breath and asked the question I was too scared to ask my mum: 'Will we really not see her at all? Ever again?'

Gran sat very still. 'Stranger things have happened.' She lifted her eyes to mine. 'I've no rights at all. Not legally. Neither does your mum, as Sara's gran. As for Alan... well, it depends.' She peered at me. 'Has no one talked to you about what's going on?'

I shook my head.

She considered me. 'Well, you're old enough to know. Just don't go telling your mum we've talked about it, okay?'

I nodded.

'Jackie says she doesn't want a thing from Alan, even if she's entitled. No maintenance. Nothing. She's doing well in nursing. She reckons she'll get a good enough job to manage on her own. Another year or so, and Sara'll be starting school, anyway.'

She paused, as if the thought of it caused her a sudden stab of pain. I sensed why. She was thinking about Sara, dressed up in a smart new uniform, hair scraped back into cute bunches, heading off for her first day at school, and none of us there to share it.

'Can't he fight back? Go to the police or something?'

'It wouldn't be the police.' She hesitated. 'He could go to court. Your dad's been looking at that. But it's quite a performance, getting access. They favour mums, mostly. And then, if Jackie gets a good job some place that's hundreds of miles away, how's he going to go and see them there?'

I consider. 'He could drive.'

'How often though, really? Once a month? Maybe not even that? He'll be a stranger to her, that's all. Not a real dad. He can't be.' She shook her head. 'It's cruel, what she's doing. I can't forgive her. Neither can your mum. We welcomed her into our family, we really did. Helped them out every way we could, especially once Sara came along. And this is what we get in return.' She frowned, thinking. 'It's breaking our hearts in pieces, the thought of losing that little girl. You can't imagine.

Me and your mum.' Her voice faltered, and she stopped and struggled to collect herself.

She sat very still for a few moments, far away. Finally, she sat up straight and squared her shoulders, as if she were drawing a line, then wiped her eyes and stowed her handkerchief away in her cardigan pocket.

'Anyway, no use moping, is there?' She planted her hands on the two arms of the chair and shifted her weight, ready to heave herself to her feet. 'I'm stopping you working. Cup of tea, lovely?'

I sat in silence, pretending to read, but actually listening as Gran pottered in the kitchen. It didn't seem real, the prospect of Jackie and Sara just disappearing from our lives in a matter of weeks.

I thought about Alan. The way he'd changed in the hope of winning Jackie. How stunned he'd looked on his wedding day, as if he couldn't quite believe life could deal him such good fortune. The way he'd held Sara when she was a newborn, his thick muscular arms wrapped around such a tiny, fragile bundle, his expression embarrassed but proud.

By the time Gran carried in the tray, a plate of cookies knocking against the mugs, I was in tears.

She said, 'Oh, no, oh, dear, I didn't mean—' She set the tray down and pressed beside me on the sofa, warm against my side, smelling of lavender, wrapping an arm around my shoulders and drawing me to her. 'Life is full of surprises,' she said. 'You'll see. They won't always be nasty ones.'

I let myself cry on her, grateful to be held. 'It's so awful,' I said through my tears. 'Everyone's so miserable. How can we bear it?'

She tutted and stroked my hair, the same way she used to stroke it when I was a much younger child, crying on her knee. 'Sometimes, you just have to,' she said quietly, and I had a sudden sense of Grandad dying, all those years ago, and all the times she must have cried here in this room, all alone, desolate, when I was too small even to realise.

And now she was having her heart broken all over again.

I looked down the row of photographs, there on the mantelpiece, pictures of the people she most loved. She'd already lost Grandad. Now Sara was disappearing too.

I thought of all the times I'd moaned about Sara, flounced into the next room because she was absorbing all Gran's attention, sat in silence while Gran tried to coax her to eat her vegetables, ignoring me.

'What if it's my fault?' I burst out. 'I never liked her being here. I was jealous, Gran. Is that why? Is that why she's leaving?'

'Of course not.' She pulled me to her more tightly, in a squeeze. 'Don't ever think that. It's nothing to do with us.' She paused, searching for the words. 'Marriages are funny things. It's sad, desperately sad, especially when there's a kiddie involved, but sometimes, they just don't work out. She says she's not happy.' Her shoulders shrugged, as if she couldn't quite believe it. 'They married very young – too young, really. There isn't much we can do apart from be brave and look out for Alan. He'll get over it. You'll see. It might just take him a little time.'

Gran plucked out her handkerchief again and mopped my face.

'As for never seeing that little girl again, who knows? I'll tell you a secret. But promise me you won't tell your mother. She'll think I'm silly.'

I blinked up at her into her soft eyes and stammered, 'I won't.'

'After she's gone, I'm going to pray every night that she comes back to us some day. Every night when I have my little word with Him Upstairs and ask him to keep an eye on Grandad for me and to look after you and Alan and your mum down here.' She smiled. 'There's always hope, Paula. While there's still life, anyway. And I'm not dead yet.'

She considered me, reading my expression. I looked sceptical, I suppose, about the idea of her praying every night, about those prayers being answered.

She kissed my damp forehead, giving her blessing. 'I know your mum doesn't hold with all that, not really,' she said, reading me as she always could. 'But I do. Maybe you should too.'

9

PRESENT DAY

Where do you start, after all that? How do you pick up the pieces?

After Sara strode over and joined us, we just sat, rigid, at the café table, surrounded by bustling shoppers and the clashing of cutlery and crockery and the tinny bounce of piped music.

Gran sat very still, her face, beneath her make-up, drained of colour, and stared at Sara. Her look was dazed and almost religious in its intensity; the sort of wondrous gaze a Renaissance Mary might bestow on her infant son.

I looked too, trying to see in the young woman the little girl I remembered from long ago. She was attractive, rather than pretty, with strong cheekbones, poker-straight hair and grey-green eyes. Jackie's eyes. But her nails were bitten down and her hands worked each other in her lap, all nervous tension. No wedding ring.

Finally, Gran broke the spell, leaning forward and pulling at the wrapping of the sandwich nearest to her. 'You must eat something' – she paused, as if the next word cost her an impossible effort – 'Sara.'

Gran lifted out one of the ham sandwiches she'd planned to

eat herself, put it on a napkin and pushed it across the table to Sara. 'You need feeding up, lovely.'

Sara shook her head, her eyes pinned to the table. 'I'm alright, thanks, Granny.'

Granny? Was that what three-year-old Sara had called her great-grandma? I couldn't recall.

'Cup of tea, then.' Gran rallied, picking up the metal teapot and trying to pour. Her hands shook, and tea splashed into the saucer.

'I can buy my own.' She pulled a battered wallet out of her jacket pocket and brandished it, embarrassed, as if it proved something.

'That's ok.' I took charge, giving Gran a strong cup first, then setting the second cup – the one that would have been mine – in front of Sara. 'Here.'

She nodded thanks and set the wallet on the table between the two of us. I stole a glance at it. There was a clear plastic pocket on the outside with an official-looking card inside.

I handed Hannah her hot chocolate and set a sandwich on a plate for her, nodding at her to eat. She picked it up, but without enthusiasm. She was scrutinising Sara, an eight-year-old child struggling to work out who this stranger was and why the adults in her life were acting so strangely.

'So...' I made a point of opening my packet of sandwiches and starting to eat. I'd lost all appetite, but I tried to swallow something down. 'How did you find us?' I was trying to keep my tone light, but I saw Hannah's eyes flick to me, reflecting the tension. 'Where've you been all these years?'

Gran sat forward, expectant.

'With Mum,' Sara said simply.

Gran joined in. Her voice was eager, as if she were finally being offered the pieces to a puzzle that had plagued her for so many years. 'But where? Where've you been living?'

'All over the place.' Sara pulled a face. 'I can't remember

them all. Cornwall, when I was little. I remember the beach. Then Cardiff. Newcastle. Glasgow, for a while. Wherever Mum's job took us, really.'

I considered. 'That's a lot of moving.' I imagined her as a child, changing schools every few years. A new area. New classroom. New children to befriend.

'It was.' She shrugged. 'I didn't know any different.'

She had one of those neutral English voices without a particular accent, as if she'd spent her life adapting, never belonging to any particular place or tribe, rich or poor, north or south. Just anonymous.

Gran said, 'Where's your mum now?'

Sara hesitated. 'She died. A few months ago.' There was a catch in her voice. 'Heart attack. She wasn't well for a long time, long before that.' She lifted her eyes to Gran's and some current of feeling passed between them. 'She had MS. She used to say she couldn't remember what it was like not to be in pain. It was like a worm, eating its way through her body. She kept working as long as she could, but it got too much for her in the end. You've got to be fit and strong to nurse, haven't you? Lifting. Carrying. On your feet all the time.'

She paused as if she were remembering. 'I went back to live with her after college and helped out.' She stuck out her chin, defiant. 'She didn't ask me to. She was always telling me to go off and live my own life and all that. She was brave. But then she had a stroke, and I knew she mightn't have long. I wanted to be with her while I could.'

Gran wiped her eyes. 'You poor love. We had no idea. Any of us.'

Sara said simply, 'I know.'

All the time she'd been talking, I'd been surreptitiously trying to get a better look at the card in her wallet. It was a student ID for the University of Nottingham. The photo certainly looked like her. And the name was right: *Sara Turner*.

It would be enough to convince Gran, I knew, if we asked Sara to prove who she was. I just wasn't sure. It wasn't hard to order fake IDs online. I'd heard of a friend doing it years ago so she could get into clubs. I hesitated, thinking.

'Why didn't you get in touch earlier?' I said, trying to keep my tone light. 'We might've helped.'

Sara hesitated. Her fingers pick, pick, picked at each other in her lap.

'You're family,' I continued. 'It was your mum who dropped contact, not us.' I wasn't trying to blame Jackie, just to make sure Sara knew the truth. 'It broke your dad's heart, losing the two of you. And my mum's. And Gran's.'

Gran murmured, 'Paula.'

I said softly, 'Well, it did.'

Gran reached across the table towards Sara, offering her hand. 'You poor love. I'm so sorry.'

Sara didn't move. Her expression was hard to read.

I thought of Jackie, slim and lovely, walking down the aisle towards Alan, and the dazed, grateful look on his face as he turned and saw her. I tried to work out how old she must have been when she died. Around the same as Alan probably: forty-four. *That's no age*, as my mum used to say. At least my mum had made it into her fifties before she died. Dad had just turned sixty when we lost him. That was bad enough.

I took a deep breath. 'I'm sorry about your mum.' I nodded, remembering. 'I lost mine too. Cancer.' I swallowed hard. 'You don't expect it, do you? You think they'll go on forever.'

Gran said, 'What about your dad? Does he know you're here?'

Sara shook her head. 'Not yet. I wasn't sure...' She tailed off, uncertain, and looked from Gran's earnest expression to mine. 'I wasn't sure if you'd be pleased to see me after all this time. Mum didn't want me contacting any of you. I tried. When she was really ill and couldn't work and worried so much about bills and everything, I said maybe I could go and see my dad, maybe he'd help. She was so angry. She made me promise not to.'

I thought of Alan and the mess he'd made of his life. He could have had his own business by now, bought his own garage, if he'd worked hard and saved. He was a great mechanic, everyone said so. But he always messed things up: arguing with the boss or getting into fights, drinking with his shady friends. I wondered what he and Sara would make of each other.

Sara lifted her cup with a shaking hand and swallowed down some tea. 'I went through her things after she died. Found an old address book from years ago. I was going to write. I started a few times. I just couldn't work out what to say.' She paused. 'Then I thought I might as well come down here and see for myself. I went to the old house in Shorewell Road first. It was the last address she had for Gran and Grandad Turner.' She nodded at me. 'Your mum and dad. It took me two days to get the courage to knock on the door. There's someone else living there. An Italian family.'

I nodded. 'We sold it after Dad died.'

'Right.' She hesitated. 'The only other address from round here was Granny's. Denby Road.' She nodded across at Gran. 'I was going to come and knock on your door too. I came a few times. Stood under those trees, just across from you. But I couldn't do it. Couldn't think what to say.'

I remembered the shifting shadows under the branches when I strode down Gran's street with her shopping, my mind on the art school job. Had Sara been there then, watching the comings and goings but too frightened to knock?

Gran reached out and patted her hand. 'It's alright, lovely. We understand. It would've been fine, though, if you had. I'd have pulled you right inside.'

I was still thinking, trying to make sense of it. It wasn't just a coincidence then, that she'd found us here at the shops. She'd followed us from the house. Trying to find courage to talk to us.

I remembered the sense I had earlier, when Gran was trying on shoes, that someone's eyes were on us.

Gran looked thoughtful too. 'Where are you living now?'

Sara looked embarrassed. 'I've got a room in a house on Harlow Road, just for a week. Airbnb. I figured by then...'

Gran smiled. 'Don't go spending your money like that. Stay with me for a bit, while you're here. I've got a spare room. There are always clean sheets on the bed, just in case. Aren't there, Paula?' She gestured to the sandwich. 'Anyway, eat up. You look half-starved. We can sort all that out later.'

I frowned, glancing again at the ID card, still uncertain. I picked up my own half-eaten sandwich and nibbled at it. I thought about Alan and how he'd react to the news that his daughter was back. She was so different now, transformed from a three-year-old child to a young woman.

Sara's shoulders were still tight with tension. For a few moments, we all sat silently, sipping our tea and swallowing down as much as we could, thinking about the past.

I thought about Jackie's family. Her mum and dad and the little sister who'd walked down the aisle beside me. Beatrice, wasn't it?

'What about your mum's family?'

Gran gave me a warning look, as if I'd said the wrong thing.

I stuttered on. 'I mean, how are they? Are they still around?'

Sara spoke to the table, unable to look me in the eye. 'Auntie Bea went to live in Canada years ago. As for Grandma and Grandpa, they never wanted us. They never forgave Mum for leaving Dad, the way she did. They couldn't understand it. She caused quite a scandal, I suppose, in their little lives.' She swallowed. 'Mum sent them a Christmas card every year, and they sent me one or two presents at Christmas when I was a kid.' She paused and her face clouded. 'Stupid things. Key rings and make-up bags and photo frames. They didn't even come to Mum's funeral. They said it was too far to travel at their age.' Her grey-green eyes shone, clear as a cat's. 'So, I've got no one.'

Gran tutted and reached out. Her veined hands, with their swollen knuckles and neatly kept nails, closed over Sara's young, smooth ones. 'You've got us, lovely.'

Hannah, watching Gran, finally seemed to realise what was going on. 'So, she's that little girl in the photo?' she said to Gran. 'The one on your mantelpiece?'

Sara raised her eyebrows at Gran, and she nodded and smiled.

'Then you're my long-lost cousin? Cool!' Hannah looked thrilled. She jiggled about on her seat with excitement. 'I'm Hannah. I'm eight.'

'Hello, cousin Hannah.' Sara lifted her hand, and they slapped a high five, the tension suddenly broken. 'I'm Sara. It *is* pretty cool, isn't it? I don't know about "long-lost", though...' She smiled. 'I guess we can't say that any more. Now that I'm found.'

10

I stood at the sink, pausing halfway through washing glasses, rubber gloves squeaking as I ran my fingertips round the rims in the soapy water, and looked out over the patio and the garden beyond.

At the far end, on the neat square of lawn, Hannah and Lizzie were playing makeshift badminton, biffing the plastic shuttlecock high into the air, one to another. Now and then, their shrill voices cut through from outside as they shrieked. They seemed to be getting on at the moment. That was a blessing. Hannah had been desperate to invite Lizzie round to show off her new cousin, trying to score points in the painful competition to be Lizzie's best friend.

To one side of the patio, Will was poking chicken breasts and turning sausages on the barbecue. He wasn't taking an active part in their conversation, not at the moment anyway. His eyes stayed calmly on the cooking. But I could tell from his expression that he was listening and enjoying it all.

I smiled to myself. He worked hard, not just seeing patients but steadily building the practice. It was good to see him so relaxed. He looked handsome too. He'd taken up running again recently, inspired by some medical paper he'd read about the benefits of exercise. It suited him. He looked broad-shouldered and effortlessly stylish, as he always did, in neatly pressed black jeans and a dark blue polo shirt, open at the collar. I liked to joke that he spent far more money on his clothes than I did, and it was probably true.

Beside him, Sara and Gran were sitting at the patio table, the umbrella furled between them. Gran had arrived looking even smarter than usual; I didn't remember seeing that dress before. It was spiked with bright colours and the extra detail at the collar and cuffs caught the eye and drew it away from her slackened waist, a feature she so hated. Her cheeks were flushed, her eyes on Sara as she explained something to her. I wondered what they were talking about. Gran looked younger and happier than I'd seen her for a long time.

And Sara. I hesitated. It was so strange, seeing her sitting there on the patio, as if she'd never been away. Her straight hair, tied back in a high ponytail, flicked lightly as she talked. She used her hands a lot, waving them about in mid-air to make a point, then bunching her fingertips delicately round her drinking straw when she leaned forward to take a sip of sparkling water. I tried to remember if Jackie had had the same gestures, but it was all too long ago.

But there was something else too. A clench to Sara's jaw. A tightness in her smile. She was wearing those narrow jeans again, the same ones she wore yesterday when she accosted us in the department store café. A prettier top, though, more feminine, a rich blue cotton with tiny white flowers and three-quarter-length sleeves. Light make-up, skilfully applied.

I imagined Sara picking through her clothes earlier in the day, trying to decide what to wear to meet her dad. She must be nervous. Who wouldn't be? I couldn't imagine how much she'd really remember him. She was so young the last time they met.

I wondered what the room was like, the one she was renting. Gran was still full of plans for Sara to stay with her, to save money. Sara had just smiled and said very little. Maybe she didn't want to get too involved, or was wary of imposing. We all had a lot of catching up to do.

I'd told Gran that morning, before Sara arrived, that maybe we should take things slowly. We needed to get to know Sara, I said. Give her time.

'Time?' Gran had looked cross. 'I'm eighty-eight, lovely. How much time do you think I've got?'

Now, I reached for the last dirty glass and plunged it into the suds, washed it, rinsed it in cold water at the twin sink and set it upside down to drain. The lounge clock chimed. I peered out again at the soft, steamy smoke rising from the barbecue, trying to judge if the food was nearly ready.

Will looked up and caught my eye at the same moment. He always seemed to know when I was watching him. It was the same at parties. I'd look across a crowded room to see him deep in conversation and, as if by magic, he'd turn and meet my gaze and give me that shy half-smile that still knotted my stomach, even now. He just felt my eyes, he said. Maybe it was magic, that force that crackled between us. Maybe it was just because we'd been married for so long.

Now, he winked at me across the patio and brandished his tongs. He pointed to the meat, then raised and spread his hand to tell me we were five minutes away from take-off.

It was time to peel off my gloves and start carrying the bowls of salad outside. I looked at the wet wine glasses. I'd just leave them there to dry. There was already a jug of iced water on the table, and tumblers. That would do for now. Will could offer another round of proper drinks once the food was dished up.

The doorbell rang and I snatched off the gloves, smoothed down my hair and hurried to answer it.

. . .

'Are you alright?'

Alan's face was pale and sheened with sweat. His hair, thinning now, stuck out at odd angles as if he'd forgotten to comb it this morning. He didn't answer, just held out a bottle of wine in a brown paper bag.

I took it. 'Thanks.' I looked at him more closely, trying to tell from his eyes, the smell of his breath, if he'd already started drinking. 'Where've you been? Work?'

He nodded. 'Sorry I'm late, sis. Busy morning.'

I shrugged, not entirely convinced he was telling the truth. He'd got this latest job through a mate – the way it always seemed to work in his business – but he was already complaining about the boss, saying he treated Alan like a kid and ordered him about. Alan had years of experience. There wasn't much he couldn't fix. I just hoped he'd keep his powder dry this time.

He followed me down the hall. I hesitated before we reached the kitchen at the far end and turned back to him, taking advantage of the fact we were still hidden from view.

'How are you feeling?'

'I don't know.' He shrugged. 'Weird.'

I nodded, taking him in. 'You'll be fine. I think she's nervous too.'

He pulled a face. I thought of his quiet misery over the years since Jackie had left. The humiliation of moving back home for a while, to live with his parents and kid sister again. We'd all watched him slowly lose respect for himself, lose interest in his life.

How was he supposed to pick up again now, after all that time, and be a father to a young woman he hadn't been allowed to see grow up?

I reached forward and gave him a hug. 'Just don't drink too much, okay?'

He rolled his eyes.

I took his hand and led him out, through the kitchen and into the garden.

He stepped onto the patio, then stopped and froze.

Hannah and Lizzie were turning ragged cartwheels, screaming every time they collapsed on the lawn. Sara and Gran, still sitting, were turned away from the patio doors, watching the girls. Will raised a spatula in welcome. 'Alan! Right on cue!' He reached for a plate and started flipping burgers onto it.

Sara turned, then jumped up, banging her knee against the table. She looked flustered, steadying herself with a hand on the tabletop.

For a moment, she and Alan both stood there, eyes on each other, time suspended.

Finally, Alan nodded and went across, held out his hand to her. It was such a formal greeting, it stopped my heart. I had a flood of memory of all the love he'd felt for his little girl, all the hurt that had crippled him since she left.

Sara, awkward too, gave a pecking nod in reply and put her slim hand in his. 'Hi.' Her voice was a squeak. 'Thanks for coming.' She blushed. 'I mean, good to see you. Sorry, it's all a bit, you know, unexpected.'

I swept back into the kitchen to hide, pretending to be busy with salads and cutlery. Anything was better than watching the two of them. It was unbearable. What did I expect? For father and daughter to fall into each other's arms, to cling to each other and weep? For her to call him 'Daddy' and for him to stroke her hair and proclaim her his little girl, all grown up. Anything would be better than this careful emptiness.

By the time I carried out the bowls of salad, Alan had taken a seat and was concentrating on pouring out the water. Sara was sitting very stiffly, eyes on the table.

'Well, the rain's held off.' Gran was all false cheeriness,

filling the silence. 'Aren't we blessed with the weather? You've hardly had the barbecue out this year, have you, Will?'

I called across the garden to the girls to go and wash their hands and then join us, and they ran over, noisy and hungry, helping, without realising it, to paper over the cracks.

'Now, Sara.' I passed her a plate from the stack. 'What would you like to start with? I marinated the chicken overnight, just a hint of garlic, hope that's okay. Do you eat beef? What about a burger, then? They're minced steak. From an organic butcher. Grass-fed cattle, no hormones.'

Will gave my shoulder a warm, reassuring squeeze and kissed the top of my head. 'Give her a chance, Paula, she can't get a word in.' He smiled down at Sara. 'Just help yourself. There's plenty.' He turned to Hannah and Lizzie as they reappeared again from the kitchen and hung round the table, checking out the food. 'Now girls, what about you two? How about starting off with a sausage each and half a burger? And you do need to eat some salad, please, not just meat and bread.' He gave Gran a charming smile. 'What can I get you, Gran? Chicken?'

There was a sudden flurry of movement as the girls crowded round and Sara helped Gran pick out what she wanted.

Only Alan seemed still.

I bent close to him to hand him a plate. His voice was barely a murmur.

'All that time.' He sounded desolate. 'All those years.'

11

Later, after they'd all finally left, I shooed Hannah upstairs to get ready for bed.

I stacked the dishwasher and stretched plastic wrap over the remnants of meat and salad. Will poured two generous glasses of Chianti from an open bottle and placed one of the glasses on the counter beside me.

I paused and lifted it, savoured a sip, thoughtful. Rich and mellow. I'd stayed on soft drinks all afternoon, keeping my head. Now, something inside me softened at last and gave.

I turned to watch Will as he polished a wine glass with his tea towel, his hands strong and capable. A doctor's hands. His eyes were on the glass but vaguely, as if he were lost in thought.

'Thanks for this afternoon.' I wanted to bring him back, to have his attention, just for the pleasure of it. After all, I'd shared him all day.

He looked up and gave me a slow smile. 'You did most of it.'

I shrugged. 'You did the barbecue. Drinks. Kept it all going.'

'I'm not sure that's true.' He turned to put the glass away in the top cupboard where it belonged, then reached for the next one to polish.

I took another sip of wine. Something was bothering me. I looked around the kitchen with its modern tiled floor and clean lines, its broad counters and shiny twin sinks. I loved it. I loved this whole house. Our life there hadn't been without its sorrows, but I loved Will, I loved our daughter. I shivered. Why did I suddenly feel so uneasy, as if a shadow had fallen over us all?

Will finished polishing the next glass and stowed it safely away. I took a larger draught of wine.

I ignored for a moment the salad I still needed to put away and leaned back against the far counter, glass in hand. 'What did you think?'

'About what?'

I tutted. 'About her? Sara?'

He said evenly, 'She seemed okay. Bit nervous, maybe.'

'She was, wasn't she?' I remembered the tightness in her jaw, her nervous habit of picking at her fingers. She'd relaxed a little as the barbecue wore on, but not completely.

Will's eyes were on the glass in his hands. 'She's been through a lot. Losing her mum. She's still very young.'

I nodded, thinking. She did seem young. By her age, I was already married and working at the bank. I'd never liked it there. I was glad to leave once Hannah came along. But Sara felt different from the person I'd been. Not just young, but somehow rootless.

'Did you talk to her much?'

Will shrugged. 'Not really. Just chit-chat. You?'

'A bit.' I hesitated. 'I don't feel I've got to really know her yet.'

He picked up his wine and leaned back against the kitchen counter, his face turned away from me as he looked out at the blackness of the garden.

I went on, talking half to him and half to myself. 'It's so odd. She's part of the family. One of us. But she's also a stranger. It's going to take time, isn't it? And effort.'

'Let's see.' He sipped his wine. 'She may not stick around long.'

'What makes you say that?'

His expression was half-hidden. 'Just that. From what you've said, she's not used to staying long in one place, that's all. It's a big world out there.'

I put my wine glass down and went back to spooning rice salad out of a bowl into a plastic container, clipped on the lid and spent a minute finding room for it in the overcrowded fridge. Finally, I turned back to him.

'Well, I hope she does. It would hurt Gran terribly if she disappeared again. She's besotted.' I hesitated, remembering what Alan had murmured. 'And there's Alan too. It's not easy for him, having all that stuff raked up again. He's not as tough as he likes to think.'

Will shrugged. 'Well, maybe I'm wrong.' He drank off his wine as if it were water and went to wash up the glass. 'Just a feeling, that's all. She may just be touching base here, then she'll be off again.'

'Maybe.' I paused, thinking back. 'I wonder how much she even remembers? She was only three when she left.' I nodded to myself. 'She was a great kid. Alan adored her. Full of fun. And chatty as anything. She and Gran used to bake a lot. Flour everywhere. And I remember taking her to feed the ducks, down at the river. I wonder if she remembers that? I must ask her.'

Will dried the glass and put it away. I sensed he wasn't really listening.

'Everything okay?'

'Yep.'

I ploughed on. 'Fancy a film this evening? I'm not sure I can eat much, but there's wine and plenty of leftovers.'

'I might head upstairs. Work's pressing in again.' He poured himself a mug of coffee from the pot. 'You don't mind, do you?'

'Mind about what?' Hannah dashed into the kitchen in a streak of pink nightshirt. She reached past me for a tortilla chip as I started to pour them back into the packet from the bowl.

'Haven't you just cleaned your teeth?'

'Mummy! Mind about what?' she repeated.

Will brushed past us both with his coffee, heading out of the kitchen.

'Where's Daddy going?'

'Upstairs, sweetheart.' He stooped and kissed her cheek. 'I've got paperwork to do. Very, very boring.'

Hannah protested at once, 'But Daddy! It's so late!'

He called back over his shoulder. 'I know, but I get homework too, you know. Got to be done.'

The stairs creaked under his soft tread as he headed up to his study.

Hannah pulled a face. 'Stupid work.'

'I know.' I opened my arms to her for a hug. 'You go and find a book and snuggle down in bed, and I'll be up in two minutes to read to you. Deal?'

She ran off. I wiped over the worktops. Will was under a lot of pressure at the practice. I knew that. But I was still disappointed. I'd wanted to talk to him about the arts school job. It wouldn't be an easy conversation, I knew that. There was too much emotion involved – not in the job itself, but in what it meant for us. It wasn't something I wanted to rush, but there never seemed to be time to talk properly, just the two of us.

I switched off the kitchen light, frowning to myself, and headed upstairs to Hannah's room.

12

It still seemed a miracle to me that Will and I had ended up together. I'd adored him for so long, years before he even noticed me.

Will liked to joke with Hannah that it was actually Uncle Alan he'd liked best in the beginning, and getting to know Mummy had come later. It was actually true. He'd been one of Alan's best mates when they were teenagers, and eventually surprised everyone years later by falling for his friend's little sister.

I liked to imagine that he first became aware of me on the day Alan and Jackie got married. I felt so special, walking down the aisle behind Jackie in my pink, pouffey dress, her sister at my side, holding my back ramrod straight, posy in my hands. My dark hair was loose down my back. A circlet of flowers wobbled on top of my head.

At the age of nine, I imagined that I was the one the whole church was turning to admire. In fact, there may have been an elderly aunt here or there who thought I was adorable, but Alan and his friends were far too old for me then. Will was lanky and impossibly sophisticated in a dark suit and tie. He and the rest of Alan's crowd danced and goofed around at the reception and I, a gangly schoolgirl, sat quietly with my mum and dad, invisible to them all, ashamed of the fact I was still just a kid.

Will was the brainy one in their gang, the posh one – the one with prospects. His mother and father were both doctors and everyone just assumed he'd study medicine, too, when the time came. My parents had always approved of him. Steady lad. A good influence on Alan. The kind of young man who'd make something of himself.

No, Will didn't notice me until years later. He'd moved back to the area after he'd qualified and joined a local practice as a family doctor. We bumped into each other in town one Saturday. He didn't recognise me at first, but I knew him. I was nineteen at the time and nursing a broken heart. He and Alan were both twenty-nine. He must have heard what had happened with Jackie from his parents, of course he had. There was no keeping anything quiet for long in our home town.

He asked after Alan, once he'd realised who I was, and made an effort to come round and see him at Mum and Dad's. He took him off to a cricket match or a football match or just out to a bar, anything to get him out of the house. Mum acted as if the Messiah had appeared, she was so grateful.

Then he did his best for us a few years later when we found out about Mum's cancer. He went with Alan and my parents to some of the meetings at the hospital. Alan must have asked him to, I suppose. He listened and talked medical jargon with the consultants and, afterwards, tried to explain the treatment options to us in simple terms.

Later, when it came to it, he drove round with my parents to look at hospices. So, it was no surprise that his was the broad, capable, grown-up shoulder I wanted to cry on when Mum finally died and my world split into pieces. I was twenty-three, struggling to concentrate on my boring job at a bank, and adrift. My dad was in too many pieces himself to put me back together.

He never really recovered. When he died himself – just three years after her, the same year Hannah was born – the doctors called it a massive cardiac arrest. I used a simpler term: a broken heart.

Will became a constant, comforting presence in our grieving home. When he finally did kiss me, late one evening, he seemed overcome with remorse, saying he hadn't meant to, he'd promised himself he'd wait much longer, until I was calmer, until I could be sure of my feelings.

I was sure. I'd been sure since I was nine years old, walking down the aisle with a floral coronet pinned on my hair. I just never thought it would really happen.

I cried on our wedding day, but only because I wished Mum were there too. I wanted her to know. As I walked down the aisle on Dad's arm, I could almost see her there in the front pew, resplendent in a wide-brimmed hat, twisting back to look, her face flushed with emotion and blinking back tears, trying not to ruin her make-up.

She'd have been so pleased, so proud. Not just because I was marrying a doctor, but because it was Will – ten years older than me, strong and safe and settled – and just the sight of him, waiting for me there at the altar, made me so happy I could burst.

13

'Do the admin for them, by all means. But use it as a springboard. Take more courses yourself. Build your contacts.'

Iris led me up the art school's steep stairs to the rooftop studio, her voice drifting down over her shoulder, echoing slightly in the stairwell. 'You're good.'

Iris and I had been talking about the job as we walked over together. I hadn't meant to burden her with it, not in so much detail, but Iris was such a good listener. She drew me out, just by paying attention and giving me the space to think aloud.

'I do love drawing.' I hesitated. 'But it's just a hobby, really, isn't it? I mean, I'll never make a proper career out of it.'

Iris paused on the top landing, getting her breath back and letting me catch up. 'Lots of the artists who come here make money. Through exhibitions, obviously, and selling their work. But there are other routes too. Some do book illustrations or adverts or work with greetings cards' companies. All sorts. You'll find out if you get to know them better.'

She read my expression and didn't push me any further. She was good at that, gently encouraging me without being domineering, as if she knew I needed to find my own way.

We found our seats inside the studio and settled in front of our easels. Morning light was filtering through the picture windows, spilling in pools across the floor. The class was fuller than usual, with almost every seat taken. It was mostly older women, close to Iris's age: retired teachers and accountants and a doctor, their children grown, all finally getting the chance to spend Mondays as they pleased.

The teacher, Nick, appeared in the centre of the circle of easels, pushing back his floppy mane of greying hair. 'Morning, everyone.' He fixed his gaze past us, somewhere towards the back of the studio, awkward in front of groups. 'Karen can't sit for us for a few weeks, so we've got a new model today. Two thirty-minute poses please, quick pencil work, with a classical theme. Right, on you come, Hugo.'

I was fiddling with the bundle of paper on my easel, trying to straighten it. Iris turned to look as the model strode in, and her eyes opened wide in exaggerated shock.

She mouthed, 'Blimey!'

I grinned. That was for my benefit, to make me laugh. She liked to ham it up sometimes, pretending to be a prudish older woman when in fact she was anything but. But she wasn't the only one reacting. The studio was gripped by a sudden silence as the women around me shifted in their seats or coughed behind their hands. Or just stared.

Nick cleared his throat for attention. I peered over the top of my easel to see what all the fuss was about and felt myself flush. Nick, in his baggy woolly jumper, looked diminished by the muscular young man who was stepping onto the podium beside him. The man paused, then theatrically removed his knee-length robe to reveal a taut body, clad only in Speedos. He was gorgeous. He held his shoulders proudly, his skin smooth over a broad chest and taut stomach.

Every woman in the room, whatever age, gaped.

'Hi, Hugo!' One of the retired teachers called out.

'Nice to see you,' said another, drawing titters.

Others murmured to each other in low voices.

Nick mumbled instructions to Hugo to take up his first pose, draping a sheet around his body and across one outstretched arm. A perfect Roman statue.

'Thirty minutes, class!'

Iris gave me a comical sideways look, followed by some fast blinking, as if the sight of this handsome man-god were blinding her, then we reached for our pencils and began to draw.

He turned at once from man to model as I concentrated on the lines.

Usually, in the coffee break, Karen put her robe on and joined us in the café for a chat and a coffee. She'd been sitting for the group for a long time, and we'd got to know her pretty well. But this time, when we picked up our bags and shuffled out, Hugo stayed behind, alone.

Iris made a face at me. 'Well,' she said. 'Better not tell Will.'

I smiled and nodded at the gaggle of women crowding by the serving hatch. They seemed more skittish, more giggly than usual. 'He's caused quite a stir, hasn't he?'

'Are you surprised? He'll be the talk of the school.' Iris pressed forward towards the tea and coffee. 'I've been coming for twenty years and he's the first model under fifty.'

I laughed. 'You think it's Nick's way of keeping his numbers up? He'll have a waiting list once word gets out.'

Iris looked back towards the studio. 'Poor lad. Let's take him a coffee, yeah?'

'Well, I'm not sure—'

But she was already weighing into the group, reaching for one of the coffee pots and pouring. She handed a cup out to me, then reappeared with two more.

'Full speed ahead!'

She led me back into the studio.

Hugo was sitting on his own by the open window, his short

robe loosely knotted around his waist, smoking and looking out over the suburban rooftops.

Iris set the coffee down beside him with a clatter. 'Well done,' she said. 'It's harder than it looks, isn't it? Keeping still for that long.'

He looked round. 'I thought my arm was going to fall off. Do you think he'd let me sit down for the second half?' His voice ambushed me. Deep, rich and resonant.

Iris said, 'So what else do you do? Are you into art?'

He tapped the ash off the end of his cigarette and shook his head. 'Actor,' he said. 'TV, mostly.'

Of course. He'd have to be an actor with that voice.

Iris brightened up. 'What've you been in? Anything we might have seen?'

He named a few TV soaps and dramas, then a washing-up liquid commercial. We nodded, but he seemed to realise we were bluffing. I'd no memory of seeing him in anything.

'Small parts, so far.' He looked endearingly crestfallen. 'I'm hoping for a break. It takes a while.'

Iris nodded encouragement. 'You've got presence, though.' She turned to me. 'Hasn't he, Paula? You could've cut the air with a knife when you stepped up on that podium.'

He took a final drag of his cigarette, then stubbed it out. The shards of tobacco glowed red, then spread and cooled to blackness. 'I was being Julius Caesar. Could you tell? We did it at school years ago. It was one of the plays that got me into acting.' He took a deep breath. 'It's pretty weird, you know, walking into a room like that and taking your kit off.' He glanced at Iris, then looked quickly away. 'I thought it might help to make a performance of it, you know. Pretend I was on stage.'

'Well, it worked,' said Iris firmly. 'You're doing fine.' She glanced across to the studio clock. 'Now drink your coffee and sort yourself out. You're back on in about five minutes.'

'You're a born director.' He winked at her, then drained his cup in one and got to his feet.

As he passed me, he nodded over at my easel. My rough pencil sketch of him was still pinned to it.

'That yours?'

I nodded.

'Could I possibly buy it off you? It's just... well, it's really good.'

I hesitated, awkward, trying to think what to say.

He flushed slightly. 'Have I said the wrong thing? Sorry. I didn't mean to—'

'No, have it, please.' I pulled the paper off the easel, ripping the corner off in my haste, and pushed it at him. 'It really isn't that good.'

'Thanks!' He grinned and rested it back on the easel. 'I owe you. Will you sign it for me? It might be worth a lot someday.'

'I very much doubt it.'

Already, the others in the class were arriving back into the studio, taking their seats. Several of the women looked over, checking Hugo out. I scribbled my name at the bottom of the sheet and handed it back again.

Nick entered the circle, clapping his hands and gesturing at Hugo to join him.

This time, as Hugo undid his robe, his pose was more Chippendale than Caesar and his eyes, playful, found mine as he grinned.

I ducked behind my easel, feeling my cheeks flame.

Iris gave me an amused look.

I whispered, 'Stop it.' It felt as if the whole room was staring at me, and she wasn't helping.

Iris shrugged and smiled to herself.

Nick swung a chair onto the podium and organised Hugo into a seated pose. The silence settled as we all started to draw.

Hugo's head was turned now, his gaze directed at the

window. The sunlight streamed across his face, accentuating the bones and hollows of his forehead, his cheeks, his chin. It gave me the freedom to look, to study him, knowing he couldn't look back. Blood pounded in my ears. I tried to steady my breathing and relax, but my pencil movements were stiff and wooden.

What was the matter with me? Maybe it was the contrast he made with Will. There was an edginess about Hugo, a bad-boy vibe. Will was charismatic, but he turned heads for totally different reasons. He was handsome, yes, but successful and stylish. Hugo looked naughty and a lot of fun.

I was flattered too by the fact Hugo had taken an interest in what I'd drawn. Taken an interest in me. Perhaps it was only a passing interest, but still, I'd forgotten what that felt like. It had been a long time since a stranger had flirted with me, especially one with a body like that.

A moment later, Hugo twisted his head, just for a moment, to scratch behind his ear. He looked right at me and raised his eyebrows teasingly, as if he could tell exactly what I was thinking. I flushed and fixed my eyes on my drawing.

At the end of the class, I mouthed an excuse to Iris, grabbed my things and was the first out of the door, clattering down the stairs as if the building were on fire. I hurried out through the atrium and into the fresh air, breathing deeply, feeling my cheeks cool and my embarrassment slowly drain away.

Hopefully, it would be someone else on the podium next week.

Hopefully, I'd never have to face Hugo again.

14

The next day, I got another surprise.

I picked up Hannah from school, as usual, and we popped round to see Gran. I let myself in and then hesitated. The hall smelled strange. Of something perfumed. Shampoo, maybe, or bubble bath.

'Gran? It's me, Paula.'

Fast footsteps sounded overhead. I tensed. Was it that European guy – what was his name, Tomas? – back for another bath?

A slim figure in a black T-shirt and jeans appeared at the top of the stairs.

'Sara!' Hannah ran forward, thrilled.

Sara grinned down at her as she came down, two at a time. She was wearing different jeans today: baggy ones with frayed hems. 'Hey, little cousin. You want to come up and see my room? I can fix us a snack to take up, if you like.'

Hannah twisted back to look at me. 'Can I?'

'Sure. Just say hi to Gran first, would you?'

'Gran!' Hannah ran into the lounge to find her, leaving me to follow.

Gran was in her armchair, bright-eyed, her arms open for Hannah's hug. 'My, you are in a rush.' Gran's face lit up with pleasure. 'Did I hear something about a snack?'

'Is that alright, Gran?' Hannah beamed. 'We're going up to her room. Does she live here now?'

'Well, she's staying here, petal. Keeping me company. I've never liked rattling round here on my own. Too many rooms for one person.'

Hannah pulled away, ready to run out again.

I said, 'Don't be too long up there. Remember you've got homework.'

'Don't worry.' Sara called through from the kitchen, butting in. 'I'll help. It'll be fun.'

Their voices drifted through as they met again in the hall and hurried up the stairs together, chattering about the spelling sentences Hannah needed to write.

When I turned back to Gran, she was watching me. 'Those two get on well.' She nodded a little to herself. 'Cup of tea? Sara just made me a pot.'

I fetched a cup and saucer from the kitchen cupboard, noting a few changes. A loaf of seeded brown bread had appeared, not something Gran ate, and, in the fridge, there were cartons of hummus and low-fat cream cheese. The biscuit tin and breadboard and block of knives were askew, as if someone had moved them to wipe over the surface and been in too much of a hurry to put them back neatly.

Gran's earthenware milk jug, usually out of sight at the back of a cupboard, was standing on the kitchen table with a bunch of pink carnations in it. I peered at them. They were ragged blooms, already past their best, the outside petals brown and moulting. Presumably, Sara didn't have much money at the moment.

Back in the lounge, I settled down near Gran with my tea. 'So, she's moved in? When did that happen?'

'Yesterday afternoon.'

'You should have said. We could have helped.'

Gran shrugged. 'She hasn't got much. Just a suitcase and a couple of bags.'

I considered. Gran had lived alone for so long. It was a big change. 'Are you sure you're okay with this, Gran?'

Gran smiled. 'She's family, Paula. Do you think I'd turn you away, if you needed a roof over your head?'

I sipped my tea. Footsteps sounded upstairs. Hannah's muffled giggles. I wondered how much homework would actually get done.

I turned to Gran, thinking. 'What's she planning to do? Has she said?'

Gran shook her head. 'She hasn't, and I haven't asked. She's got a degree in English, did you know? She's clearly got brains. She just needs a break. She's been through a lot, looking after her mum and everything. And in the meantime' – she shrugged – 'I've told her I don't want money from her. She did offer.'

'I'm sure she'll be able to get a decent job, once she decides what she wants to do.' I paused. 'I've applied for that job, by the way. At the art school.'

'Good.' She gave me a searching look. 'What did Will say?'

I squirmed. 'I haven't actually told him yet. I haven't had the chance.'

She hesitated. 'It doesn't mean you're giving up. It might even help. Take your mind off it.'

I bit down on my lip. 'It's just been a while, you know, since Hannah was born.'

'I know.' Gran nodded. 'But you're still young. It's not over yet.'

I nodded. 'Hannah needs a lot of support. Schools push kids so hard nowadays. She's already getting stressed about getting into a decent secondary school, and that's two years off.'

There was a thud upstairs, followed by more giggling. Gran

gave the ceiling a wry look, before saying, 'Sara might help, if you need someone to pick Hannah up now and then, do her homework with her. Bet she's great with kids.'

I hesitated. 'That's a thought.' Sara was family, even if we hadn't seen her for years. So why did the thought of handing Hannah over to her make me feel uneasy? I thought about Will's warning, that I mustn't expect her to stick around long. Maybe he was right. I didn't want Hannah to get hurt.

'I can see Sara teaching, can't you? There are some lovely schools round here. A bit of tutoring would be good practice.'

'Gran, stop scheming.'

We sat in silence for a moment. I remembered the flowers in the kitchen.

'Nice carnations, by the way.'

'Aren't they?' Gran nodded. 'Bit past their best, but a lovely thought.'

'Yes, sweet of her.'

Gran looked round, eyes wide. 'Oh, they're not from Sara! Is that what you thought? No, dear, they're from Tony.'

'Tony?' I stared at her. Who the hell was Tony?

She nodded. 'He came round the other day, selling dusters and dishcloths and whatnot. I bought some very nice oven gloves. Ten pounds. They're in the kitchen somewhere.'

I did some rapid thinking. 'He was selling at the door?'

'Yes, lovely. He had one of those plastic tray things, you know, so you can see everything. It reminded me of the great wooden ones they used to carry in the street when I was a girl, round their necks. They used them for hawking shoe polish or pies, all sorts of things. Anyway, he said he'd been up and down these streets, knocking on doors, for five hours and I was the first person who'd bought anything. Poor lad. How can people be so mean?'

I shook my head at her in disbelief. 'People are just careful,

Gran. A lot of these men are straight out of prison. You shouldn't even open the door to them.'

Gran carried on. 'Tony *was* in prison, actually. He was quite open about it. Fraud, he said. He conned people out of their savings. He told me all about it. But he's determined to go straight now. How can he get back on his feet if no one gives him a chance?' She paused, remembering. 'I got a rather good dishcloth as well, actually. It's in the sink. He saw the state of my old one and had a rummage in his tray and Bob's your uncle.' She saw my face. 'You needn't worry. He gave me a good deal.'

'What do you mean, he saw your old one?' I was still working it out. 'Gran, you didn't ask him in, did you?'

Her face clouded. 'Honestly, Paula. You've got to stop fussing. I'm a grown woman.'

'You had him in the house? In the kitchen?'

'It was raining.' Gran shook her head at me as if I were the one being unreasonable. 'He looked so cold and wet. He wouldn't let me feed him – just a quick cup of tea and a biscuit. He started off in the police, he said, when he left school. But that all went wrong – I forget what happened. And then he got into debt.' She sighed. 'He's got a kid of his own somewhere, but they won't have anything to do with him. You know, Paula, we've got a lot to be grateful for.'

I couldn't answer for a moment. I was too stunned. Gran must really have befriended him if he'd popped back with a bunch of wilting flowers. 'Gran, you promised me. You said you'd stop asking people in off the street. It's not safe.'

She hesitated, looking into mid-air as she practised something in her head. Finally, she said, 'Be not forgetful to entertain strangers.'

I blinked. 'Pardon?'

She nodded. 'That's what I wanted to say the other day when you and I had our little chat about Maria. It was something my mother used to say. Sara helped me look it up on the iPad.' She cleared her throat and recited: '*Be not forgetful to entertain strangers, for thereby some have entertained angels unawares.*'

'Shakespeare?'

She shook her head. 'Hebrews' – then added, knowing I'd never attended Sunday School as she and my mother had – 'the Bible.'

I gave her a look. 'And what does it say in the Bible about staying safe?'

She smiled. 'Well, there's a lot about trust, put it that way.'

I was about to retort when the door opened, and Hannah burst in. She was giggling and slightly out of breath as if she'd pelted downstairs.

'Look! Do you like it?' She did a twirl, showing herself off.

Sara hovered in the doorway, watching her, a smile on her face.

Hannah's hair was expertly plaited into an intricate French braid. It made her look instantly older, her neck suddenly elegant, her cheek bones more pronounced. I peered more closely. Her eyes were rimmed with kohl, her lips shone with gloss.

'Well, look at you! You look so grown up, Hannah!' Gran clapped her hands, delighted.

'Isn't she a stunner? Eight going on eighteen, eh?' Sara lounged against the door frame. 'I can teach you how to do the braid, if you like, Paula? It's not hard. Just fiddly.'

I didn't know what to say. She looked so different in make-up. It was hard to see my little girl suddenly looking like a teenager.

Finally, I managed a smile. 'You look amazing! Thanks, Sara!'

Hannah beamed and worked out her excitement by doing a ragged handstand on Gran's rug.

'Watch out!' Sara waited until Hannah was the right way up again, then held out her hand. 'Now, what did we say? Beauty parlours first, then homework. That was the deal.'

Hannah groaned as Sara led her out. Sara looked back as she closed the door and gave me a complicit wink.

'See what I mean?' Gran leaned towards me. 'Born teacher.'

15

Alan was my brother, but he wasn't an easy man to read, especially not where emotions were concerned.

Gran called him a man's man. An old-fashioned term, but I knew what she meant. He took refuge in practical tasks and his conversation revolved around sport and drinking. When it came to talking about his feelings, he was a closed book. He bottled. Always had.

He didn't often tell us he loved us, but he showed it by quietly fixing our cars, or sorting out a dodgy shelf for Gran or taking her out shopping. I wondered sometimes what he'd have been like if Jackie and Sara had never left. Less damaged, perhaps.

I'd watched him, on and off, at the barbecue on Sunday. He hadn't said very much; so little, in fact, that I wondered what Sara made of him. I hoped she hadn't mistaken his solid quietness for a lack of caring. He'd eaten his way through a burger and sausages and knocked back a few beers. But his eyes had been sharp, homing in on Sara's expression whenever she was busy speaking to Gran or Will, as if he were silently searching for something, seeking out a trace of the child he'd loved.

As he'd left, I'd whispered in his ear, 'You okay?'

He'd just kissed me on the cheek and headed out into the dusk for the walk home. I wondered if he'd stop off at a bar or a late-night supermarket on the way for more drink.

Since then, I'd texted him twice, asking him how he was doing, just trying to check in. No reply.

By Wednesday, I decided to call round to the garage, on the pretext of taking him some lunch. I packed up a plastic box with a load of sandwiches and cold chicken and some leftover rice salad and checked the address on my phone before I headed over.

I hadn't been there since Alan got the job several months ago. The boss, a stout, hard-faced man in a shiny suit, came out of the showroom to greet me. The smile slid from his face when I explained who I was, as if he only had a limited supply of bonhomie and it was strictly reserved for paying customers.

He pointed me grumpily to the workshop around the back of the showroom.

'Alan?' It was dingy in there. The boss must be as stingy with electricity as he was with goodwill.

'Paula?' Alan slid out from under a car, flat on his back on a wheeled trolley. His overalls were grubby, his hands black with oil. He sat up, back rounded, and wiped them off on a bit of rag.

'I bought you some lunch. We're still eating leftovers from Sunday.' I pulled the lid off the container and showed him. He looked without much interest.

I said, 'How are things?'

He shrugged. 'Okay.' He nodded at the car. 'Big job.'

I tried to look sympathetic and hide the fact I didn't care about the car's problems, only his.

'Any chance of a cup of tea?'

Alan pulled back his cuff to check his watch. 'Quick one.'

He rolled his eyes. 'The boss is in a bad mood today. Just for a change.'

I nodded. 'So I gathered. Charm on legs, that one.'

He disappeared through a door at the back of the workshop. I looked around for somewhere to sit. Everything looked filthy. In the end, I spread a carrier bag over a large tyre and perched on top.

Alan came back with two mugs of strong tea and sat next to me, offering me one of the sandwiches from the box, then helping himself to one. He ate in large hungry bites.

'Don't you get a lunch break, then?'

'Technically.' He answered thickly through the bread and ham. 'Just not in reality. Too much work on.'

We sat in silence for a little while, eating. The workshop, one in a row of three, was a poky concrete box. Rusting metal girders stretched overhead, looking down on a mess of dented metal fittings and tools, used parts and heaped tyres. A set of strip lights buzzed. The smell of oil and petrol was overwhelming. It was such a contrast to the bright, airy showroom at the front. I didn't know how Alan could stand spending all day cooped up in here.

He reached for another sandwich and said, 'Go on, then.'

'What?'

He gave me a knowing look. 'Well, you didn't pop round just to feed me, did you? Not that I'm not grateful.'

I opened my mouth to deny it, then said instead, 'I just wondered how you were. About her coming back.' I paused. I couldn't quite say her name to him yet. 'Bit of a bolt from the blue, isn't it?'

He munched hard without looking at me. 'I don't know, really.'

I hesitated. These weren't easy things to talk about. I understood that. But he didn't have long, and I needed to try. 'She's moved in with Gran. Had you heard?'

He didn't react, just carried on eating, his eyes on the car. I couldn't tell if he'd known or not.

'Gran thinks she might go in for teaching.' I picked at a bit of cold rice salad and waited a while. 'So, what did you make of her?'

'Make of her?' His broad, strong shoulders seemed to sag. 'Dunno. It's all a bit of a shock.'

I leaned in and patted his arm. 'I know. It must be. But she's your daughter, Alan. I know you've missed a lot of years. You can't get them back. But this is a fresh start. A chance to get to know her.'

He didn't answer. He looked tired. The dirt had slid into the creases on his face and drawn deep black lines across his forehead and along the sides of his nose and mouth, like a young child's picture of a man.

'If there's anything I can do, ask me, won't you?'

He looked past me towards the front of the workshop, as if he were frightened the boss might be on the way over.

'Thanks, little sis. Message received.' He gestured to the car. 'Anyway, I'd better get on.'

He hauled himself up and headed over to the car again. I watched him lower himself onto his back onto the wheeled platform and slide underneath.

I stood there for a moment, looking down at the oil-streaked bottoms of his trousers, the workman's boots with their frayed laces, one sole flapping where it was peeling away from the toe, all sticking out lifelessly like the legs of the felled witch in *The Wizard of Oz*. Then I clipped the lid back on the leftover sandwiches and left the box there for him, for later.

As I walked away, I thought again of Jackie and what a mess they'd made of their marriage.

If only things had been different. He could have been so much happier. He could have been so much more.

SARA

16

It was weird, being there.

She wasn't sure they'd believe her when she walked up to them in that café and announced she was Sara. Paula seemed uncertain, at first. Sara had seen her furtively checking out the University ID card in her wallet. But, after that, they all seemed to have taken her on board, no questions asked.

She wondered about that: about that need in them for her to be their long-lost girl. About Hannah, so desperate for a friend. About Granny, who opened her arms to her, opened her home, without a qualm. Even Paula, who was so protective of them both, had welcomed her into the family. She was surprised by that. Of all of them, Paula had the most to lose.

Granny had this way of saying something massive in the midst of the utterly mundane. The other day, they'd been chatting about something and nothing over tea, about all the fancy cleaning products on the market nowadays and how much they cost. Granny had been saying that when she was a girl, her mum had used cooking salt to get the burnt bits off pans, and vinegar and old newspaper to clean the windows. Then, from nowhere, she suddenly said, 'You have to understand, lovely, that deception isn't only about cheating another person, it's a betrayal of yourself and, worst of all, it's a betrayal of God.'

Where did that come from? Sara had been too stunned to say a word. She just gaped at Granny who looked calmly right back at her, as if she could see through to her soul. All Sara could think was: *Is Granny trying to say she doesn't trust me?*

A moment later, Granny was on about newspapers again, saying she'd learned recently that old newspaper was actually rather warm, which was why it could act as a sort of blanket for people who were sleeping on the street, as long as it stayed dry.

And then just the other day, Granny had come downstairs with a bundle of dirty tissue paper in her hands. She was holding it with such reverence, Sara thought it must be a sacred relic or something.

Granny had looked over at Sara and given a grin. Impish. 'Come over here a minute, would you?'

Sara put her magazine down and went over to see what she had.

Granny plopped down into a chair, puffing, and opened up the tissue paper in her lap. It was dusty and yellowed with age. Nestled in it was a bit of thin cardboard, about five inches square. It looked as if it had been hacked out of a cereal packet, roughly cut with scissors. A piece of paper, the same size, was glued to the other side. 'Know what that is?' Granny's eyes rose to Sara's face.

It was a tiny orange handprint. A bit smudgy and uneven, the little finger indistinct as if it hadn't been properly pressed down on the paper. So small.

'Do you remember?'

Sara took a breath, then shook her head.

Granny nodded. 'Well, you were very little. Long time ago. Look at those big hands of yours now!'

Sara swallowed hard. She didn't know what to say. The old woman had kept that bit of paper and cardboard for more than two decades, hidden away in the back of some drawer or cupboard. Waiting. She imagined Granny taking it out now and then and sitting with it in her lap, just like this but alone, remembering. She imagined her old heart aching in the quiet. She'd have a cry, probably, and then tell herself not to be so silly, fold the past back in its tissue paper and go to put the kettle on.

All that love.

Granny set it on the arm of the chair and rummaged again in the paper.

Sara didn't see what it was, at first. She thought it was just a scrap of fading ribbon. Granny lifted it to show her. A lock of fine, blonde hair, tied up tightly.

'That was from your first haircut. You were only two and a half. Don't suppose you remember?' She looked at Sara hopefully, but she shook her head. 'You were a bit frightened. All the bustle and big mirrors and the noisy hairdryers. They perched you up on a cushion so you could see and gave you a trim. I begged this bit from your dad.' She held it up, close to Sara's. 'Changed a lot, hasn't it?'

Sara held her breath, suddenly tense, wondering where she was going with this.

'You were such a little blondie in those days. That's how I always imagined you.' She didn't seem to realise how stiff Sara had become. 'Still, things change. That's the way of the world.'

She folded the lock of hair and the handprint back into the tissue paper and set it to one side, to put away later, when she went back upstairs.

Sara went back to her chair and picked up the magazine again, pretending to read, wondering what Granny was really thinking.

Once, when Sara had gone up to bed and closed her bedroom door and could finally be herself, she'd heard

Granny saying her prayers before she settled down to sleep. She didn't mean to eavesdrop, Granny just said them loudly. Maybe she was getting a bit hard of hearing and didn't realise how far her voice travelled. Or maybe, it occurred to Sara, Granny intended her to hear. Granny thanked Him for answering her prayers and sending Sara to her and asked Him to guide and bless her. It gave Sara the shivers to realise she'd prayed for all those years for her long-lost great-grandchild to appear in her life and now she was thanking God that she was there.

It told Sara all she needed to know about Granny's trust. If she literally thought God had sent her, how could she doubt her? It would be downright ungrateful.

Granny had gone on praying for ages. No wonder she was always tired. When she'd finished on Sara, she started on all the lost souls out in the night, the homeless and hungry, the destitute and despairing, and asked Him to help and comfort them too, and to guide home those who were separated from the people they loved. Afterwards, she got going on everyone in the family, one by one, dead and living, but her voice had become gradually softer until Sara couldn't really hear.

Sara sat for a long time, afterwards, looking out at the dark, empty street and the black shadows under the trees where she'd once stood and kept watch on the house, trying to sum up the courage to knock on the door. Granny was right. There were a lot of desperate people out there. She'd already got far more than she'd expected, living there rent-free. She should keep her head down and be grateful to be safe and warm.

It wasn't completely one-sided. Granny didn't take money from Sara, but she did ask her to do jobs around the house, chores that she clearly couldn't manage any more herself. The other day, Sara had to go from room to room taking the lightshades down and washing them all in soapy water. They were filthy, thick with grime and plastered with trapped flies.

She'd asked her to clean all her silver one afternoon – all the stuff she had out on the sideboard, just for show. She never used any of it. Posh silver teapot and little pieces on a tray with fiddly lids and a load of goblets that looked as if they hadn't been used for about a century. Maybe longer. Sara's hands were black by the time she'd finished.

And she ran errands for her, now and then, to get some shopping or pick up medicine from the pharmacy. It was getting harder for her to go out and about herself, she said. It was certainly true that she only left the house now and then: if Alan came round to take her out somewhere, or Paula.

They didn't seem to realise how short of breath Granny got. She went red in the face and wheezed just going up the stairs. Sometimes, Sara found her in the hall, propping herself upright against the banisters or the radiator shelf, fighting for breath. Granny would bat her off with her hand if she tried to help her, miming annoyance because it was too much effort to speak.

In the afternoons, after she'd had lunch, she dozed in her chair, her head nodding, then eventually woke with a jolt and a big pretence of, 'Goodness me, did I drop off?' as if it had never happened before and she was astonished. She was always in bed by ten.

And then there was Alan. Sara couldn't bring herself to call him 'Dad' and, so far, he hadn't asked her to. He seemed knocked sideways by the apparent reappearance of his long-lost girl.

Sara had caught him looking at her that first time they met at the barbecue. He had such a confused expression on his face, as if he couldn't quite figure out where she'd come from after all that time; how it was possible that a three-year-old could have gone away and a fully grown twenty-four-year-old come back in her place.

She had no idea how she was supposed to behave with him, or even what he wanted to talk about.

With Granny, at least she felt she wanted to believe in Sara, that the idea of her precious girl returning from the past was bringing her joy.

It wasn't like that with Alan. He seemed just as much at a loss with Sara as she was with him.

RUTH

17

SIXTY YEARS AGO

Everything they said about me was true. There was no denying it.

I've spent a lifetime going over it. How it happened, why it happened.

I've tried to look back and see with my older eye the young girl I was then, naïve and excitable. Silly, I suppose. Why did I do it? It's the question they all kept asking, in their different ways. The one question I couldn't answer.

I came from a decent, respectable family. That was almost part of the problem, though they'd never understand if I tried to explain. We lived proudly on a neat suburban street, a tidy front yard in a long row of tidy front yards. Pebbledash on the walls that we children were forbidden from picking off (we tried), and a glassed-in porch round the front door which sported a fern plant and a blue and white china umbrella stand with two frilly, permanently furled umbrellas inside, purely for show.

Everything in the house had a history. That table in the lounge came from Great Aunt Nell's. Those dishes once belonged to Nan and Grandad. They bought those wardrobes from Harding's department store when they got married, funded by the pot of money they'd saved together, so many shillings put away each week for two years, scraped out of Mum's shop wages and Dad's job in the bank. They knew how to do without.

I'm making them sound stuffy, aren't I, or pious? That's not fair. They were good, kind, steady people who'd seen plenty of families around them in far worse circumstances than their own and were grateful for the little they had.

They grew up on stories from their parents about the First World War, thankful such horrors would never come again. They were dazed when they found themselves plunged into the Second World War, my dad sent off to India to build bridges and maintain trucks. I've still got a grainy black and white portrait of him in uniform, looking like a film star. He never talked about it much, and I suppose I never asked.

I was eleven when the war ended. I remember bunting in the street and parties with jellies and my mum sitting in the kitchen, crying. I didn't feel much when Dad came home. I pretended, but he seemed such a stranger. I'd got used to it being just me and Mum, I suppose, for all those years. I'd shared her bed if I was scared at night. We ate an early dinner together after school. It was odd when we suddenly had to make room for a grown man in the house.

Looking back now, I can see we didn't have much. But my parents always told me how lucky we were. Having our own neat house with the pocket handkerchief of back garden for Mum's washing and Dad's vegetable plot, and where I could play. Having enough to eat, even if butter and meat and chocolate were still rationed treats. Having Dad, safely home, when so many others we knew had lost fathers and uncles, husbands and fiancés, brothers and sons.

Generation after generation, members of our family had worked hard, endured and paid it forward: each set of children born to stand on their parents' shoulders, able to see a little further into the world, to have a little more.

So, I grew up feeling grateful and maybe a little special – and there was no escaping the guilt too. Ghosts were everywhere, in the bombed-out buildings not yet cleared for redevelopment, in the spaces and silences inside the families we knew, up and down the local streets.

If I try to explain all this, don't think it's an excuse. There is no excuse.

You see, it was a thrilling time too, for those of us growing up after the war. The world was opening up, exploding from black and white to a streaming, vibrant colour in a way my parents didn't seem to understand in our small, sheltered corner of England.

It leaked into my life illicitly. When we were sixteen, Kate at school, with her long, straight hair and secretly painted toenails, started bringing in picture magazines printed on cheap, crinkly sheets, filched from her big sister who'd started work as a secretary and owned everything we dreamed of. We pored over them at dinner time, ogling the film stars with their perfect looks and teeth, lolling against American cars or lying by swimming pools in Hollywood sunshine. The men, so handsome, made my stomach twist, my palms sweat. Afterwards, in class, our fingers were print-stained and, when we put them to our noses, smelled of chemicals and danger.

When I went to Kate's house after school, we pinned the waistbands on our school skirts so tightly we could barely breathe and padded out our hips and shoulders to give us curves, then smeared traces of her sister's lipstick on our mouths and pouted in the mirror. We imagined dates and dancing, sailing to New York on a cruise liner and marrying Americans with money and cars, eating out at restaurants and owning whole drawers of silk stockings. We talked and dreamed, full of unfulfilled longing for things we couldn't even name.

Then Kate dared me. A friend of a friend of hers had told her that some people she knew were getting together for a party. A proper party with drinks and smoking and music and boys. She was going to go, she said, her eyes shining. What about it?

It was thrilling just to think about it. That was enough – the excitement of imagining, of pretending. I didn't really want to go, but all week we whispered in corners, plotting a way to manage it.

'Tell your mum you're coming to my place to do homework,' Kate said. 'Say I've asked you to stay the night.'

I opened my eyes wide. 'She'll be suspicious. She'll never say yes.'

Kate shrugged. 'Just use your brains, can't you? Think of something.'

It was easy, in the end. Too easy. Mum and Dad were having people round for dinner that Saturday evening, entertaining someone important from the bank where Dad worked. Mum was already in a tizz about the cooking, stretching herself to make some fancy dumplings to go with the beef stew and an apple pie with flavoured cream that she clearly hoped would impress them.

'You're planning a midnight feast?' She was sitting at the kitchen table with her fancy colour cookery book open in front of her, making lists. 'And Kate's parents don't mind having you? Well, just don't get crumbs everywhere, will you? And clean your teeth properly before you go to sleep. And remember your manners. Say "Thank you for having me" when you say goodbye. I'd like you home for Sunday lunch.'

She spoke without turning to look at me. I stood there in the kitchen doorway, willing her to be suspicious, to ask more questions, feeling my heart thud. I wanted to be found out, then, before it was too late.

That would be my get-out. 'I'm in big trouble,' I could moan to Kate. 'They didn't believe me. No way I can come now.'

But it turned out, in my case, that all our talk about convincing our parents, covering our tracks, had been redundant. Mine trusted me. My mother, head bowed, muttering to herself as she wrote out ingredients, didn't seem to realise what danger I was facing, that I was poised on the edge of an abyss.

I opened my mouth, ready to blurt it out, to tell her the truth.

She scraped back her chair and crossed the kitchen to rummage for dishes, checking what she had. Nan and Grandad's cut-glass dessert bowl. Great Aunt Lucy's best plates. She started as she turned back, as if she'd forgotten I was there. 'Are you going down with something?' She blinked at me, finally taking notice. 'You look a bit flushed.'

I didn't have the heart to explain it was guilt tinged with excitement because I was telling such terrible lies.

18

Kate's mum was younger than mine and more relaxed. On Saturday afternoon, she washed her hair and then put it in rollers, sitting in the garden in her dressing gown while it dried in the last, long fingers of sunshine. She smoked lazily, her cigarette dangling in the corner of her mouth as she painted her nails, her long, shapely legs propped up on the edge of the patio step.

Kate and I hung around, nervous.

'Where are you off to tonight, Mum?'

Her mum shrugged. Kate said her mum and dad always went out somewhere on a Saturday night – to the pictures, usually, with fish and chips on the way home.

'What are you two up to?'

Kate shrugged. 'Homework. Can she stay over, Mum? Keep me company while you're out.'

She peered, considering. 'If it's alright with her mum and dad.'

I nodded. 'It is, Mrs Wilson. They don't mind.'

She pulled a face. 'Well, if you like. Don't stay up late, you two. Help yourself to biscuits if you get peckish. You'll be alright on the floor, love?'

They kept a dank mattress under Kate's bed for visitors. I'd stayed before.

'Perfectly alright, thank you, Mrs Wilson.'

We sat in Kate's bedroom with our books open on her carpet, pretending to concentrate on homework, and listened to first her big sister, then her parents, get ready to go out. Shouts rang up and down the stairs. Her sister's high-pitched shriek as she hunted for her hairbrush, her new jacket. She was courting, Kate said. A young man she'd met at a dance. Then the thick smell of her mum's floral perfume creeping through the gaps round the bedroom door. Finally, they all hollered goodbye and the front door slammed behind them.

Silence. We sat very still, pens arrested in our hands, listening. Kate fixed me with large, excited eyes. 'Well?'

We rummaged through Kate's wardrobe for clothes, handed down from her sister, that made us feel older, belting our waists as tightly as we could stand and padding our bras with socks. We took it in turns to rummage through her sister's make-up and paint each other's faces: kohl-lined eyes and red lips. Kate brushed out her hair and left it loose, flowing like champagne round her shoulders. She twisted mine into a bun and stuck it with kirby grips. In the mirror, I barely knew myself.

Kate had it all planned out. She stuck a chair under the handle of her bedroom door to make sure her mum couldn't check on us if she came home early, then we climbed out of the window, steadying each other, and down the apple tree, giggling like eight-year-olds, trying not to snag our skirts.

Kate marched me down the street. My heart pounded. I imagined every curtain twitching to look out at us, every front door ready to pop open and a friend of her parents to shout: 'Where do you think you're going, dressed like that?'

We headed for a district on the far side of the parade of shops where Mum went shopping for food every few days. It was more rundown that our road, a rougher part of town. At the end, Kate led me down a narrow alley, thick with shadows, then across an estate.

'Come on!' She rolled her eyes at me. 'Keep up.'

Without even realising, my pace had slackened as I hung back. 'Where is it?'

She shrugged. 'Nearly there.'

We emerged onto a dark road. Ahead, a gap between the houses showed a cutting, opening onto a piece of waste ground. I forced myself to follow her, feeling my clumpy school shoes sink into the grass. From a copse of trees, over to one side, a male laugh drifted on the cool evening air.

Kate said, 'I think that's them.' She sounded uncertain.

'I thought it was a party?' I grabbed her arm, cold and tight in my stomach. I just wanted to say: *Let's go home.*

But before I could speak, Kate pulled away. 'That's her. Daphne. Look!'

Daphne was perched on a fallen tree, swigging from a bottle of cider. She lifted a lazy hand to greet us as we approached. She was older than us, or at least looked it, and more worldly-wise, dressed in slacks and a low-cut blouse that hinted at the pale mounds of large breasts. Her hair was thick and wavy, and her eyes shone in the half-light.

'You came, then. Wasn't sure you would.' Her voice was deep, and her words sounded like a taunt.

Kate indicated me over her shoulder with her thumb. 'This is my friend.'

'Hello, friend of Kate.'

I shifted my weight from one foot to the other, dying with embarrassment. Young men, standing round under the trees, had turned to stare. Their eyes scalded me, I felt it, even as my cheeks burned, too shy to look.

'This is Ted and Adam and that's John and that guy over there, he's Stephen. The dearly departing.'

Kate made an odd sound, a sort of strangled laugh, and reached out a hand for the cider bottle. She took a few swallows, then handed it to me.

I didn't drink cider. I didn't drink anything in those days. I put it to my lips and felt it burn its way down my throat, tried not to splutter as I handed it back.

'Smoke?' Daphne offered her cigarette to Kate. I watched as she took a drag, then blew the smoke straight out again. She didn't gag or cough. I was impressed.

A mocking male voice said, 'You need to breathe it in, love. Not much point, otherwise.'

Daphne said, 'Oh, shut up, Adam. Leave her alone.'

Kate found a place to sit, further along the tree trunk, and settled herself, gesturing to me to come and sit beside her. I scurried to her side, wondering why I was there, what I'd do if one of them tried to talk to me, how soon we could get home again.

Kate said, 'What did you mean? Dearly departing?'

Daphne nodded across. 'Poor Stephen's off to do his duty. Next week.'

Kate blinked. 'Duty?'

Daphne tipped back her head, showing a long stretch of white throat, and blew out smoke. 'National Service. Crawling through ditches and firing guns and all that.'

One of the young men said, 'Poor bugger.'

Another cuffed him lightly on the shoulder. 'Yeah, alright for you, Ted. College boy.'

Daphne said softly, 'Ted's exempt. He's off to study engineering.'

I concentrated on trying to hide my dowdy school shoes and white socks under dried leaves, dying with awkwardness. I wanted to get up and go home, but I couldn't. I was stuck,

pinioned here for as long as Kate wanted to stay. I was so terri-
fied, I shook.

Kate had kept her word. We were out with cider and cigarettes and real young men. What had I expected? A grown-up
party in a house, I suppose, like the pictures in the magazines,
with music and dancing and snacks served by ladies with tiny
waists that exploded into full skirts. Clean-cut young men in
suits.

Kate and Daphne were engaging with Ted and Adam, an
aggressive process of small-arms fire back and forth, short sharp
retorts and jibes, designed to sound cool and clever. They
seemed good at it.

I shrank against the log, my body rigid, and prayed no one
would notice me. If I could just get out of this. If I could just get
home without humiliation. I thought of Mum, serving her beef
stew and Dad, in his best suit, making small talk. I ached for
them. I'd never lie again.

The log creaked. I started. One of the young men had
approached quietly from behind us and sat now on the other
side, but facing out the other way, his shoulder almost touching
mine.

'So... you're friends with Daphne?'

His voice was soft. I forced myself to turn to look at him. He
looked away at once and, despite the darkness, he seemed to
flush. I realised with a rush that he was as nervous as I was.

'Kind of.' I shrugged. 'And you're Stephen.'

Kate and Daphne were focused on the others, their loud
voices drowning us out.

I took a deep breath. 'So, you're going away?'

'Worse luck.' He scuffed at the ground, his back rounded.
'What's the point, now the war's over? Running around playing
soldiers for two years.'

I thought about that. 'You never know. It might be alright.'

He twisted further round to me and handed me the bottle

he'd been drinking from. He nodded at Kate. 'You two are friends then?' He narrowed his eyes. 'You're different. Quieter.' He gestured at Kate and open and shut his thumb against his fingers in a comic blah-blah-blah gesture which only I could see, then grinned. 'Not my type.'

In books I'd read, when a girl and boy hit it off, they chatted all evening; the conversation never flagging as they delightedly discovered how much they had in common: books, films, ideas, marvelling at how easy it felt to share their innermost thoughts. I'd like to say it was like that with Stephen, but it wasn't at all.

We just sat there, listening to Daphne and Kate burbling on in their talking match with the other lads, feeling the chill rise from the ground as the evening wore on, stealing small shy glances at each other, close enough that I could smell the alcohol on his breath, the sweat that stuck his shirt to his chest.

I found myself grinning for no reason. The occasional swigs of cider warmed me from inside and made my fingers numb and tingling. I tried to learn his features, so I'd remember them. He had short dark hair that stuck up from his scalp in spikes and a thin face with large brown eyes. Intelligent eyes, I decided. We didn't say much.

Later, Daphne got abruptly to her feet and disappeared into the trees with Ted. Then Adam came over and said, 'Shove up, then,' to me. He took my place beside Kate, his arm snaking along the back of the log so it was almost around her. It only seemed natural for me to climb over to the other side of the log and perch beside Stephen.

My body stayed rigid with tension, alert to every sound, every movement, but he didn't try anything on. We just sat there, happy to be silent, the line of his thigh warm beside mine.

'What time is it?' Behind me, Kate jumped to her feet.

Stephen checked his watch, squinting in the darkness. 'Can't see. Ten, maybe? Ten to ten?'

'Ten! Bloody hell!' Kate waved at me. Her face was flushed

and her movements slightly uncoordinated. 'We've got to go. My mum'll kill me if she finds out.'

I jumped up too and the trees around me swayed.

'Steady.' Stephen reached out a hand, a firm grip on my arm. 'I'll walk you back if you like—?'

'That's okay.'

'It's no bother.'

Kate had already gone striding off across the grass. I hurried after her, and Stephen lolloped along at my side. He was broader and taller than I'd realised, and I felt a sudden shiver, feeling him so close.

He said, 'Here!' and when I paused and half turned to see what he meant, he caught hold of my hand in his and we carried on walking like that, strangely and stiffly joined. My hand, unaccustomed to being in someone else's, seemed separate from me, my arm tense. I didn't dare look at him, he was too close. I kept my gaze fixed on the space between Kate's shoulder blades.

When we reached the end of Kate's street, I said, 'I've got to go now.'

He tugged on my hand, jerking me back, off guard.

'Can I see you again?' His voice was husky with nerves.

I blinked at him, speechless.

'I mean, before I go,' he said. 'Monday, maybe?'

I hesitated, not wanting to say no but wondering how I'd ever contrive to get away a second time.

He said, finally, 'Well, I'll be there, at the log, at seven on Monday evening. It's up to you.'

He lunged for me and kissed me clumsily on the lips. It wasn't the romance I'd imagined. His lips were dry and a line of bristle just above them scraped my skin.

But it was a kiss, just the same. My first.

19

We made it. Back up the tree and in through the window. The chair was still in place. The house was silent. No one knew.

We wiped off the smudged make-up and got ready for bed, then made up the mattress on the floor with sheets and scratchy blankets and an old eiderdown.

We lay near each other in the dark. The light fitting above my head blurred and swam as I blinked up at it.

Kate said, 'I liked Adam, did you? He got a bit forward, though. He tried to put his hand up my skirt. Cheeky. That's why I left in such a hurry.'

I considered this. She didn't sound upset. She sounded excited.

She leaned out of bed towards me and said, 'What about yours?'

My stomach twisted. *Mine.* 'He's called Stephen,' I said dreamily. 'I liked him.'

I liked too the fact he was going away very soon. He seemed the perfect boy to meet. Someone I could think about in the evenings. Someone whose name I could carve inside my desk. Someone I could talk to the other girls about, wistfully, as if I had secrets to keep. But someone who wasn't actually around to make demands on me and complicate my life.

Kate said carefully, 'Did he like you? Did he say?'

I smiled to myself in the shifting darkness. 'He wants to see me again. On Monday.'

'No!' Kate hung further out of bed, trying to see my face. 'Really? You're joking!'

I shrugged, trying to act nonchalant but glowing with pleasure. I didn't often impress Kate. 'Seven o'clock. That's what he said.'

'On Monday?' Kate was thinking it over. 'But that's so soon. He must be really keen.'

'He hasn't got long. He's going away. National Service.'

Kate clapped her hands together. 'That's so romantic. Lucky you. Just think – you can write him love letters, and he'll carry your photo close to his heart.'

'Hardly.' I rolled my eyes. 'He's not going into battle. He'll be doing five-mile runs or digging ditches or something, silly.'

'Even so.' A rustle of bedclothes told me that Kate had pulled herself back into bed.

After a while, I said, 'Anyway, I might not go.'

'What do you mean?' She sat upright, silhouetted against the curtains. 'You must!' She twisted back to me, propped up on her elbow, her hair cascading. 'What's the matter? You said you liked him.' She hesitated, considering. 'Did he try it on?'

'No.' Then I hesitated, thinking I'd sounded too prudish, that I'd underplayed my hand. 'Well, we kissed.'

'Really? What was it like?'

'Alright.' I thought again of his dry lips and scratchy stubble. Did I want him to kiss me again? I wasn't sure I did, really. He might try if I went to meet him.

'Only alright?'

'What do you want me to say? It's private!'

We fell silent for a few moments. I was beginning to wish I

hadn't told her. She had a habit of taking things over, and I needed to make up my own mind. Besides, my eyes were closing. I wanted to get some sleep.

'Is it your mum you're worried about?' Kate went on. 'Tell her you're coming round to mine. I'll cover for you. Say we've got to work on something together.' She considered. 'Just don't stay out too late, will you, or they'll come here looking for you and the game'll be up.'

My stomach fluttered. I tried to remember exactly what he looked like. What he sounded like. What he smelled like. I wondered if he was thinking about me, right that minute. I wondered if he was imagining kissing me, maybe for a little longer next time. Maybe he was shy too. It took a lot of guts for a boy to ask a girl out, everyone said so. It wasn't kind to stand someone up.

'I'll think about it,' I said. 'I'm not sure.'

I closed my eyes and start to float into sleep. I wasn't sure I would go on Monday. But right then, it was exciting to imagine. It made me feel special. Chosen, at last.

'Well, I am.' Above me, Kate's bed creaked as she settled. 'Poor lad. Of course you're going.'

PAULA

20

PRESENT DAY

'By the way, I've got an interview.'

Will looked up from his meal. 'An interview?'

'For a job. At the art school.' I shrugged my shoulders. 'I probably won't get it, but still...'

Will was watching me closely. 'You didn't tell me you were applying for jobs.'

I shrugged. 'Not *jobs*. A job. Assistant manager. It only just came up.'

He focused his eyes on the mess of half-eaten cottage pie and salad on his plate. He looked thoughtful, frowning slightly.

'I've been meaning to tell you. I know it's a big step. I wanted to talk about it.' My voice softened. 'But there hasn't been a good time. I feel as if I've hardly seen you.'

He loaded another forkful of mince and potato, then lifted it to his mouth. I knew that closed look, that steady blink. He was processing something, something he didn't want to share.

Maybe he felt under attack. But it was true. I *had* hardly seen him.

He'd come home late the last few evenings, his face tight, hardly speaking to Hannah or me. He'd eaten dinner quickly, often with the news on, then disappeared to his study. It was only because I'd made a point of setting the table in the kitchen tonight that we were talking now. What was I supposed to do – relate with him by text message?

I took a deep breath. 'It's admin, basically, part-time, three days a week. I think I could fit the hours round Hannah. I just thought it was worth putting my hand up for it, you know.'

He carried on eating for another mouthful. Finally, he said, 'But why? Why now? I thought—'

'It's not a big deal.' I set down my knife and fork. I guessed what he was probably thinking, but I couldn't spell it out. Not if it was about having another child. It was too difficult. 'I just think I'd enjoy it. I could get to know the artists properly and maybe take another class or two. It's cheap if you're on staff.'

'I didn't know you wanted to take more classes.' Will's voice had suddenly gone very quiet. As if we were discussing something far more serious than a few art classes.

I swallowed. 'It's just something I'm thinking about. Now Hannah's that bit older.'

He gave me an odd look. 'You should have said.'

I blew out my cheeks, exasperated. 'When? You're hardly here.'

Will didn't answer. He just finished his meal, scraped back his chair and stacked our plates in the dishwasher.

I got up too and cleared away our empty water glasses. 'Anything else? Fruit?'

He shook his head, already reaching for the coffee pot and pouring himself a mug. 'Just coffee. I'm going to have to work this evening.' He turned and tried to smile, but the effort it took was worse than if he'd just frowned.

'Again?' I hesitated. 'What's going on at work?'

'Everything.' He shook his head. 'We've got an audit coming up, apparently. I'm trying to help Penny sort out the paperwork. Rachel left everything in a mess when she walked out. Staff records, building accounts...' He sighed. 'We need to get every-thing up to date.'

I nodded sympathetically. Paperwork wasn't exactly Will's passion. 'Anything I can do?'

He leaned back against the worktop for a moment and sipped his coffee. 'Not really.' He paused, then added as an afterthought, 'Thanks, anyway.'

He looked haunted. He'd always been passionate about medicine, about keeping abreast of new research, and he really cared about his patients. But the business side of the practice left him cold. It didn't help that they'd had a run of bad luck with administrators. Rachel was the latest in a series who'd simply given notice after a year or so and walked out.

I hesitated. This just wasn't right. We needed time together, all three of us. A break. 'Maybe we could get away this week-end? Take off on Friday and stay a couple of nights at the coast? What do you think? Brighton, maybe? Hannah would love it.'

Will answered at once, too quickly. 'I can't, I'm afraid. I'm out Friday night, remember?'

I stared. 'Are you?'

'That medical conference on Friday. One of the drugs companies is organising a dinner afterwards, remember?' His eyes were fixed on his coffee. 'I'm sort of expected to attend.' His eyes flicked briefly to my face, then back to his coffee. 'I did mention it.'

I didn't remember. Already, Will was pushing away from the counter and heading for the door, coffee in hand.

As he left, I said, 'Try not to work too late.'

He didn't answer. His feet sounded heavily on the stairs as he headed up to his study.

21

Hannah's mood changed as we approached the school gates. We'd walked hand in hand, as always, and she'd chattered away about computer class and an art project she was working on, her backpack bouncing lightly on her back.

The playground cacophony hit us as we turned the final corner. A heady mix of screams and shrieks and the slap and pounding of dozens of pairs of running feet. A heap of school-bags sat at the far end of the tarmac. Small bodies flew back and forth, swirling, arms flailing and wheeling as they chased each other. There was a football or two in the mix somewhere, thumped back and forth in the midst of the chaos. Some of those playing Tag had pulled their arms out of their coats and jammed them on their heads, flowing free behind them, like superhero capes.

Hannah's flow of chat stopped abruptly. She clutched my hand a little harder and shrank against me. We slowed our pace, heading towards the gates and the teacher on duty there. Hannah and her friends seemed so old at times, when they gossiped about fashion or pop music. Here, charging around outside, they all looked like infants again.

Lizzie's mum, Moira, already turning away from the gates, gave us a cheery smile. 'Morning!' She nodded down at Hannah. 'Hi, Hannah!'

I grinned back as she passed. 'Hey, Moira. How are things?'

We were acquaintances, rather than friends, but I knew Moira better than some of the others. She usually made the effort to come along to the coffee meetups I helped organise, and had served on the summer fair committee at the end of last year.

We reached the teacher. I crouched down to Hannah to kiss her and say goodbye. Other children were pelting in past us. Hannah's eyes were anxiously scanning the playground. She hung back, still holding my hand tightly.

'Okay?' I smoothed her hair from her forehead and kissed her cheek. 'Have a super day.'

She didn't answer. We looked together at the mass of moving children.

I said, 'Are you looking for Lizzie?'

Hannah nodded, then said quietly, 'She's over there. With Susie.'

I looked. The two girls were marching across the playground, hand in hand, giggling. They exuded confidence. I could see why Hannah, always easily hurt, seemed wary of dashing over to them. I wondered how they'd greet her – if she'd be embraced and included in whatever game they were playing, or if she'd be shut out.

'Lorna's over there, on her own, look.' I pointed towards another girl from their year, a more studious child who was sitting cross-legged, reading. 'Why not go and say hi to her?'

Hannah shook her head, took a deep breath and let go of my hand. She mumbled 'Good morning' to the teacher on the gate, then pushed herself out into the crowd, heading for Lizzie and Susie.

I lingered, trying to see how it went. Susie and Lizzie had

threaded their arms around each other's waists. They were too far away for me to hear what was said as Hannah joined them, but I saw them turn, noted the brassy look on Susie's face and Lizzie's sudden smirk and felt the painful hesitation in Hannah as she stood there, shifting her weight from foot to foot. Everything about her seemed to be pleading with them to be kind, to let her join in.

I turned and walked slowly away, thinking back to when I was that age myself. It wasn't easy, learning how to navigate friendships. I wondered how I could help Hannah to build her confidence or maybe get closer to other girls in her year. Lorna seemed a sweet kid. I liked her mum too.

I headed over early to the art school to get ready for my stint volunteering in the café. The baker's crate was already sitting in the entrance hall, packed with fresh muffins and pastries. I was just hoisting it up when Jorge hurried past.

'You get my email?' He gave me a cheery grin. 'About the interview?'

I nodded. 'I'll be there. Thanks, Jorge.'

He called back over his shoulder as he disappeared into the far corridor. 'Nothing to worry about.'

I set off up the flights of stairs to the rooftop studio and the café, soothed by the smell of the warm muffins rising through the paper. I wished Jorge hadn't dashed off so soon. I'd have liked to ask him a few questions about it all, including how many people were shortlisted. I shook my head. Maybe if I bumped into one of the regulars in the café, I'd ask them. I didn't want the whole school to know I'd applied, but, on the other hand, they might have good intel.

I put the radio on and listened to music as I went through the motions, opening up the shutter that closed off the hatch when the café wasn't open, switching on the boiler to heat hot water for tea and coffee, getting out the serving plates and baskets and filling them with the fresh bakery products I'd just lugged up all those stairs. I arranged those to one side of the counter and, on the other, put out trays with all the usual cupboard items: crisps and wrapped biscuits and chocolate bars.

We ought to expand the café. That was one of my ideas in the pitch I was already planning in my head to present at interview. What we had now was basically a glorified tea-trolley, crammed into a space not much bigger than a walk-in cupboard and served through a hatch. But we could easily develop it.

There were plenty of decent tables and chairs on the other side of the hatch and, off to one side, along the edge of the studio, a narrow balcony with views over the railway and the backs of the houses that looked onto the tracks. The art school could actually make a bit of money if we made more effort and served simple lunches here: most of the women who came were more interested in deli salads and fresh fruit than brownies and packets of peanuts.

I carried on setting up. There was a familiar rhythm to these mornings. They started with a flurry of activity before the main class started, as students emerged from the top of the stairs, some panting and red-faced after the climb. Now, some early arrivals stopped off at the hatch for a coffee and occasionally a pastry, then gradually they all funnelled in through the studio door.

Once class started, I tidied up and made myself a coffee, then set out rows of empty cups, saucers and teaspoons along the counter, filled a jug with milk and then readied the tea and coffee pots. With everything ready for the next rush, I wandered over to the balcony door and gazed out across the rooftops, killing time until nearer the mid-lesson break.

The sky was dull with cloud. I stood close to the glass and watched a plane, too far away for its roaring engines to be heard, climb steadily as it made its ascent from Heathrow Airport.

Will hadn't come to bed until after two last night. I'd stirred as he slid silently under the covers. He lay still, keeping to his own side of the bed. I'd reached an arm to the bedside table to check the time and he'd turned his back on me, a dark hunched shape in the gloom.

I hadn't said anything. I'd pretended to sink straight into sleep again. His breathing had deepened and thickened. I stayed awake for a while, anxious, worrying about what was happening between us. We hadn't had the most dynamic sex life since Hannah came along, but we always used to hold each other at night, even if we were both too tired to do much more. Now we seemed to be giving up on that too.

'Are you open?'

A deep male voice from behind me startled me out of my thoughts.

It was so unexpected I nearly dropped my coffee, but I knew exactly who it was as, flustered, I turned around to reply.

22

Hugo the life model was clothed now, in faded jeans and a well-worn leather jacket. 'Sorry.' He looked as taken aback as I was. His cheeks flushed. His hair flopped across his forehead, and he lifted an automatic hand to push it away, then pointed vaguely at the café. 'I mean, did I...? Um, are you...'

I nodded, suddenly brisk. 'Yes, of course. Sorry. I was miles away.' I strode back into the café booth and reappeared from behind the hatch. 'What can I get you?'

'Just a black coffee, please.'

I turned my back to him as I made his coffee, but my face stayed hot. I felt his eyes.

'Anything to eat?' I set the coffee down on the counter in front of him.

'No, thanks.' He pulled a bank card out of his back pocket, but I wafted it away.

'On the house. It's only a coffee. Anyway, you're kind of staff, aren't you?'

'Thanks.' He looked pleased and put his card away again. 'I didn't know you worked here.'

I leaned forward, elbows on the counter, as he sat down at

the nearest table. 'I don't really. I'm just a volunteer, once a week.'

'Anyway, I'm glad I bumped into you.' He sipped at his coffee. 'I didn't get the chance to say thank you for the drawing.'

'You're welcome.' I remembered the way I'd fled, like Cinderella, at the end of the class. 'No one's ever wanted one before.'

'You're good. I'm not just saying that.' He looked thoughtful. 'Well, I'm no expert, but, you know, I think so.'

There was a short silence. I looked past him to the wall clock. Another twenty minutes before they came pouring out of class for break.

I picked up a cloth and did some spurious wiping. 'So, what are you doing here? Don't tell me that lot's booked you to model for them in the second half.' I nodded at the closed studio doors. 'They're usually more interested in vases of flowers and bowls of fruit than anything with a pulse.'

He grinned. 'No, I just needed somewhere quiet for an hour or so. Somewhere to hide.'

I raised my eyebrows. 'Have you robbed a bank?'

'Not exactly.' He pulled a face and hesitated. 'I've got a big audition tomorrow.'

'More TV?'

'Stage.' He leaned closer, as if he were sharing a secret. His eyes were alight. 'It's only a tiny part, but it's West End. They won't say who's the lead. Rumour is, might be Daniel Radcliffe.'

'Harry Potter!' I laughed, and he grimaced as if to say: *Bet the poor guy gets that all the time.*

'He's good. And if it is him, it's bound to get a lot of press.'

I nodded. 'So you're a bit nervous?'

'Nervous? Me?' He made a comic show of bravado, then let it collapse. 'Yeah. I thought I might find a quiet corner here to practise a few audition pieces. My flatmate's a cellist and, lovely as he is, if I hear scales one more time, I may strangle him.'

'That wouldn't be good.'

'Exactly.' He tipped back his head to drink. His jawline was dark with emerging bristle, the skin of his throat smooth. I found myself smiling. He made me feel lighter, somehow. Youthful. Fun.

He pulled a sheaf of crumpled papers out of his jacket pocket and smoothed them out on the tabletop. 'You wouldn't mind, would you, if I had a read-through? I'll keep the volume down.' He turned a dog-eared page. 'I'm thinking, bit of Shakespeare? Maybe *Richard III*?' He hunched his back and cocked his head on one side, hamming it up. '*Now is the winter of—*'

'Maybe not.'

'Ah.' He turned to the next page. 'Bit of Stoppard? I've got a speech from *Arcadia*. Quite intense.'

I narrowed my eyes. 'Haven't you got a standard audition piece?'

He took another sip of coffee. 'It's been adverts, mostly. I mean, recently. They're a bit less fussed. More interested in how you look than how you act. Within reason.'

I hesitated. 'Do the Shakespeare for me. Properly. No hunchback.'

He blew out his cheeks. 'I was kidding about *Richard III*. Just wanted to make you laugh.' He picked up the first sheet of paper again and stared at it. 'It's Romeo, actually. I know it backwards, but, I dunno, maybe I'm a bit old now?' His hand lifted to flick away the floppy hair from his eyes. He did it so often, he barely seemed to notice.

'Give it a go.'

He cleared his throat, then set down the sheet and turned his gaze on me.

'But, soft! What light through yonder window breaks?
It is the east and Juliet is the sun. Arise, fair sun, and—'

His voice was gentle and caressing. I shivered. It was the intensity in his eyes, as well as the beauty of the poetry. He didn't sound as if he were reciting well-worn lines. He spoke as if he were really thinking aloud, a young man falling desperately, hopelessly in love for the first time. With me.

I broke eye contact and stared down at the counter, straightening the packets of biscuits, closing my ears to the hypnotic rhythm of the language.

At the end of the speech, he stopped. An awkward silence. When I looked up, the spell broken now, his eyes were anxious.

'Was it awful?' He seemed so hesitant. 'It was, wasn't it?' He shook his head. 'I knew it. I need something more mature, older. It's just a sort of comfort speech for me – I've been doing it since drama school.' He went back to rustling through his papers.

'I thought it was wonderful.' I swallowed hard. 'I don't know what they're looking for but...' I tailed off.

He grinned at me, and I held his gaze, then smiled back. From behind him, in the art studio, a sudden movement caught my eye. The women were shifting in their seats, getting ready for break time.

'Hey! I've got to get going.' I turned and started filling the tea and coffee pots from the hot water boiler. 'You ought to know, those artists are pretty vicious if you stand between them and their free hot beverage.'

'Ah.' He scraped back his chair and got to his feet. 'Got it. I'd better look for another spot.'

I bustled about, checking everything was ready. 'Ask at reception. They'll point you to an empty studio, if they can. Say you work here.'

'Thank you.'

I looked up. He was still there, standing at the counter, watching me.

'There was something else I wanted to ask.' He paused. 'Something I might have asked on Monday, if you hadn't raced screaming from the building.'

'Not exactly screaming but—'

He spoke over me. 'Can I take you for a coffee sometime? I mean properly, not just here. Somewhere they'll actually take my money.'

Inside the studio, chairs were scratching the flooring as eighteen students moved from their places. A low hum of chatter grew as they neared the door.

His eyes were on mine. I thought of his broad, muscular body and blinked hard.

'Well,' I stuttered, 'I don't know...'

He pulled out a pen and scribbled a number across one of the napkins, then thrust it at me. 'Take that, just in case. No pressure. I just—'

The studio door burst open. The sounds of animated voices and hurrying feet crashed over us both. I pushed the napkin hastily in my pocket, out of sight.

'Good luck tomorrow!'

I didn't know if he'd even heard. He'd already turned abruptly and disappeared, and the hatch was suddenly swamped with customers, reaching for cups, for tea and coffee pots, for jugs of cold milk.

23

At the end of the morning, I handed over café duty to the afternoon volunteer and headed home. My thoughts drifted as I made my way through almost deserted roads towards the high street.

I wondered how Hannah was getting on at school, if she was happy and had someone to play with at lunchtime. I thought about Will and how oddly he'd been behaving all week. And I thought about Hugo.

He'd unsettled me. I wouldn't see him, of course. I hesitated – well, not outside the art school. That wouldn't be right. But I couldn't help it if our paths crossed naturally inside the school, if he modelled for the class again or came to the café. The bulge of the folded napkin, his number scrawled across it, rubbed my hip as I moved.

I'd just reached the corner and was turning to enter the high street when I caught sight of a familiar figure on the far side of the road. Sara was standing outside the bank, waiting for her turn at the cash machine.

I slowed down, wondering whether to cross the road to say

hello. Something furtive in the hunch of her shoulders made me hesitate. Her hands were thrust deep in her pockets.

The man in front of her moved away, stowing cash in his wallet and folding it into his jacket. Sara stepped briskly forward, pushed in a bank card and stabbed in a code. She was dressed in the same jeans as always, a vivid red cotton top just visible beneath her jacket.

A moment later, the card popped out again and she waited as the machine whirred and rolled out a stash of cash. I was too far away to see what denomination the notes were, but it looked like a lot of money. Sara zipped it quickly away in the inside pocket of her jacket, then turned and headed off down the road at a brisk trot.

I was walking home in the same direction on the other side of the road and glanced in her direction now and then, expecting her to see me eventually. She didn't. She walked so quickly, she soon outpaced me. Her head bobbed off into the crowd and disappeared. I hurried on, telling myself it was none of my business, that I should think no more about it.

I had a long wait further down the high street at the pedestrian crossing, where the lights took forever to change. She suddenly reappeared on the far pavement. She was carrying a bulging shopping bag, as if she'd just stacked up on groceries. For her and Gran, I assumed. The lights changed at last, and I crossed over, slotting into the stream of pedestrians some way behind her.

I didn't have the energy to run and catch her up, but I kept her in view in the crowd. There was something intent in the way she moved, dodging around anyone moving more slowly than she was, pushing past women with buggies.

At the top of the street, she turned off to the right, heading away from the road that led towards Gran's house. In the opposite direction, in fact. When I reached the same corner, I hesitated and stood looking after her. I didn't need to go down there, it was out of my way, but I was puzzled. Something just seemed odd about her manner, her tension, her hurry.

I turned and started to follow, curious to see where she was going.

As she led me away from the main shops, the outlets gradually expanded. A carpet store as big as a warehouse. A double-fronted independent pharmacy. A Thai restaurant with a take-away attached.

Sara turned sharply left into a steep road that would, partway down, rise in a hump as it crossed the railway, then lead on towards the Catholic school and a corner newsagent and, beyond, to a latticework of suburban residential streets. These were Victorian terraces too, a row of tall, thin houses huddled tightly together, but the area was more rundown than Gran's.

A little girl, peddling frantically on a tiny tricycle, came speeding towards me on the pavement. A young woman, presumably her mother, ran to catch up as the child hurtled down the slope. I stepped out of the way as the girl rattled past, her eyes shining.

When I lifted my eyes to start walking again, Sara had disappeared.

I paused and blinked. The road stretched ahead, empty.

Where was she? There was nowhere for her to go. No shops ahead, and the school's gates were closed. Had she darted into one of the houses? I'd have seen her, surely? Blood banged in my ears. Had she realised I was following her? Had she slipped away from me on purpose?

I carried on along the road, half expecting her to jump out at me from somewhere. I felt suddenly foolish. Why was I even following her? She had every right to ask the same question, to be indignant. I'd carry on along this road until the next corner, I decided, on the far side of the railway bridge, and then turn left and head back to the high street and home.

I was crossing over the railway when my eyes were caught by a movement down below, alongside the tracks. I stood against the low wall and peered over.

A gaggle of people stood down there, spilling out from under the bridge, pressed together on a flattened strip of wasteland at the bottom of a steep grassy bank. A narrow, muddy path led down, like a snaking rope, from the side of the bridge where I stood.

Three of them, two stout women and a man, were perched in an untidy row on the steep bank, knees bent, slightly above the rest. They looked dishevelled and unkempt, their bodies padded out by extraneous layers of greyed clothes. One of the women had a woollen hat planted on her head, despite the fact it wasn't cold enough to justify one. Tendrils of silvery-grey hair stuck out from under the rim.

Another two, a man and a woman, were on their haunches close to the track, crouched over a weak, makeshift fire. One poked it listlessly with a stick. A thread of grimy smoke rose in a thin column above their heads. An abandoned shopping trolley sat behind them, half-filled with bulging plastic bags. There was an air of languid squalor hanging over the whole scene. The sight made me wince. I could almost smell the stale sweat and filthy, unwashed clothes.

They were turning in the same direction, away from me, faces lifted towards the slim figure now picking her way down the mud path to join them, shopping bag dangling from one hand.

As Sara stepped down onto the flattened earth beside the trolley, the group shifted and made space for her amongst them, as if they were expecting her, as if they were greeting an old friend.

A moment later, there was a rattle and hum along the rails. A train approached, bursting around the bend towards us, gathering speed rapidly as it travelled away from our local station and on down the line to the next. A piercing whistle sounded. I blinked as it threaded itself through the tunnel beneath me and instinctively drew back. Once it had passed and the silence mended, I peered down again.

The group hadn't moved. Sara was dipping into the bag, handing out bread and packets of biscuits to one and then another, chatting as she handed them round. The only change was the column of rising smoke from their meagre fire which, agitated by the sudden movement of the train, was swarming this way and that, expanding into thinning clouds as it dispersed.

24

It was a strange encounter and it stayed with me all afternoon.

I'd got the impression Sara didn't have much money. That was Gran's thinking, surely, when she invited her to move in and refused to charge her rent. I thought again about the wad of cash she'd taken from the dispenser. Why would she be so free with it, buying all that food and doling it out to the homeless and destitute? It was wonderful to be charitable, but how could she even afford it?

When I picked up Hannah at the end of the school day, I walked her round to Gran's house. She skipped along, excited, and I knew why. It wasn't Gran she was desperate to see, it was Sara.

'What do you think of Sara?'

Hannah shrugged. 'Nice.'

'She did a great job of your hair the other day.'

Hannah didn't respond.

I tried again: 'I know she helps you do your homework, doesn't she? What else do you two do up there in her room?'

'She lets me play *Magiclands*. Everyone at school's got it.'

She gave me a sharp sideways glance, reading my expression. 'It's really good.'

'What's *Magiclands*?'

'Mum!' She rolled her eyes. 'The computer game. I've told you about it a million times. Can we get it? Please? It's not a lot of money.' She screwed up her face and considered. 'About three pounds, I think. Or maybe thirteen.'

I hesitated. 'I don't want you spending more time on the computer. You're on it enough as it is.'

She reached for my hand and clasped it dramatically. 'I won't! Honestly! I'll stop whenever you say.'

We turned into Gran's road.

Hannah said, 'Please, Mum? Please?'

'Let me have a think about it.'

Sara came to greet us as soon as she heard my key in the door, and she and Hannah went chasing up the stairs together. I hoped they'd get some homework done before they started on this game. Computer games had come on so much since I was a kid. I hated to admit it, but I was totally out of touch. I'd better ask some other mums and find out what this new one was all about and how addictive it seemed.

Gran was puffing as she shuffled through to the kitchen. She looked back and caught sight of me, still standing, staring up the stairs after them.

'Hello, lovely.' The water swooshed out of the tap as she filled the kettle and put it on, then clattered in the cupboard for china mugs. 'Come and have a cuppa with me.'

I wandered through. 'They're playing computer games, apparently.' I picked up a tea towel and idly dried off the dishes on the drainer while Gran fussed round, making the tea. 'I don't know. Hannah still seems young for all that, but she says her friends at school play them. The cool set, anyway.'

Gran pulled out a tea tray and arranged the mugs and the milk jug. 'You've said she's struggling to fit in.'

'She is.'

'Do you remember begging your mum to let you get some game that you had to plug into the TV? Your mum gave in, in the end, but she was quite worried. There'd been something in the news that year about children's health being damaged. Sore thumbs or bad eyesight or something.' She turned to grin at me. 'Didn't seem to do you any harm.' Gran poured boiling water into the teapot and gestured to me to carry the tray through. She made her way slowly back into the lounge, ahead of me. She didn't seem to be moving as easily as usual. Maybe she was just having a bad day.

When we were settled and the tea was poured, I said, 'How's it going, Gran? With Sara.'

Gran didn't look me in the eye. 'Fine. Nice to have a bit of company.'

I thought about the bank and the wad of cash. 'Do you know how she's managing? For money, I mean.'

Gran seemed evasive. 'I'm still not charging her rent, if that's what you're asking.' She paused. 'I haven't been feeling myself just lately. I'm grateful she's here, to be honest.'

I looked around the neat room, the carefully dusted mantelpiece. 'You manage fine, Gran. Everywhere's spotless.'

'She's the one who ran the vacuum round this morning, not me.'

The late afternoon sunlight, streaming in through the kitchen, caught the array of silver on the sideboard and set it sparkling. I got to my feet and strolled across for a closer look.

Gran, watching me, said, 'She did a good job, didn't she?'

I hesitated, looking over the familiar pieces arranged just as they always were. 'I used to love playing with these little sugar tongs.' I lifted the lid of one of the three small pots. I played with those too. And those silver goblets. I admired them now, neatly lined up in two rows. I used to pretend I was a knight who'd come back victorious in battle and was honoured at a great feast. I smiled to myself. I'd never known Gran actually used any of the silver, but it was still part of my childhood, just as it must have been part of hers. 'I'd have polished it for you,' I said. Something roiled deep inside me. An unease. A feeling that something wasn't quite right. 'You should've said.'

Gran shrugged and reached for her mug. 'I know you would, lovely. But you've got enough to do. You've got your own home to run.'

I went back to sit with her and sipped my tea. I thought about Sara. Why had she withdrawn all that cash and headed down to the railway track to the homeless crowd there?

I was just wondering how to raise it with Gran when she abruptly changed the subject.

'Alan popped round last night.' She leaned in meaningfully and lowered her voice. 'All spruced up.'

I raised my eyebrows to invite more. 'Really?' We both knew it wasn't like Alan to bother with his appearance.

'He's taking Sara out this weekend. Saturday night. Dinner.'

I widened my eyes and smiled. 'Good for him.' It sounded as if he'd taken my advice to heart, but it must have been a real effort for him to ask her. 'Any idea where?'

Gran shook her head. 'He didn't say.'

I smiled. 'Hopefully not the King's Arms.' Gran and I both thought he spent far too much time and money in his local pub, a dingy place with stained carpets and the sour stench of hops.

Gran sat for a moment over her tea, considering, looking into middle distance. I waited.

'It might do him a lot of good, you know, if they get on together.' Gran looked thoughtful. 'He's been so lost all these years, since they upped sticks and disappeared. It was a cruel thing to do to him. I always said so. He took it very hard.'

I didn't answer. I was imagining Alan and Sara spending an evening together on their own.

'It might just be the making of him,' Gran went on. 'Having his daughter back.'

I wondered if Alan would welcome advice on things to talk about. Small talk wasn't his forte, and he needed some topics in mind that avoided the one subject they'd both surely find so difficult to discuss: the past.

25

Hannah nagged me all the way home.

'Can we get it, Mum? Please? Please? Sara looked up how much it is and it's only two pounds ninety-nine. I could pay for it with my pocket money if you say yes. Please, Mum? It's really cool. EVERYONE at school's got it.'

I squeezed her hand. 'I just want to find out a bit more about it. You've got to be careful online, Hannah.'

'I KNOW, Mum!' She stamped a few paces with frustration. 'It's perfectly safe. Look, first of all, everyone uses a screen name, see? So, Lizzie is Munchkin34 and Sara is BatGirl345 and I'd be PixieGirl22.'

I smiled, despite myself. 'What if someone else already has that?'

She squirmed. 'So, er, actually Sara checked it out for me. Mum, don't be cross. It's fine. I can choose something else if you like.'

'No, I'm fine with PixieGirl whatever. I'd just need to be sure you're sensible, Hannah. Keep safe and don't run up any big bills.' I raised my hand to stop her as she opened her mouth to interrupt. 'I know, but it can happen by accident. I read about a girl who spent a fortune – tens of thousands of pounds – buying extras in a game and no one even knew about it until it popped up on her mum's bank statement.' I remembered the article. Seventy thousand, gone in a matter of days. The poor girl had no idea what she'd done until it was too late. 'They wouldn't give the money back, either.'

Hannah hurried in front of me, turned and walked backwards, doing her managing-the-parent-face-to-face routine. 'Mum, listen. Seriously. I'm not stupid. I would NOT buy stuff. You don't need to. Firstly, there's tons of fun stuff you can do without all the add-ons. Secondly' – she marked off her points on her fingers as if she were addressing a lecture hall – 'I would not friend anyone I didn't know. I'd only chat to people I know in the *real* world. Like people in our class. You don't have to worry.' She seemed to see something in my expression soften and clasped her hands together with glee. 'So can I? Mum, can we download it right now, as soon as we get home?'

'Calm down, Hannah.'

Already she was squealing to herself and hopping about on the pavement like a demented rabbit.

'Let me have a chat to Daddy about it first, okay? See what he thinks.'

She gave a hectic nod, trying to contain herself in front of me, then ran back to grab my hand again and squeeze it. 'Best mum in the world!' she said.

I smiled. 'I haven't said yes yet.'

26

Will was late home from work again.

He sent a short text, telling me to go ahead and eat without him. No more explanation than that.

That evening, after Hannah had gone to bed, I pottered around the house, folding laundry and distributing it in the bedrooms, unable to settle. I still hadn't emailed the art school to confirm I could attend the interview. I needed to, if I was going ahead. But something was stopping me. Maybe it was just too soon.

I crept into Hannah's room to put away her clean clothes, easing open the drawers and sliding in folded T-shirts, vests and pants. The room was soft with the sound of her breathing. I closed the drawers and crept over to her bed, crouched beside her and gazed. My clever, wonderful, beautiful girl.

Her hair was splayed untidily across the sheet, one side of her face pressed into the pillow. One arm was wrapped around her battered teddy, holding it close. Her legs were bent and tangled up in her duvet so that her bare feet stuck out in the cool. I realised I was smiling, just at the pleasure of seeing her. She seemed so old sometimes, so knowing and yet, at moments like these, unguarded and innocent in sleep, she looked so vulnerable.

I still craved another baby. Will and I both did. Another little girl, just like Hannah. Or a little brother. I didn't mind.

I'd fallen pregnant twice since Hannah was born. The first time, Hannah was only two. I remembered feeling overwhelmed at first at the thought of coping with both her and a new baby. I only realised how much I'd got used to the idea, how much I wanted that second child, when I lost it, only weeks after I'd taken the pregnancy test. Will seemed as gutted as I was. It was all we could do to grieve quietly together, holding each other tightly at night, crying into each other's warm bodies, trying to keep the sadness a secret from Hannah.

The second time, I didn't tell Will. I took the home pregnancy test on my own, cried with joy when I saw the little blue line. It had hurt so much, losing the last baby. This time, I wanted to protect him as well. I imagined how stunned he'd be, how happy when I reached the safety of three months and tearfully broke the news. But that never happened. I lost that baby too and ended up grieving alone.

I hadn't given up, not completely. I still dared to hope, every time my period was slightly late. I still cried when it finally did start. Will and I couldn't talk about it anymore. We were each too afraid of upsetting the other. I tried to be grateful for what we had. Hannah ought to be blessing enough.

I bent down now and kissed her lightly on her warm forehead.

And that was why it seemed so final to go ahead and get a proper job. It felt as if I might be closing the door at last, finally filling the space in my life that I'd kept empty for that other child who never came. Maybe that's how Will felt about it too.

I worked the duvet free from Hannah's legs and she stirred and protested while I rearranged it and covered her up properly again, then crept from the room.

It was almost nine thirty by the time Will's key rattled in the door. I emerged from the kitchen. He looked drawn, setting down his briefcase, then shrugging off his broad-shouldered coat and hanging it in the hall.

'Have you eaten?'

He looked up and it seemed an effort for him to work out what I'd said. 'I'm fine. I might make myself a sandwich. That's all.'

'I'll put the kettle on.'

I hovered around him as he washed his hands at the kitchen sink, soaping palms and backs, between his fingers, with precision, as if he were about to perform open heart surgery and a life might depend on his cleanliness. He seemed barely aware of me, lost in thought.

'How's the paperwork?'

He shrugged and started buttering himself two slices of bread, then opened the fridge door with a sudden suck of rubber and rummaged inside for cheese and pickle. 'Still a mess,' he said. 'How about you? Good day?'

I considered all the things I wanted to talk through with him. Sara and the railway bridge. Hannah and the computer game. The job interview and whether it would really mean we were trying to move on.

I hesitated, looking at the slow stretch of the muscles down his back, the heaviness of his movements, and held it all in.

'Not bad.'

He dropped his sandwich onto a plate and headed through to the lounge. On the sofa, he reached for the TV remote and switched on the set.

'Hannah okay?'

I nodded. 'Fine. Desperate for some online game they're all playing at school. *Magiclands*.'

'Okay.' He made a point of breaking eye contact with the

screen and glancing up at me, but I could tell he wasn't really listening.

I sat beside him as he started flicking through the channels, checking out different programmes for a minute or two before moving on.

'Do you want anything else?' I pointed to his sandwich. 'Cup of tea?'

He shook his head without looking. 'That's okay, thanks.'

I sat close to him. His cheek was speckled with stubble. His eyes were tired.

I said, 'Early start tomorrow?'

'Pretty early.' His eyes slid from the TV to the clock, checking the time. 'It's a full programme.'

I leaned over and touched his face, pulling it round to me, then kissed him lightly on the lips.

'You're working too hard,' I said.

He gave a weary half-smile. 'Something like that.'

'I wish we were having dinner out together tomorrow,' I said. 'Just the two of us.'

'I know,' he said, after what seemed to me to be a moment too long. 'Me too.' He patted my leg, closing off the conversation, and turned back to his sandwich and the TV.

27

I woke in the night with a start and felt across the bed. Empty. No Will. I groped for the phone on the bedside table and checked the time. It was after two. I forced myself out of bed, pulled on a dressing gown and padded out onto the landing. A line of light showed under his study door.

I pushed it open. He was sitting in the armchair in the corner and started when I walked in, as if he'd been dozing or deep in thought. His shirt collar was unbuttoned. A discarded tie lay coiled on his desk.

'You okay?' I took a few steps across the room towards him.

'Fine. Just thinking.' He reached for my hands and kissed them. 'You go back to bed. I'm coming soon.'

I bent down and kissed him on the top of the head, then sloped back to the bedroom, puzzled.

I lay still, willing my heartbeat to slow again, trying to relax so I could drift off back to sleep. I'd be tired in the morning. I thought about Will and how lost he was in work. About Hannah.

The room started to dissolve. I closed my eyes and hung there, drifting, slipping from wakefulness into sleep.

Then it burst into my mind, and the nagging thought that had been eluding me all evening, the sense of something being wrong, the something I couldn't quite identify, exploded into focus.

I opened my eyes and sat up with a jolt, trembling and alert.

RUTH

28

If it hadn't been for Kate, I might never have gone to meet him that second time.

I'd deceived my parents once and got away with it. I didn't want to do that again. It wasn't me. Besides, by the end of the weekend I could barely remember what he looked like. When I thought back, the most I could summon up was the stale smell of cigarettes and his soft voice and the feel of his dry lips scraping mine.

It wasn't love, I decided. Not true love. But, even so, I wrote his name at the back of my pocket diary, row after row of little Stephens, decorated with love hearts. Just looking at them made me tingle.

But Kate was more excited than I was, and she was determined not to let it go.

At school on Monday, we glowed with planning, whispering together every chance we stole. What was I going to wear? How was I going to handle my mum? What should I talk to him about, to make him like me? Our humdrum lives shone with colour.

I didn't really mean to go through with it. It was just

thrilling to have a secret. I didn't want a real boyfriend, just the idea of one to giggle about.

I thought a lot about that later. What if I hadn't gone through with it, after all? I could have pretended. I could have stayed at home and invented a story for Kate, about meeting him. That would have been enough. She'd never have known. But that never occurred to me. I wasn't a girl who was used to lying to anyone. Doesn't that give a sense of how young I was, how very naïve?

I wore my navy-blue school skirt, in the end, as I didn't have much else. I rolled down my socks and untucked my blouse, hoping it made me look devil-may-care. I sucked on my lips and pinched my cheeks and set off to the waste ground with trembling limbs.

I was there early. The log was empty, the area deserted. There was drizzle in the air and a low, light wind creeping through the trees from the river. I sat on the log and settled in for a dutiful wait. I decided I'd count to one hundred and then go home.

One. I was a fool. *Two.* He'd never come. *Three.* Maybe someone had dared him to ask me, just for a joke. *Four.* Maybe he was there, hiding somewhere, watching, sniggering about me with his mates. I peered about, trying to make them out in the shadows between the bushes and trees, flushing with embarrassment at the thought.

Someone was coming. I stiffened. The crack of a twig, ahead. A heavy male footstep. I held my breath. A middle-aged man in a dark overcoat came bustling along, walking his dog. I shrank back, still as a statue, willing him not to see me. The dog snuffled, then caught a scent and ran ahead and they passed. The sound of the man's humming lingered in the air like perfume.

I shifted my weight and made to get up. My legs were cold, my bottom damp from the mossy wood. That was it, then. I'd go home. Kate might laugh at me when she heard, but I could trust her to keep it to herself, I was sure. More fool him, she'd say, or something like that. She'd be secretly pleased. In the race to grow up, to have a real boyfriend, I hadn't pulled ahead, after all.

'Sorry!'

He appeared from nowhere, running out from the trees, panting, red-faced. I stood, staring. I'd almost forgotten what he looked like, stopped believing he was real. He struck me suddenly as very physical, his spiky hair damp with sweat, his jacket flapping loose around his waist, showing a tan leather belt in dark brown trousers. I pulled my eyes away from his groin as if I'd been slapped.

I shrugged, trying to look nonchalant. 'That's okay. I wasn't sure, you know.'

He nodded. 'I ran all the way.' His voice was choppy with breathlessness. 'I wasn't sure you'd come.'

'Well, then.'

Now we were both here, so close to each other, it was all dreadfully awkward. I stood there, looking down at my shoes, studying the wet leaves that clung to the polished toes.

'You look lovely. Pretty.'

I bit my lip. I couldn't look at him. I wanted to remember everything he said, to learn him for the future, for the evenings I'd be alone in my messy bedroom, bored and thinking about him, reliving this evening.

'Come on then.'

He reached out a hand and I offered mine and we walked together, hands clasped, along the path, deeper into the copse. His fingers were strong but slippery with sweat, and we grasped each other, drowning together. I couldn't speak and he didn't either. He led the way, slightly ahead, tugging me through the trees behind him. The only sounds were the soft puff of our breathing and the swish and crack of grass and stick as we hurried forward.

The trees broke open after a while and gave onto the river. He stopped on a stubby patch of grass, overlooking the water, and let go of my hand to take off his jacket and spread it out on the ground.

I hesitated, wondering if he expected me to sit on it. It was romantic but also impractical. I thought about grass stains and the fact his jacket was really big enough only for one. But he seemed expectant, so I sat down anyway. He sat down with a bump beside me, almost knocking me sideways.

He turned to face me. 'I kept thinking about you.' He reached out a hand and lifted hair from my face, tucked it back behind my ear. 'I even had a dream about you last night.'

'Not a nightmare, I hope?' My voice sounded high-pitched and silly.

His breath smelled of beer. 'I really like you.'

It sounded odd, hearing him say that. I shivered, thrilled. He leaned in and I closed my eyes, and, a moment later, his mouth was on mine and it was a different kiss this time, his lips parting mine and his tongue pushing into my mouth.

I flicked my eyes open and pulled back, shocked.

He looked worried. 'Okay?' Somehow – I wasn't sure when it had happened – he'd insinuated an arm round me. I only realised because his hand pressed into the small of my back, steadying me. 'You do like me too, don't you?'

'Of course.' I nodded a little too hard.

The hand in the small of my back stopped me from squirming away, nudged me gently closer towards him. His skin was heady with the smell of fresh male sweat, undercut with a whiff of carbolic soap.

He nodded. The darkness was thickening but passing glimmers of light flew in from the moving surface of the river, making his lips gleam, the whites of his eyes shine.

Stephen. This is Stephen. None of it seemed real. I wanted to ask him if I was his girlfriend now, if he was my boyfriend?

I blinked as he came at me again. This time, I tried not to mind the probing tongue. It was too wet to be pleasant, but maybe this was normal. I'd have to ask Kate. He mustn't realise I didn't know how to kiss. He'd think me a baby.

He stopped after a while and we sat side by side, looking out across the inky water streaking with the last rays of the sun. The breeze was becoming cold, and I started to shiver. He tightened his arm round me and pulled me closer. His body was hard and warm through his shirt, warming mine.

He murmured in my ear, 'I love you, little girlie. You know that, don't you? You drive me crazy.'

Little girlie? I almost giggled. He eased me backwards onto the ground, his arms firm. My head found grass, ticklish round my neck, against the side of my ear. I thought about insects. He needed a larger jacket. It was sweet, really, the fact he hadn't thought that through.

He had an odd look in his eyes as his head lowered, following mine. Intense. His chest came down on mine, squashing the breath from me, and his mouth was on mine again, all tongue, harder now, and suddenly his hands were roaming about, sliding up under my skirt. I was pinned fast, I could barely inhale, let alone move. Words flashed in and out of my mind as I struggled for breath. *Disarray. Carrying on. Courting.*

He'd said he loved me. I didn't want to make a fuss. I didn't want to make a scene and embarrass myself, do anything that might make him realise how inexperienced I was with boys and besides, I trusted him, he was my boyfriend, wasn't he? He liked me. He loved me. He wouldn't hurt me.

Whatever he was doing, it must be alright.

PAULA

29

The next morning, I dropped Hannah off at school and hurried straight to Gran's.

Gran was only just up, puffing round the kitchen as she made up her breakfast tray with triangles of toast and a pot of tea. She looked up, surprised. 'You're here early, lovely, Everything okay?'

'Fine. Just thought I'd call by.' I glanced through to the empty lounge. 'No Sara?'

'Think she's out. I thought I heard the door when I was in the bathroom.' She grinned. 'I try not to ask too much about her comings and goings. Don't want to cramp her style.'

'I'll get that for you, Gran.' I gestured to the tray. 'Pop the teapot on and I'll carry it through.'

On my way into the lounge, I paused by the sideboard. My stomach contracted. I was right.

'Looks quite nice out,' Gran called from behind me. 'What are you up to today?'

I waited until she was settled in her chair with her mug of milky tea poured and her toast buttered before I tackled her.

'You know your silver goblets?' I said at last. 'Weren't there always six?'

She blinked at me, trying to focus. 'The goblets? Well, yes, there are. It's a set, you see. Great Aunt Elsie passed them on to me. They'll be yours one day, lovely. Or Alan's.'

I took a deep breath. 'There are only five there, Gran.'

She frowned, puzzled. 'Really?' She gazed absently over towards the sideboard at the far end of the room as if she could count them from her chair. 'You're sure?'

I leaned in. 'I thought something was wrong yesterday, but I couldn't put my finger on it. Do you remember, I went over there to look when you told me about Sara polishing the silver? You always have them in two rows of three, don't you?'

She chewed slowly, listening. 'Maybe she just put them back wrong. She wasn't to know.'

I shook my head. 'There's one missing.'

Gran shrugged. 'She probably got mixed up and put one away with the polishing rags by accident. It'll be something like that, Paula. It'll turn up.' She smiled. 'Remember when you lost your bus pass and your mum found it in the oven? Charred to a cinder. We never did work out how it got in there, did we?'

I sat very still, thinking.

I looked at Gran as she munched her toast and sipped her tea, her eyes still merry with the memory of the missing bus pass. She made such an effort every morning, even if she didn't expect to see anyone. It wasn't only the fact her hair was neatly brushed and her clothes crisp and neat, it was the extra touches. The hint of perfume. The face powder and the careful arch of her eyebrows and her perfectly applied lipstick.

It was as if she woke each morning expecting the best from the day. The same way she saw the best in the people around her. Even the ex-cons selling dishcloths. Even Sara.

'You will be sensible today, won't you?' My voice was more

pleading than ordering. 'Don't go entertaining any more of your strangers. Not inside the house, eh? Just in case they don't turn out to be angels, Gran.'

'Don't worry so much, Paula.' She shook her head at me, fondly. 'I can look after myself.'

30

Back at home, I sat in the silence of the lounge, looking sightlessly towards the window, thinking.

My insides churned. Before I'd left Gran's, I'd searched all the places we could think of: under the sideboard, in the cupboard where Gran kept the cleaning rags, even in the bin.

Gran didn't realise, but I'd also taken a quick look around Sara's bedroom when I went upstairs, pretending I needed to use the bathroom. I checked under the bed and rummaged through drawers and the battered backpack and open suitcase, spilling clothes, my hands trembling, constantly looking over my shoulder and imagining Sara standing there, in the doorway, watching me rifle through her possessions. No sign of the goblet there either.

Now, sitting there, my heart pounded so hard it made me feel sick. It had been there just a few days ago. I was sure of it. I'd have noticed. But was Sara really capable of stealing from Gran? My hands twisted in my lap. I thought about the way Sara had spied on Gran's house from across the road. The way she'd followed us to the shops and watched us as we tried on shoes, then finally revealed herself in the café.

My insides went cold. How much did we really know about her, anyway? How did we know for sure that she really was Sara, our long-lost girl? We'd taken it on trust. We'd opened our hearts and homes to her because we wanted to believe her; we wanted so desperately to have her home again.

I shivered. But what if she'd deceived us? What if it wasn't her at all?

Gran would never believe me if I voiced suspicions. And it wasn't fair. That's all they were at the moment, suspicions. I needed to put some effort in. I needed to do some digging and find out the truth.

I pulled out my phone and did a search for local antique shops that might buy and sell silver, then reached for the phone to start calling.

The first number I tried just went repeatedly to voicemail. In the end, I left a message with my name and number and moved on.

A gruff male voice took my call at the second shop. He sounded well-educated but out of breath. I imagined him wading through packing cases in a stockroom or climbing down from a stepladder to reach the phone. He didn't deal much in silver, he said. It was a specialist market. He gave me the feeling I was a nuisance, rather than a potential customer.

I put on a fake smile, took a deep breath and span him my story about my dear sister and brother-in-law's silver wedding anniversary and the special silver goblets I wanted to find them as a present and by the time I'd finished, he'd given me contact details for two local businesses who dealt in antique silver and would sell at a fair price. I think he just wanted to get rid of me.

The first of these was a delightful lady. She sounded only too pleased to answer questions about silver goblets, although by the time she'd finished explaining about hallmarks and silver-smiths and the different periods and styles, I realised the subject was far more complicated than I'd ever thought. I took frantic notes, but when she asked me questions about exactly what I was looking for, I saw how little I really knew about Gran's set. I wasn't even certain how old her silverware was. At least a hundred years, certainly, but how much older, I wasn't sure.

The specialist ended by saying she didn't have anything suitable in stock at the moment, but she'd certainly take my details and keep an eye out and what a pleasure it had been talking to me.

I made myself a cup of tea and paced around the kitchen. The patio needed sweeping.

I remembered looking out at Gran and Sara and Alan, sitting at the table together, making earnest but awkward conversation. I wished I felt closer to Alan. I'd have liked to know more about how he felt about all this, this sudden reappearance of a young woman who said she was his daughter, after all these sad, difficult years alone.

Gran was right. It had been cruel, the way Jackie had cut him off and made it so difficult for him to maintain any contact. Changing phone numbers and addresses so often. Not answering when we tried to send letters and cards. Perhaps a different sort of man would have gone to court and demanded access, or even taken matters into his own hands and stalked them. Alan just wasn't like that. He'd accepted defeat and withdrawn into himself, hurt and humiliated, and let them leave. I'd never really understood why he didn't try to fight back. Maybe his feelings about it all were so complicated, he didn't really understand them himself.

I finished my tea and dragged myself back to the phone to try the other antiques business that dealt in silverware.

A man answered the phone, business-like in tone but not unfriendly. He listened calmly while I told my story and outlined the kind of thing I was looking for. His pen scratched as if he were taking notes. I imagined him standing at a polished desk, walnut perhaps, at the back of a dimly lit shop, the interior crowded with glass-fronted display cabinets, Victorian knick-knacks and polished, dark furniture, musty with the smells of another age.

When I finished, he hesitated. The light scuff of a turning page.

He said, 'You said you were looking for a pair, or possibly a single?'

'Yes.' My heart pumped.

'My partner took in a single yesterday afternoon. Very similar to the style you've described. It's silver-plated, not solid, circa 1900. Not a terribly expensive piece, but it's in good condition, it's been well cared for. Would that be of interest?'

I swallowed hard. 'It might be. Are you open now? Could I come round to have a look?'

The shop was tucked down a cobbled side road, a few minutes' walk from the high street. I must have passed near there, striding along the main road, a thousand times, but I couldn't remember ever turning off and going down the cobbles. There was no reason to cut through.

It was mostly residential but, halfway down, I discovered a small run of retailers. None of them looked very prosperous. A Thai noodle takeaway, a fly-blown newsagents with a cluttered forecourt, and the antiques shop.

It looked like an antique itself with a dark wooden door and window frames so thick they left little room for displaying goods. An old-fashioned bell jangled as I wrestled with the brass handle and managed to shove open the door.

I stood for a moment, blinking, letting my eyes adjust to the gloom. The smells reached me at once: brass and furniture polish, dust and mildew, leather and horsehair. It was like stepping back into the Victorian era. It was crowded with furniture, dining chairs stacked in batches, tables piled with carriage clocks and ornaments, umbrella stands and vases.

'Can I help?'

A young man stepped out of the darkness of the back. He looked so normal I was taken aback. He was dressed in smart jeans and a crisp blue and white striped shirt, the sleeves neatly rolled back to the elbows to show muscular forearms, lightly furred with dark hair. I suppose I'd expected him to look Victorian too, with a waistcoat and pocket watch and a full beard.

'I phoned about the goblet,' I said. 'You said you had one in.'

'Ah, yes, for your sister's anniversary!' He grinned. 'I've got it right here.'

He clicked on the lamp beside him, lifted a shape from under the counter and buffed it up with a cloth, then angled it in the stream of strong light so it gleamed. He had an air of pleased reverence, as if the sight of an object of beauty caused him personal delight. My breath stuck in my throat at the sight of it.

'You're in luck!' he said. 'We don't get them in very often. House clearances, mostly. This one's been well kept. It's not solid silver, only plated. Late Victorian, around the turn of the century, I'd say. English made. Almost certainly part of a set.'

My heart was thudding. I moved closer for a better look and tipped it slightly to one side.

'You're looking at the pattern under the rim?' He seemed oblivious to the fact I was so unsettled. 'That lattice design was quite common, I've come across it before. Nowadays, we put them on display, but in those days, they really did drink from them. Well, on special occasions, anyway.'

I thought about the way I used to arrange the goblets on the carpet when I was a child, playing pretend feasts. I knew that pattern only too well. 'Where did you say you got it from?'

He was still preoccupied, turning the goblet in the air, examining the curve of the bowl.

'A walk-in,' he said. 'Just yesterday. We get that quite a lot. People inherit silverware, clocks, paintings, you know the kind of thing. My grandparents' houses are packed full of them. Most of it isn't worth much and not many people have the house-room nowadays. So they pop in here for a valuation and, often as not, it's a quick sale, cash in hand.'

I hesitated. I wanted to know more, but I wasn't sure how to ask without raising his suspicions.

'Do you know who it was? Who brought it in?' I managed a tense smile. 'It's just, I really like it, but I'd love a pair, ideally. Because it's an anniversary present. You said it was probably from a set. I just thought, maybe if it's a regular customer, you could ask...?'

He nodded, set down the goblet and flicked over the page of a large, old-fashioned ledger on the desk, running his finger down the page. 'Sorry. She didn't take a name.' He looked at me thoughtfully. 'I could take your number and give you a call if another one does come in. Would that work?' He hesitated. 'I don't want to get your hopes up, though. This one might just be a stray.'

I nodded. 'And how much are you asking for this one?'

He sucked on his teeth for a moment, his eyes on the goblet, calculating. 'It's a nice piece. I'd normally say sixty. But, seeing as you're local and it's a present and everything, how about fifty-five?'

31

I missed Will so much on Friday evening.

As soon as Hannah and I got home from school, she rushed to the laptop to download *Magiclands*. I sat beside her, trying to show an interest as she chattered away excitedly, roaming through the multi-coloured graphics, hunting mythical animals and building a digital home for her avatar.

My mind drifted as she sent friend requests to classmates whose screen names she knew. Soon messages were pinging back and forth. I could see why she wanted to join in, if this was how everyone else at school was spending their spare time.

Later, when she was settled in bed, I crept down to the silent kitchen, put together a plate of cheese and biscuits and poured myself a glass of wine. I sat at the table, looking out at the darkness, at the stretch of black lawn set around with stirring trees, and tried to imagine Will at his conference dinner, looking smart in his best suit.

I wished he were there, at home. I wanted to draw the curtains, shut the world out and be with him, just the two of us. To hear him talk about his week and tell me what was on his mind. I knew something was.

I wanted to confide in him too. To share my concerns about Sara and whether she really was who she claimed to be. About the time I'd seen her withdrawing all that cash. About Gran's goblet and the way I'd tracked it down – I was sure it was hers – and bought it back.

If Sara had taken that, what else had she stolen? Gran's jewellery? Knick-knacks scattered around the house? We might never notice they'd gone.

Will hadn't said what time he'd be back. I pulled out my phone and typed him a short message:

Miss u.

I drank off the wine and poured myself a second glass. Since I'd recovered the goblet, I'd been agonising about what to do next. I didn't want to upset Gran or Alan, not until I was really sure of my facts. It wasn't fair to accuse Sara without evidence.

I switched on my laptop and started to do some quick research, teaching myself the basics as I went. Again, I found myself wishing Will were there. He'd be able to answer my questions.

I shook my head. Will didn't need to know, not yet. This was something I'd have to pursue alone.

By the time the lounge clock struck eleven, I'd bought what I needed. The only issue now would be figuring out how to carry it out, once the package arrived.

Before I switched off my bedside light, I checked my phone a final time. I was hoping for a message from Will that said he missed me too, that he was on his way home.

But there was still no reply.

32

Hannah's Saturday afternoon art class was held in the same rooftop studio where I took my life-drawing class on Mondays. She chattered away as we walked there, her small hand warm in mine. Her head was still full of the online game.

I let her chatter on, only half listening. I'd been asleep by the time Will came home the previous night. I'd stirred in the small hours and stretched out a hand to feel him there, his warm bulk comforting on his side of the bed. But his breathing had been quiet, too quiet. He was lying awake in the darkness, I could tell.

I'd whispered, 'You okay?'

He'd sighed, feigning sleep, and turned away from me, onto his side, without answering.

Hannah tugged at my hand. 'Can I go on it again later? PLEASE, Mum? It's Saturday. All the others will be playing. PLEASE say yes. Can I?'

As soon as we arrived at the studio, she went running in, pulling an apron from the pegs and setting up her workspace with paper and paints. I smiled and turned away, knowing there was little chance of getting a goodbye kiss or even a wave. I was already forgotten.

Hannah had always been the sort of kid who dived head-first into things. I remembered when I first left her at nursery. She was only three and I'd planned, for the previous day or two, what words to use to reassure her when we got there, especially at the crucial moment when it was time for me to turn and leave.

Other mums suffered the trauma of distressed children clinging to their knees, sobbing. I couldn't bear to watch. But Hannah didn't even let me give my rehearsed speech. She ran straight in through the door without hesitation, arms pumping with excitement, and when I peeped in through the window a few minutes later, just to check she wasn't crying miserably in a corner, she was already sitting on a tiny chair at a toddler table, head bent forward, happily lost in frantic crayoning, the tip of her tongue poking out as she concentrated. Gran said I'd been just as independent.

I was heading back to the entrance hall, still worrying about Will, when someone called, 'Paula!'

A deep, velvety voice.

I turned around.

Hugo was lolling against the archway that led to the ground-floor studios and workshops, wearing jeans and his battered leather jacket. He drew lazily on a cigarette as I approached, then tilted his head back to let out a stream of smoke. 'Fancy meeting you here!'

I gave him a knowing look. 'You knew I'd be dropping Hannah off, didn't you?'

I didn't know who'd told him. It could be any number of people in the art school crowd. The teachers were as bad as the students when it came to gossip.

He pushed himself upright and fell into step at my side as I headed out through the automatic door and down the stone steps. Outside, he stubbed out the end of his cigarette on the wall, scattering fragments of spent, cooling tobacco. 'You have a very suspicious nature, you know that?'

I didn't answer. I was surprised by how pleased I was to see him. I was a married woman, a happily married one. I wasn't the sort to risk all that on a fling, however attractive he was. I turned the corner and headed back towards the high street again.

Hugo had to hurry to keep pace. 'Well, aren't you going to ask?'

'Ask what?'

'Excuse me?' He stopped dead and I found myself stopping too. He pulled a face, making a show of looking devastated. 'My audition. Er, "How did it go?" maybe?'

I nodded, conceding the point. 'Okay. Your audition – how did it go, Hugo?'

He slapped his forehead. 'No, no, no, darling. That was so *flat*. Try again. As if you really MEAN it.'

'Oh, please.' I turned away from him and carried on briskly.

He rushed to catch up with me again. 'Okay, so we can't all be actors. I'll take the question.' He cleared his throat. 'Actually—'

I grinned. 'You got the part!'

'Wait! No. Actually, not so much as a callback. Curtains. Nada.'

'I'm sorry.' I patted his sleeve. 'Did you do the Romeo?'

He shook his head. 'Stoppard. And a ton of improv. It didn't go well.'

I shrugged. 'Well, the boy wizard doesn't know what he's missing.'

'Exactly.' He shrugged too. 'Theatre's loss is life drawing's gain. At least for another week or two.'

We reached the intersection with the high street, hectic with Saturday afternoon shoppers.

He pointed to a café down the road. 'Come for a quick coffee. My treat. Won't take long, I promise.'

I faltered. 'I don't know. I've got a lot to do, you know, shopping and—'

'Please?' He hesitated, his face suddenly tense, as if it really mattered to him that I agreed.

We stood there on the corner, awkward, getting in everyone's way.

I said, 'Hugo, I'm not sure I—'

He raised a hand and cut me off. 'I know what you're thinking, but stop it. It's all above board. Promise. I just want to help you get the job, that's all.'

'The job?'

'Yes. The job.' He laughed and added in a stagey American accent: 'As one pope said to the other, "Don't play the innocent with me!"'

He steered me into the café two doors down and grabbed a free table in the window, settling me there while he went up to the counter to buy our coffees.

I twisted round to watch him as he lined up. He was so different from Will. It wasn't only the age difference. It was their attitude to life.

Will was solid and responsible. A doctor, for heaven's sake. A man who always paid the bills on time. Someone I could trust and rely on. That meant a lot.

Hugo was slightly crazy. I couldn't make him out. He'd seemed so focused on his audition last time we met; now he was acting as if he never took anything very seriously. And he was so full of energy, just being with him made me feel different. I was trying on another version of myself, the one who hadn't got married early and had a daughter and settled down in a stylish, middle-class house. The one who thought, as Hugo seemed to think, that life was a game and we owed it to ourselves to have fun.

He reached the counter, and I watched him chat up the young female barista. She smiled and flushed slightly as he bantered with her. He was attractive, there was no doubt about it.

He carried back the brim-full coffees with exaggerated care, the tip of his tongue poking between his teeth. It reminded me of Hannah's face when she drew.

'So, the interview is a week on Tuesday.' He slipped into the chair beside mine.

'I know.'

'Three candidates. Did you know that?'

I shook my head.

He counted off the first. 'Elizabeth Farnborough.'

'Elizabeth!' She was another long-term volunteer, well into her seventies and terribly disorganised.

'She'd be a disaster. I know. But they had to give her an interview, didn't they? She's been volunteering for centuries. So, basically, it's Elizabeth, you and a guy from the library. Word is, he knows nothing about art, but his Dewey decimals are a thing of joy.' He paused. 'He's the one to beat.'

I stared at him. 'How do you know all this?'

He tapped the side of his nose and said in a deep, dramatic voice, 'I have ways, my child.'

He pulled a sheaf of crumpled paper from his jacket pocket. For a moment, I thought they were his dog-eared audition pieces, but when he spread them out on the table, gritty with spilled sugar, I saw they were notes, scrawled in a messy hand.

His writing could hardly have made a greater contrast with Will's neat, methodical script. I felt a sudden pang. What would Will think if he could see me now, sitting thigh against thigh with Hugo, inhaling the sexy smell rising from him: cigarettes and leather suffused with warm male sweat?

'I've put together some notes. Hope you don't mind. You

don't have to read them.' He gave me a look. 'But I may cry if you don't.'

'But why? I mean...' I was lost for words.

He shrugged. 'It's always easier doing it for someone else, isn't it? Besides, it's entirely selfish. You'd be really good.'

He leaned forward and pointed, talking me through one sheet after another. He seemed to have consulted half the art school about the way things were being run, what worked well, what they'd like to see changed, ideas for new courses and ways of reaching out more to the community. I had a feeling he was right: these were all issues which were bound to come up at interview.

I tried to focus and listen, but my mind kept veering off in other directions. Mostly, I was preoccupied with the fact Hugo was sitting so close to me that I could feel the heat along the edge of his body. Now and then, as he talked, his hair fell forward onto his forehead and he raised a hand to brush it back.

I shouldn't be doing this. It should be Will who was taking an interest in my interview and helping me by brainstorming ideas. But that was just it. Will had shown so little interest, I still wasn't sure what he really thought about the fact I might go back to work.

'Can you read this okay?' Hugo tipped his face to mine, and I started, aware at once how close he was to me.

I nodded and pointed him back to the table.

As he carried on, I remembered what he'd said about modelling again for the life-drawing class. I bit my lip. I wasn't sure I could cope with that. I wasn't sure I could sit there and stare at his near naked body without embarrassing myself. Not now that I was getting to know him.

I took a deep breath. 'Hugo?'

He broke off and looked at me, surprised.

'I'm happily married. You do know that, don't you? I mean, I'm really not...' My cheeks burned.

He grinned. 'I know. Married to Doctor Will. Pillar of the community. Quite a catch, by all accounts. One daughter, Hannah. Adorable, by the way. Looks just like you.'

I stared. 'How do you know all this?'

He shrugged, pointed to the papers strewn across the table. 'I do my homework.'

My heart raced. I felt wrong-footed. He knew things about me. I knew so little about him.

He lowered his voice and leaned in closer. His eyes were soft. 'Look, I'll be honest. I like you. If you were free, well, who knows? But you're not. I respect that. That's why I'm doing all this, trying to help you with the job stuff. To show you I'm a good guy. Let's be friends. Right?' He put his hand fleetingly on my knee. Warm and strong. 'You don't have to worry about me, Paula.'

He gave me a long look. I should have been reassured, but there was something too careful, too measured in his expression. He smiled and I sensed, for the first time, what a constant performer he was. I had no idea, I realised with a shiver, how much of what he said, what he did, was real... and how much was just part of an elaborate, habitual act.

33

Hugo left first.

I sat on in the window, looking over the pages of notes he'd left for me as preparation for the interview and thinking about him. Something had shifted as soon as he'd said he'd been asking around about me, about my family. It was my own fault. I'd been a fool to encourage him, to let him turn my head. Now it felt as if he'd gone too far, by spying on me. My stomach clenched. What if Will heard about him?

I sipped the final dregs of cold coffee, feeling suddenly sick. I still had half an hour before I needed to pick up Hannah. I should get going, run a few errands, but I couldn't find the energy. I was too lost in thought. Life seemed suddenly very tangled. *Hugo. Will. Sara. The stolen goblet.*

I gazed out of the window at the scurrying passers-by. Then I started, sat up straight in my chair, craning to see further into the road.

A slim, energetic figure was coming rapidly towards me down the pavement, making her way through the Saturday shoppers, a bulging bag on her shoulder. Sara.

I grabbed my bag and headed to the café door to watch her

approach. She was walking briskly, weaving through the crowd, angling her bag with care to stop it banging into people as she squeezed through. She strode right past the café without seeing me, eyes forward, a slight frown on her face, as if she were troubled.

I nipped out and slotted into the crowd, some distance behind, keeping sight of her bobbing head as I followed. I manoeuvred down the street keeping close to shop doorways, ready to dart inside if she turned round.

Sara took a sudden left turn off the high street and headed off down a broad, leafy street into a densely built residential area. The pavements were emptier, and I hung further back, looking out for occasional shops and small businesses, dotted here and there along the way, where I could conceal myself if I needed to.

I was soon out of breath and hot-faced, as much with nerves as the pace she was setting. Why was I gripped with this urge to track her? I couldn't explain it, even to myself. It was an instinct that something wasn't right, that something was going on, and I needed to understand what.

She took another sharp turn, heading now towards a development of low-rise apartments, mostly owned by the council, which mopped up families who couldn't afford Victorian terraces like Gran's. It was a rundown estate, with a children's playground where the swings often hung, broken, on a single chain. The patch of central grass was notorious for late-night drug deals, featuring often in the crime report of the local community e-newsletter.

Sara reached the entrance gates and stopped, looking around, as if she were getting her bearings or trying to identify something. I hid behind a stone pillar, the entrance to a garage, and watched. Finally, she crossed the road and disappeared into one of the premises on the far side, part of a small, battered parade of shops.

I waited, blood roaring in my ears, to see if she reappeared. Nothing. I plucked up courage and crept forward, checking out the side streets as I approached for somewhere to run if she suddenly confronted me on the pavement.

The first shop was a laundrette, a social statement in itself. The flats inside the development must be the only homes in the area without their own washing machines. The steamy smells of wet wool and detergent seeped out through the door. The next shop was a catch-all grocer's shop with a sign saying: NO CREDIT – PLEASE DON'T ASK on prominent display inside the door. Its windows were concealed behind rusty iron grilles.

I inched forward and started as I caught sight of her. Sara had gone inside a poorly lit neighbourhood café, the wipe-clean kind with grey Formica tables, red bucket seats and a tired menu board behind the counter dominated by combinations of sausages, burgers, eggs, chips and beans.

Sara had just slid into a table near the front, her back to me. Opposite her was a rough-looking man with a short, spiky haircut and gorilla arms. A tabloid newspaper lay in front of him on the tabletop. Apart from the two of them, the café looked almost deserted.

As I watched, a balding man with an apron around his waist shuffled over from the counter to their table and set steaming mugs in front of them both. The man tore open several packets of sugar from the bowl on the table and stirred them in. Sara just watched and waited. Her hands were tightly folded in her lap. Her back was unnaturally straight.

The man sipped at his drink, then glanced across to check the counter. The balding man, who looked like the café owner, had turned his shoulder to them as he folded a stack of paper serviettes in half, scoring each fold with his thumbnail.

Sara's companion nodded to her. She reached down and pulled a slim brown envelope from the bag at her feet and slid it across the table to him. He opened the folded newspaper an inch so it swallowed the envelope, then again looked round, checking that the owner wasn't looking their way. He turned in the opposite direction and scanned the pavement, through the large glass window. I pressed myself back against the edge of the grocery store and held my breath.

When I dared to look again, the man had tilted the envelope, still half-concealed inside the folds of the newspaper, so that he could slit the seal with a stubby knife pulled from his pocket. I watched as he thumbed through the notes inside. A stack of purple banknotes: twenties. I wasn't sure how much was there altogether, but it had to be several hundred pounds at the very least. He seemed satisfied and stowed the envelope inside his jacket pocket. He sat quietly for a moment and sipped his drink, motioning to Sara to do the same.

She lifted her mug with both hands, as if she didn't quite trust her grip, and raised it to her lips. Her head faced forward in a stiff, uncomfortable pantomime of drinking.

They sat for a while, in silence from what I could see, finishing drinks that neither of them seemed to want. Eventually, the owner ambled back and dropped a saucer with their bill on top. Sara's companion pulled it towards him, looked it over, then fished in his pocket for change and dropped the coins onto the saucer before handing it over.

As the owner headed to the counter, the man reached swiftly into his coat pocket and drew out a bulky A4 envelope and pushed it in a single movement under the table into Sara's hand. She dropped it straight into her bag and zipped it up.

The man scraped back his chair and Sara did the same, hanging the straps of her bag back on her shoulder. Clearly, their business was over.

I didn't wait any longer. I turned and bolted down the nearest side street before they could come out and see me, threading my way back towards the high street and the shops.

34

Coming home from art, Hannah skipped along beside me, singing to herself under her breath.

I was grateful. She seemed suddenly lighter, happier again. Some days, she seemed so carefree, acting the fool and playing make-believe and cuddling her toys.

She'd really made me laugh the other day. She'd begged to be allowed to dry her hair all by herself after we'd washed it and I'd handed her with the hairdryer while I went to spread the damp towel over the heated rail.

When I walked back into the bedroom, a few minutes later, she was standing with her mouth wide open and the hairdryer trained on it, seeing what happened if she blew warm air at her face.

As soon as she saw me, she collapsed in giggles. 'Look, Mummy!' She'd turned the jet of air back into her mouth, ballooning her cheeks and making them wobble and distort.

At other times, she seemed to have the weight of the world on her shoulders. I'd suddenly find her hunched in a corner, knees drawn up, her face clouded with anxieties too complicated to put into words.

Now, we got home to find the package I'd ordered online had been delivered, tucked out of sight behind the dustbin. No sign of Will. I sidestepped Hannah's questions about what was inside the parcel by chatting about what she'd like for dinner. She always hoped a delivery might be something for her. It so often was. But this was an order I didn't want anyone to know about, not yet. I took it upstairs when she was distracted and hid it inside my wardrobe.

As she ate, she prattled about the project she was working on in art class. It was some sort of medieval stained-glass window involving black card and intricate pieces of tissue paper. I smiled and nodded along. My mind was still busy with Sara and her transaction with the strange, rough-looking man.

After dinner, Hannah begged for some screen time before bed and headed upstairs with the iPad. I stood at the sink, washing up, looking out at the darkening garden and thinking. Sara had looked so tense and uncomfortable in the café. What did she buy from that man? Drugs? It was possible. I had no idea how drugs were sold. In films, they were in packets, weren't they, or screws of paper? Maybe they could be hidden inside a large, thick envelope.

Forged papers, perhaps, to bolster a fake identity? I grimaced.

I wondered where Will was. I sent him a text, pretending I was just wondering what time to do dinner, rather than checking up on him. I paced around the kitchen, wiping over surfaces that were already pristine, checking through the fridge and planning meals in my head for the next day or two, too unsettled to relax.

Footsteps and the rattle of a key in the lock of the front door. I hurried into the hall. Will came in, his face drawn, his brief-case in hand.

'Everything okay?'

He didn't answer for a moment. He kept his face turned

from me, focusing on quietly closing the door and taking off his coat, then hanging it on the rack. Finally, he turned to face me. 'Absolutely.'

I hesitated. I wanted to ask where he'd been all afternoon, if he'd been at the practice catching up on paperwork and, if so, why he hadn't just brought it home and worked here, in his study? I swallowed it back.

'How was art?' He smiled, but it took him some effort.

I thought about Hugo and the smell of his leather jacket, the warmth of his thigh against mine. Maybe Will would somehow know – a trace of stale cigarette smoke on my clothes?

'Fine, I think.' I shrugged and turned to climb the stairs to Hannah's room. It was time to tell her to finish online and start getting ready for bed.

Her bedroom door was closed, but, as I neared it, a muffled sound reached for me. For a moment, it sounded like stifled laughter, then, as I pushed open the door, my chest tightened. Not laughter, not at all. The gulps of low, desperate sobbing.

'Hannah!'

She was curled in a ball on her bed, her arms wrapped round her pillow and her face pressed into it. I hurried across and sat beside her. The laptop lay abandoned on the floor.

'What's happened?' I tried to stroke her shoulder, but she tightened her grip on the pillow and tried to draw away from me. Her muscles were tight.

'Hannah?' I tried to lift her hair away from her hot, damp face.

She squirmed.

'Sweetheart, what is it?'

The sobbing lessened and I started the guessing game. 'Did you hurt yourself?'

She shook her head.

'Was it the computer game? Were you playing *Magiclands*?'

A barely perceptible nod.

I tried to remember the game and think what might have happened. 'Did one of the creatures die, one of your magic pets? Or did something attack the den you built?'

She rolled over and gave me a withering look. 'No!' Her eyes were puffy with crying and her cheeks red. I thought of all the times she'd cried in her short life, times I'd been able to pick her up, brush her down and make it better with a kiss and a rocking cuddle. I was on the edge of that magic now. She was starting to leave me, to venture into more complicated realms with problems a cuddle wouldn't solve.

I opened my arms to her, and she hesitated, then crawled into them and let herself be held.

After a while, when she seemed quieter, I tried again.

'Please tell me, Hannah. I hate to see you so upset. Something awful must have happened, I can see that.'

She mumbled something into my shoulder, and I eased her away from me to talk. Her face was miserable. Her eyelashes shone with tears.

'What was that?'

'He said something mean about me.'

'Who did?' My stomach tightened. 'Someone online?'

She bit down on her lip as if it were too awful to say aloud.

I smoothed her hair and wiped off her damp cheeks. 'Someone you know?'

She nodded, her eyes avoiding mine.

I took a deep breath. 'Someone from school?'

She pulled a face. 'I can't tell you.' She twisted away again as she started to sob.

I frowned. I didn't know what to say.

I took a deep breath. 'That sounds horrible,' I said at last. 'No wonder you're upset.' I paused. 'But can't you block them, if they're being mean?'

'WHY would I do THAT?' she exploded. 'He's my *friend.*

He LIKES me.' She glared at me, furious. 'You just don't *get* it, do you?'

I tried not to react. In a way, she was right. I didn't really get it, not the way she did. Her generation was more tech savvy than mine had been, for a start. Also, it was hard to convince an eight-year-old that blocking someone who was unkind really might be a sensible move.

'I'm sorry.' I tightened my arms around her again and she let me hold her. I kissed her damp hair. 'I'm really sorry, Hannah. That sounds very hurtful.' I wondered how much further I dared to go without infuriating her again. 'Couldn't you tell me who he is, just in case I can help?'

She roared at me. 'No!'

'Okay.' I rocked her gently, holding her warm, body close against mine. 'I love you.'

She snuffled, and something of her hardness gave a little and settled against me.

I wanted to keep asking: *Who is this boy? Why can't you tell me? Why do you care what he says, anyway? Don't you know you're worth so much more than that?*

But I didn't risk it. She'd only tell me I didn't understand, I'd got it all wrong.

So, I just rocked her, and we stayed like that for a while, glued together, trying to keep her safe, my arms wrapped tightly round her, forming a circle whose magic was steadily fading with each year she grew.

35

On Sunday, Hannah seemed subdued, mooching around the house and defying my efforts to get her out and about with me. I could tell the previous day's bad experience online was still clinging to her. She didn't even ask to go back onto the laptop, despite the fact she seemed unable to settle to anything else.

At lunch, she suddenly asked if we could go round to see Gran later and let out a 'Yay!' when I said yes. I was delighted, but I wasn't entirely fooled. I was pretty sure it wasn't Gran she wanted to see, but Sara.

My suspicions were confirmed as soon we arrived. Hannah made a beeline for Sara, oblivious to the fact she was clearly reading, curled in an armchair in the lounge.

'Can we go upstairs and hang out?' Hannah jumped about like an overexcited puppy. 'Can we?'

I tutted. 'Hannah! Can't you see Sara's trying to—'

'That's ok.' Sara set down her book and heaved herself to her feet with an amiable grin. Hannah bounded along by her side as the two of them headed for the door, seized by an energy I hadn't seen in her all day.

Gran, clad in her old cotton apron, spattered with flour,

called me through to the kitchen. She was baking scones. The smell took me straight back to childhood. I could almost see myself perched in there on a stool, barely reaching the kitchen table, helping Gran roll the dough and being given the solemn job of cutting out the rounds. She used to feed me currants or bits of dried peel now and then to keep me interested.

Gran looked flushed. I pulled out a chair to watch and she sat too, wielding her rolling pin with slow care.

'How's everything?'

She didn't answer until she'd finished rolling out the dough and set down the rolling pin.

'Busy, busy.' Gran smiled. 'How about you?'

I nodded too. There was so much I wanted to tell her, to talk through, but I couldn't. It wasn't fair to burden Gran with my worries about Will, and I was too embarrassed to tell her about Hugo. As for my suspicions about Sara, I couldn't share those until I had proof, one way or the other.

'Did I tell you I've got an interview for that art school job? A week on Tuesday.'

'I thought you would.' Gran gave me a meaningful look. 'Do you feel ready?'

She didn't have to spell out what she meant. She wasn't asking if I'd prepared well; she was asking if I was ready to move on, to accept that, whatever we'd hoped, Hannah might be our only child, after all.

'I think so.' I bit my lip. 'I think it's time.'

'Well, then. I wish you luck, lovely.' Gran picked up the cutter and started to make neat rounds from the dough. She always seemed to know the most economical way of placing the cutter so barely any dough was left over for the second rolling. I watched her hands, heavily veined now, her knuckles swollen.

I carried on, thinking about the interview. 'I've worked up a few ideas, you know, about making things more efficient and bringing more people in. We need to put more effort into applying for grants, especially for the kids' programme. They need a proper café too. One that actually makes some money.'

Gran nodded. 'Make sure you tell them about working at the bank. Not everyone's got experience like that. You've always been good at maths, as well as art.'

'I'll tell them.' I hesitated. 'Am I doing the right thing, Gran? I don't want to miss time with Hannah.' I thought about the way Hannah had sobbed, reluctant already to tell me too much. 'She's growing up so quickly.'

Gran smiled. 'They do.' She paused and turned kind, thoughtful eyes on me. 'I want someone to invent a time machine,' she said. 'Not to travel through time, that's far too complicated. More of a time bank, to store the odd bit of time, like the bits of dough you don't need the first time round.' She paused and cleaned off the inside of the cutter, dropping the stray fragments onto a saucer. 'When they're young, like Hannah is now, you could put some away. They wouldn't miss the odd half an hour nipped out here or there, would they? Then later, when they're all grown up, you can help yourself to a bit, now and then, see? As a treat.'

I thought about that. 'And maybe time with certain people too,' I said. 'The odd hug or chat that you mightn't miss at the time, when there were plenty going, but you could really do with later. Years later.'

She flipped the raw scones onto her baking tray, breathing hard.

I jumped up. 'Are those going in the oven?'

She nodded and wheezed, 'Second shelf.'

I put them in, set the timer and went to sit beside her again. 'Do you want me to roll out the rest?'

She smiled and handed me the rolling pin. It wasn't like her, giving up halfway through a batch like this.

Once she'd recovered, she said, 'Who were you thinking

about? The person whose hugs you'd have liked to bank. Your mum?'

I nodded. 'Mum and Dad. What about you?'

I expected her to say Grandpa. She didn't. 'A certain special little girl.'

I thought for a second she meant Hannah or even me. Then I saw how wistful she looked, how sad, and I realised it wasn't me at all. She was thinking about all the lost years with Sara.

I said, 'But she's come back, Gran, hasn't she? I know you missed out on a lot, all those years, but she's here now.'

Gran brightened at once and sat up straighter. 'You're right. And you know what, I think she might stay around for a while yet.'

'Really?' I tried to force my own mouth into a smile. 'What do you mean?'

Gran leaned in closer, her voice lowering. 'She's looking into teacher training. Don't say anything – she wants it kept secret for now. But I've told her, if she wants to study round here, she can stay in the house with me. It's not cheap, you know, studying. It might help if she doesn't have rent to worry about.'

I couldn't speak for a moment. Gran was so full of love. I couldn't bear to think how much it would hurt her if Sara wasn't what she seemed. My eyes fixed on the dough as I bashed the rolling pin back and forth, pounding it too hard, making a sticky mess underneath.

'She might even get a job round here, afterwards, who knows?' Gran rattled on. 'We've got some good schools.'

I said, 'She might not want to settle here, Gran.'

Gran looked surprised. 'Why not? There're worse places.' She leaned over and shook more flour onto the board to stop the dough from sticking. 'Has Alan said anything to you? About last night?'

I blinked, remembering. I'd been so wrapped up in my own

worries, I'd forgotten about Alan's plan to go out with Sara, just the two of them.

'Did they go out then, Alan and Sara?'

Gran nodded, beaming. 'She hasn't told me much. I don't like to pry. But she was in a really good mood this morning. Singing about the place.' She put a finger to her lips. 'I try not to ask her where she goes, you know. She's got her own key and she can come and go when she likes. She's old enough to look after herself.' She paused, clearly deciding how much more to disclose. 'I just said, "Did you see him last night, then? Your dad?" And she nodded and smiled and that was that.'

I kept my eyes on the board, setting down the rolling pin to reach for the cutter. 'Well, that's good.'

'She's a lovely girl.' She nodded to herself. 'It might be the making of him.'

I lifted the scones onto the second baking tray and managed, finally, to look her in the eye. 'Let's hope so,' I said at last.

RUTH

36

Kate was the one who got it, not me.

'What do you mean?' She looked stunned. It was her reaction that made it real, that made me feel sick. The dread in her eyes. 'How long, Ruth?'

We both put crosses in the back of our diaries to keep track of the curse, just so we weren't caught out at school with nothing to wear. It happened, sometimes, to girls we knew: dark, spreading patches staining their skirts when they stood up to change lessons and female teachers beckoning them over, sending them off to Matron for bulky belts and pads while the boys winked and made fun. There was little more mortifying.

But the diary spoke for itself, now. *Two months. No cross.*

I shrugged, embarrassed. 'I'm not that regular. You know me.'

She didn't laugh or tease the way she usually did. She paled. 'You don't think...? I mean, is it possible?'

'What?'

She blurted out, 'Stephen. I mean, you didn't actually do it, did you?'

'Him?' I tried to laugh. I hadn't heard from him since the night at the river. No love letters, after all.

She took a step away from me, as if she were frightened I was contagious. 'What are you going to do?'

37

Oh, the scenes. My mum, usually so stoical, so tough, crying. This woman who'd endured the war.

My father rushing to the window to close the curtains, at half past five in the afternoon.

What would people think?

Through her sobs, my mother saying, 'You were always such a good girl. I never thought... I never...'

My father, striding up and down the back of the room, face tight. 'He'll just have to marry you.'

I looked up, peering incredulously through the fog of misery and grief, and stared. Marry me? What was he talking about?

My father came to a sudden halt in front of me and bent forward, hands on thighs, as if he were playing leapfrog. 'What happened? Tell me. Who are his parents?'

I shook my head. My own dear father, this old-fashioned but kindly man, seemed suddenly ancient. His parents? What would he suggest next – a duel?

My mother looked up, a flicker of hope in her face. She seemed buoyed up by the thought of a wedding, after all.

'Answer your father, Ruth. Who are they, his family? Do we know them?'

I knew what she meant: are they respectable? Are they one of us? 'I don't know.'

'Well, what's his name?'

'Stephen.'

My father said, losing patience, 'Stephen *what*?'

I looked from one anxious face to the other. 'I don't know. He didn't say.'

They twisted to look at each other, shocked.

My mother said faintly, 'You don't know his *name*?'

For a little while, neither of them spoke. The mantelpiece clock ticked loudly through the quiet.

Finally, my mother tried again. 'Where does he live? Your father can go round to see him. You just need to help. Where does he work?'

'He's gone away.' I had no idea where, I realised. 'National Service.'

A horrible thought hit me. How could I even be sure any of it was true? What if his name wasn't even Stephen? What if he'd planned this all along?

38

I didn't have choices, not then. It's hard to explain nowadays. I understand that. It was another time, another age, almost another country. A teenage mother had nowhere to turn if her parents didn't want to support her. An unmarried mother brought shame on everyone. Her family. Her child. Herself. It wasn't only my life I might ruin; it was my unborn child's. They told me that all the time. *Think of the child. Growing up illegitimate. Think of the stigma.*

Maybe, if my parents had been determined, they could have traced Stephen. My father could have started with a visit to Kate and her parents, moving on to her friend, Daphne, and eventually tracking down the boys we'd met that first evening, one by one. It was a small community.

But that was the problem. It was a small community where gossip ran in a moment from house to house, street to street, like an ignited gunpowder trail. No one must know. Instead, my mother told the neighbours that I'd been stricken with pneumonia and needed to be sent away to rest and recover, to stay with an aunt near the seaside in Wales.

The only person who knew what had happened was Kate

and she dropped me like a rock, understanding at once as soon as word of my sudden illness reached her.

It seemed very unreal, this storm swirling around me. I spent my time sitting in my bedroom, looking out at the bustle in the road, the neat gardens and pristine gates. I put my hand on my flat stomach and wondered if it was all a lie, this idea of a baby growing there. I didn't feel anything, nothing at all.

I thought of the poking tongue and the weight of him, crushing me against the grass.

I just wanted to go back to school and never be alone with a boy again. But no one asked me what I wanted. It was too late for that. I'd done my part and look what a mess I'd made. My mother went about the house with a pinched, pale look and red eyes; my father's mouth was set in a tight line as he made the necessary arrangements.

Neither of them looked at me, let alone spoke to me.

PAULA

39

On Monday morning, I texted Iris with an excuse about missing our life-drawing class.

Food poisoning. Just need to rest.

My guilt worsened when Iris sent a kind message back, saying how sorry she was, that she'd let Nick know and was there anything she could pick up for me from the shops?

I knew I'd have to stay indoors all day, until it was time to collect Hannah, just in case Iris saw me. That was the trouble with lying to a neighbour. Too close to home.

I spent the morning thinking about Hugo, just the same. It was hard not to imagine him posing for the group, flexing his bulging muscles, his skin slick. All those women would be gazing at him, biting their lips as they struggled to concentrate, to reproduce the line of his biceps, his chest, his thighs. He clearly loved the attention.

I made myself a cup of tea and sat with my laptop at the kitchen table. I spread out Hugo's crumpled notes and started to go through them, feeling them spark ideas of my own. He'd spoken to a lot of people; he'd gone to a lot of effort, even though he knew all about Will and Hannah.

I stopped and stared out at the garden and the squirrels shaking the trees as they chased each other.

Why had he?

The following day, I bumped into Lizzie's mum, Moira, as I came away from the school gates.

'Hiya!' She was dressed in sportswear, her hair swept high in a ponytail. 'How are things?'

She fell into step beside me as I headed back towards the high street. She walked with a perky bounce, all ready to hit the day.

'All good.' I nodded, smiling, playing the mum game. 'How about you?'

'Good! I've been meaning to email you. Would Hannah like to come to us for a play date? Lizzie was asking. This Friday, maybe, after school?'

'I'm sure she would.' I was confident that Hannah would be thrilled. 'Thanks, Moira.' The two of them seemed to get along fine when they were on their own, away from school.

We chatted for a while about the new head teacher and the changes she was slowly implementing – the topic of much debate on the class chat apps. I expected we'd part company at the crossing, but Moira stuck to my side and turned to cross the road with me. Whatever exercise class she was about to join must be in that direction.

As we hit the far side of the road, she suddenly said, 'Rob said he spotted Will in the bar at Greystones on Friday night. Lucky for some, right?'

'Greystones?' I blinked. Will hadn't mentioned that the conference was being held there. I'd have remembered, surely. Greystones was a fancy spa and golfing hotel, only half an hour away. We'd been there several times for dinner, before Hannah was born, when we had something special to celebrate.

Moira rattled on, 'Rob was meeting up with the boys. His golf buddies.' She raised her eyebrows. 'You know what they're like. One round on the golf course followed by ten rounds in the boozer. What about Will?'

'Far more boring, I'm afraid. A work dinner.' I hesitated. 'I didn't think it was there, though.'

She was too busy talking to listen. 'Anyway, I told Rob, they need to take wives next time. They've opened a spa, did you know? They do the most amazing Thai massage. Not cheap, but worth every penny. Honestly, afterwards I slept like a baby.'

I pretended to look impressed. I wasn't as keen as Moira about spending a small fortune on a massage and, besides, I was still thinking about Will. 'I don't think the corporate dos are as much fun as they sound. He can't drink much, for one thing.'

'Really?' She gave me an odd look. 'Rob seemed to think he was pretty well-oiled.'

We reached the end of the road and hesitated on the corner of the high street, finishing up with polite goodbyes.

'Thanks again about Friday, Moira. Hannah will be so pleased.'

Moira was already turning to bob away, hair swinging. 'No problem. Have a great day!'

And she was off.

I frowned to myself as I headed home. I should ask Will. That was the most obvious thing to do. Rob might have got it wrong, mistaken Will for someone else after a few drinks. That might be it. It was just... what was it, exactly?

All the way round the supermarket, picking through the loose apples with care, something gnawed at me. He never drank a lot at those dinners. He was far too professional. And he'd have told me if he were going to Greystones, I'm sure he would. I'd have remembered.

I picked up some more salad for dinner and joined the line to pay.

I practised in my head.

You know Moira's husband, Rob? Well, he thought he saw you at Greystones on Friday night. Was that where you were? He seemed to think you'd definitely had a few drinks!

Why did that seem so unlikely? Why did it seem so hard to say?

The house was silent when I got home. I checked over the laundry to see what was dry, folded it and carried it upstairs – to Hannah's room first, then ours. Will's wardrobe door was ajar and, on my way out, I went to close it. I found myself pausing, my hand on the door, looking in.

I'd always prided myself on trust in our marriage. I'd never been the sort of wife to check his phone when he'd left it out and a message pinged, or to go through his emails. I didn't need to. I knew Will was rock solid. I had no cause to pry and spy, no reason to worry.

But that was before. His behaviour had never been odd in the past. He'd never seemed so distant. He'd never found it so hard to look me in the eye. Now, for the first time, rightly or not, I was worried.

I opened up both double doors and stood for a moment, looking across the array of suits and jackets. A rail of dark, dull colours. A palette that basically ranged from light brown through dark brown to black. I concentrated, trying to remember what he'd worn on Friday night, and settled on three or four contenders.

I reached in, heart racing, and lifted out the jackets, hung them on the outside of my wardrobe door and started to run my hand through the pockets, inside and out. My fingers trembled.

I felt like a thief as I pulled out crumbled receipts for a coffee here or there, the odd tissue, a stray coin, a half-completed café loyalty card. I examined each item as I went, checking dates. There was absolutely nothing to tell me where he'd been last Friday evening. I put everything back and slotted the jackets into place again.

I sat down on the edge of the bed with a bump and stared out towards the trees, emotionally strung out and somehow disappointed. What had I expected? Why did I feel so deflated? Had I wanted to catch him out in a lie?

I stood up and headed for the door. I was being ridiculous. I could stop all this right now and forget the whole thing. I could decide Rob was mistaken. Or I could decide that, even if Will had been at Greystones, there was a perfectly innocent reason that he hadn't thought to mention it. Maybe he *had* ended up having too much to drink and was embarrassed to tell me. There were all sorts of explanations. I could go right back to the way things were before and say no more about it. It was a question of mindset, of trust.

I stopped on the stairs, my hand still on the well-dusted banister.

That was the problem, though, wasn't it?

It was a question of trust.

40

I woke in the night.

The shadows crossing the ceiling were long and tapering: fingers of light bleeding in from the street lamps through a gap in the curtains. For a moment, I wasn't sure where I was, why my stomach was tight with worry. Then, in a rush, it all came back.

I turned onto my side. Will lay beside me, sprawling on his front, his face squashed into his pillow. I reached out a hand and stroked his hair. Tougher and more wiry than Hannah's. The black was flecked with grey now. I wriggled closer and threaded my arm around his shoulders, sank my face against the knot of muscle at the top of his arm and breathed in his smell. Safe. Solid. Steady. That's what I'd always thought.

He stirred, half-asleep, patted my hand, then twisted away from me, facing towards the far wall. His breathing lengthened and settled again.

In the morning, in the bustle of breakfast, as I hurried Hannah through eating her cereal, brushing her hair, teeth, I said to Will, 'Where was your conference, again? Did you say?'

He was pouring himself a coffee from the pot, his back to me. 'You don't want to know. Wheatfields or Ryefields or something. One of those purpose-built places. All concrete.'

Hannah, half-asleep, had lapsed into a trance.

'Come on, sweetheart.' I pointed her back to her cereal bowl. 'We'll be late.'

Will turned away with his coffee, heading towards the kitchen door to go upstairs.

'That's a shame,' I said. 'You'd think they'd pick somewhere a bit more inspiring.'

He hesitated, then turned back. 'Or at least a bit nicer. I'm not sure I can face that food again.'

'Again?'

He sipped his coffee, not looking me in the eye. 'I'm back there on Friday. I told you. It's in two parts – last week and this week.'

I stared at him, too shocked to reply.

Hannah, sensing the tension, lifted her head and gazed at us.

Will shrugged. 'Well, I did, but no point arguing about it. I'm there again tomorrow night. Same deal. Conference, followed by dinner. Hopefully, I won't be as late home, this time. Okay?'

I moved away from him to the worktop to stack dirty dishes in the dishwasher.

My heart thumped. *Of course he hadn't told me. We both knew he hadn't.*

If there was one thing I knew about my husband, it was this: he was a terrible liar.

SARA

41

She and Hannah were two of a kind. Sara sensed it from the start.

She'd read the yearning in the young girl's face when she came bursting through Granny's front door, eyes at once seeking Sara out, eager as a puppy as the two of them charged upstairs together. It was flattering, of course. But she recognised it too.

Hannah was loved by her mother. Terribly loved. Perhaps too much – yes, she'd come to believe that was possible for a child.

Sara made a point of drawing Hannah out as they chatted together. The girl seemed only too pleased to talk about herself, about her life. All Sara had to do was listen and take careful note, reading between the lines.

She learnt a lot. Soon, she built up a picture of a young girl who was her mother's friend and companion, as well as her daughter. She knew all about that. She'd been an only child too.

They had plenty of time alone together in Sara's room. Sara took care to heap attention on the little girl. She did her hair in precocious, princess styles. She let Hannah experiment with her make-up and nail polish, on condition it all came off before they went back downstairs. She let her try on her clothes and strut across the room in her heels. It was their secret, she said, with a smile and a quick hug.

Was it wrong to observe a needy child carefully, see what she craved, and try to fill the gaps?

In return, Hannah made it pretty clear that she adored Sara, with the idolatry of a child: all passion and loyalty and no restraining judgement.

In fact, Sara could already tell, she'd do pretty much anything to please her cool, older cousin.

PAULA

42

My phone rang when I was on my way home, after dropping Hannah at school. I nearly didn't answer it. I didn't recognise the number. 'Hello?'

'Mrs Bates?'

I hesitated. I didn't recognise the voice either. I sharpened my tone, bracing myself for a sales pitch or a scam. 'Where are you calling from, please?'

'It's Greg here. Drayton's Antiques? You were looking for a second silver-plated goblet?'

I stopped walking and moved to the side of the road to huddle over my phone, giving Greg my attention. 'I was. Only if it's a match, though. So, I can give them as a pair.'

'Well, I've got good news! I think you're in luck.' He sounded so pleased. He couldn't imagine how much his words sickened me. 'We took another one in yesterday. Same thing, a walk-in, cash in hand. I'm pretty sure—'

I interrupted, struggling to hear against the traffic on the high street. 'Who brought it in, please? Can you describe them?'

We'd spoken over each other for a moment. He hesitated, then said, 'You're asking about the seller? Sorry. I'm afraid my partner handled it again. I haven't had the chance to ask. I just came in this morning and started checking through new stock and there it was. I wanted to let you know straightaway. I'm pretty sure it's from the same set. If not, it's very similar. It's got the same decorative styling near the rim. Look, why don't you bring in the first one and we can put them side by side and compare? If it's not an exact match, it's certainly close. I'd say they'd work very well as a pair. You've been lucky!'

I couldn't speak. Shoppers blurred as they bustled past me.

'Hello? You still there?'

I managed to say, 'Thanks, Greg. That's amazing. Put it aside for me, would you? I'll come right in.'

I didn't need to fetch the first goblet so I could compare the two. I was confident that I'd know at once if this second one also belonged to Gran's set. I'd grown up with them.

And there was another reason I was eager to dash straight there. I had a hunch, deep down in my gut, that this one had been brought in by Sara too. After all, if Sara had stolen the first one from right under Gran's nose and got away with it, what reason would she have to stop?

43

I called Gran's house as soon as I got back from the antiques shop. The second goblet was safe now in my bag. They were from the same set alright.

Gran sounded so pleased when I explained I was calling to ask Sara if she fancied coming over to my place so we could have coffee, just the two of us. I'd been thinking about the fact she'd been out for dinner with Alan, I told Gran. Now it was my turn to be friendly. Besides, it was such a lovely day. We could sit in the garden and have a chat about her teaching plans, and I could share what I knew about local schools.

I went upstairs to my wardrobe and took out the package I'd hidden there. Downstairs, I set it on the patio table along with the two silver goblets, placed side by side. They made a perfect pair, polished and buffed and shining in the morning sunlight.

I reheated a coffee for myself from the pot I'd made earlier in the morning and stood at the kitchen window, looking out at the garden and at Gran's silverware, sitting ready on the table.

I sipped my drink, steadied myself with deep breaths, and waited.

. . .

Sara looked wary when I opened the door to her. She wore the expression of an animal who senses a trap has been set for it but isn't sure when and how it's going to spring.

'Coffee?'

She shrugged and came through with me to our pristine kitchen, leaning against the counter and watching me pour some into a mug and reheat it. For a minute, the only sound was the low whirr of the microwave and the soft clunk of the turning plate.

'You must be wondering why I asked you round,' I said at last, handing her the mug.

She nodded. 'Something Gran's told you?'

My hands trembled as I picked up my own mug. 'I thought it was time we had a frank chat. Just you and me.'

She didn't answer. Her eyes followed me as I crossed the kitchen towards the patio door, beckoning for her to follow.

She knew the game was up as soon as she stepped out, clear of the doorframe, and caught sight of the goblets. Her face flushed and her eyelids started fluttering with a sudden attack of nerves. Her eyes flicked to mine.

I didn't need to say a word. She knew and I knew.

I pointed her to one of the patio chairs, one of those same chairs she'd sat in when she came round for the barbecue to meet Alan, for our happy family reunion. It suddenly seemed a lifetime ago. I pulled up a chair across from her and set down my coffee.

I said softly, 'You're not Sara, are you?'

She drew in breath, and, for a moment, she looked thrown. 'Of course I am.'

'Right.' I nodded at the goblets. 'Did you take these from Gran's?'

Her eyes fell to her lap. We sat in silence for a moment. No denial. It was all the answer I needed.

After a while, she said, 'How did you find them?'

'How do you think? I went looking for them and bought them back. You thought you'd got rid of them, didn't you, flogging them to that dingy little shop?'

She couldn't look me in the eye.

'I really hope you're not Sara,' I said. 'You know why? It would be so much easier to find out you're some random person who heard what happened to us, all those years ago, and thought she'd make something out of it. Is that what happened, Sara?' I watched her closely. 'I thought that ID card in your wallet might be fake. I should have trusted my instinct. I just wanted to believe you, for Gran's sake. And Alan's.' I paused. 'What is your real name, anyway?'

She didn't answer.

'Look, you'll be doing me a favour if you just tell me,' I went on. 'Think of it from my point of view. It would hurt far more to think you really were my niece. What kind of person would steal from their own great-grandmother? Who'd do that?' I hesitated. 'So, tell me. Which is it?'

She shook her bowed head. Her hands, with their bitten-down nails, had clenched around her mug into tight fists.

I shook my head. I didn't know what I'd expected. More lies, perhaps. Angry threats. Not silence. I reached for my mug and drank down a swig of coffee. I thought about Gran and how heartbroken she'd be to find out she'd been deceived. I thought about Alan, sprucing himself up at the weekend to impress his long-lost daughter. I couldn't imagine how betrayed he'd feel. All over again.

'I hear you saw Alan on Saturday night. How did that go?'

She cautiously lifted her eyes and looked at me. 'Fine. Why?'

'I'm just wondering what you talked about, to be honest. I know what he'd want to ask. About Jackie. About every little thing she ever told you, growing up, about him, and why she just left like that. It was cruel, what she did to him. He's never got over it, not really.'

She frowned, listening.

'So, what did you tell him? That's a lot to make up, if you're not his daughter. A whole lot of lies. Is that what you did?' I took a deep breath. 'It's going to be hard to keep up. Had you realised that? If something happens, if you slip up just once, if you get found out, it'll cause a lot more hurt than if you just tell the truth now and get it over with.'

She bit down on her lip, nipping at the flesh. I didn't get the impression she was going to tell me anything.

I nodded at the goblets. 'Why did you do that? For the sake of, what, forty pounds each? Bit obvious, isn't it? Didn't you think we'd notice? They've been on Gran's sideboard since I can remember. I knew at once.' I paused. 'Have you taken anything else? Anything Gran mightn't have missed yet? Jewellery, maybe?'

'Stop it!' She sounded furious. As if the allegation that she might have pocketed jewellery was somehow terrible, but stealing goblets wasn't. 'What do you want, anyway?'

I hesitated. It wasn't an easy question to answer. It wasn't only about her. It was about the rest of the family too, and sparing them as much hurt as possible.

'I need to know for sure if you're really Sara.' I gestured to the goblets, shining between us. 'Here's the deal. I'm willing to keep this quiet for now. Until I know the truth. After that, well, let's see, shall we? One step at a time.'

I already had a good idea of what I planned to do. If she wasn't Sara, I'd consider going to the police. They wouldn't only prosecute her; they'd also establish who she really was. That might be the best way of convincing Gran. On the other hand, if she was Sara, maybe we should try to sort it out within the family and keep the police out of it.

I opened the package, took out the small box inside and pushed it towards her.

She read the side. 'A DNA test?'

I nodded. 'I could try to get a sample without you knowing. It's not that hard. But I want this done properly. With your consent.'

She looked at the test kit doubtfully. 'What do you have to do?'

'It's just a cheek swab. Doesn't hurt. You and I can both do it, then I send the samples off together and in two or three days, they email me the link to upload the results. They'll confirm if we're aunt and niece. Or complete strangers. Simple as that.'

She looked cornered. 'And if I say no?'

'Why would you, if you're telling the truth?'

Her eyes shifted to the glistening goblets. 'Until then, until you've got the results, you're not going to tell anyone about those?'

'Not a word.'

She hesitated, then seemed suddenly to come to a decision. 'Okay.' She pushed the package back to me to open. 'I'll do it.'

44

When Moira invited Hannah around after school on Friday, I hadn't realised Will would be away too – for the second part of this alleged conference of his. It only hit me late in the afternoon, as I found myself wandering round the house, straightening pillows that didn't need adjusting and contemplating what to cook: I was all alone for the evening.

I'd spent most of the day putting the finishing touches to my interview prep. They'd asked for a short presentation, and I was doing mine on plans to expand the café and show how it could generate a decent income. I'd been putting together slides, including the figures to back up my argument, and a funky new name and logo to show I understood about branding. All those years designing and running school events, raising money for the PTA, hadn't been in vain.

Afterwards, when the slides were done, I spent some time checking emails and browsing on my laptop. I pulled up the site for Greystones and flicked through the pictures. They made it look amazing, of course: images of women having treatments in the new spa and a couple enjoying a romantic dinner in the rustic Italian restaurant.

I pulled out my phone and sent Will a message:

Miss you. Hope conference going well. Love you so much. Xxx

I had a salad for dinner, sitting alone at the kitchen table. I hadn't checked with Moira what time she wanted me to collect Hannah. Last time she'd had a play date, I'd gone round at seven and Hannah was exasperated, explaining to me on the way home, in her struggling-to-be-patient voice, that I'd arrived far too early and made her look like a baby.

'It's not a school night, Mummy,' she'd said, raising her eyebrows. 'It's *so* embarrassing. We were halfway through a film! I mean, come on, literally *no* one else's mum would do that.'

This time, I waited until seven thirty and then decided to give Moira a call before I set off, just in case I was in danger of repeating the same mistake. Maybe Hannah was right. Maybe I was more protective than some of the other mums.

It took a while for Moira to come to the phone. I imagined them all sitting together in the lounge, watching a movie with snacks. Hopefully, Hannah would be having a blast.

'Sorry to interrupt the fun, Moira.'

'Hey, Paula, is that you?'

'Just wondered what time I should pop round for Hannah?'

At almost exactly the same time, Moira said, 'How's Hannah?'

There was a sudden pause. A hard fist reached into my chest and closed round my heart.

'Did you say, "How's Hannah?"' I blinked hard and speckles jumped around the cream wall opposite me.

'I thought—'

'Isn't she there?' I could barely speak. 'She's with you. For dinner.'

Moira sounded lost for words for a moment. 'Well, I know that's what we planned. But Lizzie said Hannah wasn't well at school and so she couldn't—' She pulled away from the phone and hollered: 'Lizzie!' Then she came back on, 'Lizzie said Hannah had to go home early. I've been meaning to text you to check how she's feeling but, you know...'

For a few seconds, I couldn't breathe. My stomach twisted and I put my free hand to it, bending myself forward.

Moira's voice became muffled. Lizzie must have arrived. I couldn't make out what they were saying to each other. My ears roared with panic.

Moira's voice came clearly again, 'Yes, that's what I thought. Lizzie says Hannah wasn't feeling well in the last lesson, so she went to the office and never came back to class. Naturally, we assumed they'd called you and you'd taken her home. But you're saying—'

'Does she have any idea where she might be?' My voice came in a rush, sounding more aggressive usual. It was all I could do to stop myself from shouting.

'Well, no,' Moira said. 'As I said, Hannah didn't feel—'

'No one from school called me. This is the first I've heard of it. I thought she'd been with you all this time.'

'Well, I'm sorry.' Moira's voice sounded suddenly clipped. 'I'm not sure what to suggest. If Hannah hasn't come home—'

'Please.' I forced myself to sit up straight again, to breathe as deeply as I could. 'If Lizzie thinks of anything, has any idea where she might have gone... call me, would you?'

I put the phone down, hand shaking.

45

The specks on the wall were dancing now, out of control. I made it to the bathroom just before I was sick. Afterwards, I sat on the cold floor, next to the toilet, my head pounding. *I can't do this, I don't have the strength. Please, God, make her okay. Make her safe.*

I dialled Will's number, but it went straight to voicemail. I left a garbled, frantic message, saying Hannah was missing, to call me. Then I sent him a text saying the same.

When I called Gran, she picked up at once. 'No, she's not here, lovely. Wasn't she seeing one of her friends?'

I tried to keep my voice calm, but there was no fooling Gran. 'She was, but apparently she didn't go.'

'So you don't know where she is?'

'No. I don't know. I thought maybe she's with you—?'

Gran was puffing, as if she were struggling to her feet. 'No, lovely. Not here. I just remember her saying she was going to her friend's house today.'

It was all I could do to stop myself from shouting. 'No! I mean yes, but she never went. Lizzie said she wasn't well or something. At school.'

'Not well? Is that what she said?'

'Yes. They thought I'd picked her up. But she never came home, Gran. I just...' My head throbbed. How was this possible? One minute I was happily getting ready to collect her from Lizzie's, the next I was falling apart, thinking I might never see her again.

'Calm down, Paula. Please.' Gran sounded suddenly very much in control. 'Now tell me. Exactly what's happened?'

I took a deep breath and everything Moira had told me came tumbling out. Gran didn't interrupt, she just listened.

At the end, I said breathlessly, 'Should I call the police?'

Gran said briskly, 'Do the rounds first. Just in case. Do you think you can drive? Good. Get in the car and check the route to school. Think of anywhere she likes to spend time. A park, a playground, down by the river, wherever. I'm here if you need me. Can you do that?'

I rang off in a daze. This couldn't be happening. Not Hannah.

Will still wasn't picking up. Why not? Had he switched his phone off? I couldn't bear it. It seemed impossible that Hannah could be missing, that I could be searching the streets for her, and Will didn't even know.

I shook my head. I couldn't waste time worrying about Will. I needed to get out there and find her. I pushed my phone into my pocket, grabbed the car keys and headed out into the streets.

I crawled along the roads, scanning empty pavements, tracing the route we usually took to and from school, sitting high in my seat to peer into the gloom, into shop doorways, beside bins, pulling into the side every time a car needed to overtake and hurry past. When I caught a glimpse of my face in the mirror, my eyes were red-rimmed and wild.

I'd just reached school when the phone rang.

Gran again, keeping track of me. 'Any sign?'

'This is hopeless. Where am I even going?' I was angry with

her. I needed to be angry with someone. 'If anything's happened to her, God help me, I don't know what—'

'Don't.' Gran cut me off at once. 'She'll be fine.'

I pulled in just past the school. 'I just keep thinking, what if—'

'Pull yourself together, Paula.' Gran took a deep breath, as if she was forcing herself to keep calm for both of us. 'Where are you now?'

'By the park.' It was dark. I couldn't imagine she'd be in there. But it was somewhere I sometimes took her, after school, to scoot or cycle or play in the children's playground. I switched off the engine and climbed out. The gates were already padlocked. My lip started to tremble, and I bit down on it. 'It's locked, Gran.'

'Have a quick look anyway. Just five minutes. Call me back the minute you find her.'

She sounded so sure I would. I walked along the outside of the railings, peering into the shadows. The torch on my phone was thin and weak. The beam made no in-roads into the darkness of the park. I kept low, scanning the contours of long bushes and trees, menacing in the blackness, their leaves whispering.

I started to shout, 'Hannah! Hannah! It's Mummy. Are you there?'

My voice dispersed at once on the breeze. Rain was coming. I was despairing. How could Hannah be in there, all on her own in the dark? It was madness. What was I doing?

I was level with the children's playground now, the painted lines of the tennis courts beside it gleaming eerily. I peered over the railings at the stilled swings and roundabout. No sign of movement. The place was deserted.

I turned and started to walk briskly back to the car. Where else could I try? Where could she be? I shook my head. I was wasting time. She could be anywhere. She could be hurt or being held by someone. Every minute mattered. What was I doing, roaming the streets when she could be in pain, dying? I started to sob.

I checked my phone again. No missed calls. No messages. Nothing from Will. This was it. I'd reached my limit. No more looking on my own. I was calling the police.

I was just keying in my code to call emergency services when the phone started to ring in my hand. My first thought was *Will?* Then, as I hit accept, I saw the name: Gran.

'Gran?' I could hardly speak for crying. 'I'm calling the police. Okay? She could be in terrible—'

'Listen!' Gran's voice was almost a shout, getting me to shut up and pay attention to what she was trying to tell me. 'I know where she is.'

I stopped dead, slumped against the railings, the phone pressed to my ear.

'What?'

Gran was breathing so heavily it was hard to make out the words. 'Tomas is here. At the house. He came to tell me. They've got her. Down by the railway, you know, just beyond the high street, where the road crosses over. Under there.'

46

An image of Tomas loomed in my mind as I jumped in the car and drove, too fast, down towards the railway. That muscular, stocky man, sporting tattoos, who'd appeared on Gran's stairs that day, fresh from helping himself to her shower. Or so he said. What else had he helped himself to?

I threw the car crookedly into a parking space and hurtled across the road to the edge of the bridge. It took me a moment to find the top of the path, the same steep, muddy track down towards the railway track that Sara had taken, laden down with her bag of shopping.

The air was moist with blown drizzle, wetting my nose and cheeks and making the path slippery. I shifted my weight sideways, trying to feel for stones to anchor my feet. Below, smoke wafted out from beneath the bridge in feeble, rapidly dispersing columns. As I approached it, smells reached for me: the acrid stench of burning rubber, carried in the smoke; the human stink of unwashed bodies, and excrement.

I pushed further down, thinking only about Hannah and what they might be doing to her, holding her prisoner there. I reached the flat, muddy ridge just above the level of the track.

The metal sleepers were a matter of feet away, humming with vibrations, warning of an approaching train. Figures shifted in the darkness under the brick arch. I sensed the tension, the fact they must be watching me. They had the advantage. I was clearly visible, picked out by the spillage from street lights above. They were little more than blackness for me, dark silhouettes shrouded in swirling smoke from a fading fire.

I was shaking, aware how dangerously I was exposed. I pulled out my phone and fumbled to switch on its torch. The faint beam seemed a comfort, despite the fact it barely penetrated a few feet in front of me. I crept forward.

'Hannah! Are you there?' No one answered. I was closing in on the edge of the archway now. Blood boomed in my ears. Where was she? What had they done to her? 'Have you got my daughter? What do you want? Money?' As I entered the arch, my voice changed, bouncing back to me off the stone in a mocking echo. 'Just don't hurt her, please. She's a child.'

The rails shrieked as a train came thundering towards me. Sparks flew from the wheels. The driver, beginning the final stretch to the station ahead, started to brake. Noise engulfed me, a metal screaming filled my ears.

At the same moment, as the train ripped past me, a blast of air knocked me off balance. I staggered sideways towards the wall, crashing into the cold, damp stone. Light strobed over me in waves as the carriages flashed by. Then it was gone. The sounds receded as quickly as they'd come.

I was shivering, pressing myself against the stone, shaking and close to tears. 'You alright, darling?'

Someone came shuffling towards me. I shrank back, afraid.

'You're her granddaughter, aren't you?' A woman bent towards me, peering. Her grimy face cracked into a hard smile. 'You didn't like it, did you, when we came to see your gran—? But the shoe's on the other foot now. Now you're the one coming to visit us. Funny old world, eh?'

I blinked. My heartbeat was slowly settling again. My eyes were trying to adjust to the dimness under the bridge and focus on her face. 'You're the musician, aren't you? The one in Gran's kitchen.'

'Maria. That's right. Wondered if you'd recognise me.' She stood there, regarding me, an odd look on her face. It was a damp evening, but not a cold one; nevertheless, she was swathed in a thick, padded coat, tied roughly around the middle with a frayed cord.

'Have you got her?' My voice sounded pathetic in the stillness. Frightened and powerless. 'Hurt me, if you need to hurt someone. Not her. Please. She's only eight. She's a child.'

'Hurt her?' Maria frowned. 'You hear that, guys? She thinks we're hurting her little girl.'

A high-pitched woman's voice called, 'Who does she think she is, anyway?'

Something wet hurled through the air from the darkness, and struck me on the cheek. A second pellet skimmed past my head and landed somewhere behind me.

'Oi! That's enough of that, missus!' Maria shouted back over her shoulder, then turned back to me. 'That's upsetting, that is. Making allegations.'

'Is she there?' I took a shuddering breath. 'Can I see her? Please.'

Maria gave me a steady look, then seemed to come to a decision and inclined her head, telling me to follow. She twisted round and shuffled back, further into the darkness, further under the bridge. I thought of the people passing on the road overhead, the cars and bicycles, the strolling couples and striding young professionals. They had no idea what lived down here, so close to their world and yet so separate from it. Neither had I, until now.

Another figure grew out of the gloom as I approached: a woman with stooped shoulders and a shock of grey hair, her torso thickened by layer upon layer of garments, ending with an outer wrapping of an outsized duffel coat. She had one hand squarely on the handle of an old supermarket trolley laden with plastic bags. The other hand was raised and pulled back. Her eyes, fixed on me, were fierce. She was the pellet thrower, clearly, ready to resume battle.

Maria nudged her as she passed. 'Enough of that, Sal. She's after the kid, that's all.' She turned back to me. 'Don't mind Sally. She's alright, really.'

I felt my way after her, one hand reaching now and then for the curved wall to keep my balance, the other holding my phone, its torch clicked off now, hidden inside my pocket. The ground beneath me was soft and slimy. The smell in there – of rotting food, mould and stale sweat – was overpowering.

'Hannah?' I called, peering. 'You there?'

Maria turned back. Her teeth glinted as she spoke. 'She'll not hear you.'

I swallowed back bile. My mind was sharp with terror and, underneath it all, a rumbling stream of prayer. *Please, God. Please let her be safe. I'll do anything. Anything you ask.* 'Where is she? Please.'

Maria came to a halt. We'd come so far now that light from the street above was spilling in from the other side of the bridge. She squatted down by a pile of rags and coats, then pulled one back.

Hannah's face gleamed in the half-light, her skin pale. Her eyes were closed.

Breath caught in my throat. 'What have you...? Is she...?' Suddenly, my legs were in motion, propelling me forward towards her, stumbling. *Please, God, let her be alive.*

I touched her cheek. The skin was cool, exposed to the evening breeze. I pushed my fingers deeper into the neck of her school blouse and felt the warmth there. Alive, then. Something inside me crumbled and gave way.

'What have you done to her?' I fumbled to lift Hannah's shoulders from the ground, scrabbling to free her from the filthy old coats wrapped around her. 'What happened?'

Hannah stirred and groaned. She muttered 'No!' in her sleep and pulled away from me. She tried to bury her face in a grimy jumper, to lie flat again and fall back into sleep.

'We didn't do anything to her. Apart from look after her.' Maria shook her head at me sadly. 'Didn't think of that, did you? That maybe we'd been kind, rescued your precious little girl for you.' She narrowed her eyes. 'You're nothing like your gran. Nothing.'

I blinked. I tried again to shake Hannah awake. 'Hannah! Come on, wake up. We need to go home.' I just wanted to get her away from there. Away from the dirt.

And, yes, away from them.

'She was down on the tracks. Didn't seem to know where she was going. Crying her eyes out.' Maria tilted her head back towards the woman with the trolley who was watching me, scowling. I shrank back, closer to Hannah. That woman had the wild look of a mangy dog.

'Sal found her, wandering,' Maria went on. 'We told her to go off home, but she wouldn't leave. Sobbing fit to burst.' Maria gave me a searching look. 'Question is, what did *you* do to her, to upset the poor kid so much, eh? Must've been something.'

I shook my head, frightened of her anger and said, for no particular reason, 'I'm sorry.'

I slid an arm under Hannah and concentrated on trying to raise her. She was too heavy for me to lift. I put my lips to her ear. 'Hannah. Can you hear me? It's Mummy. Wake up. Please. We need to go home.'

She opened her eyes but struggled to focus on me in the gloom. Her mind seemed far away. She seemed slowly to realise, at last, who I was, but instead of reaching for me, she tried to pull back. 'No!' She tossed her head. 'You can't make me.'

'What?' Had they hurt her? What had they done? 'Hannah, it's me. Mummy! You're safe now. I'll take you home.'

'No!' Hannah started to sob, some fresh grief breaking over her as she came back to consciousness.

'Hannah!' I tussled with her, trying to draw her close and wrap my arms around her, to comfort her, even as she pushed me away.

Maria leaned in. 'She'd have been hit by a train if we hadn't hauled her up here and bedded her down, nice and safe.' She put her face close to Hannah's. I imagined the smell of her sour breath in my child's face. 'Didn't we, darling? Kept you safe when you wouldn't go home. Sent Tomas to run off to your gran for help.'

I threaded my arm under Hannah's shoulder and half dragged her, still protesting, onto her feet. My eyes took in every movement. The distribution of her weight on each foot, the slant of her hips, the contours of her arms and shoulders as, more feebly now, she pressed me away from her. No sign of injury, that I could see. No swelling or dark blood stains. She seemed exhausted and despairing as she fought me, trying to stop me from rescuing her, from taking her home.

Had they given her something, some drug? I didn't know.

Was it really true that they had actually saved her, as Maria claimed?

I used my free hand to fumble in my pocket, trying to think how much cash I had with me. I pulled out a crumpled ten, then a twenty-pound note, folded in with my debit cards, and thrust them towards Maria. 'Here. Take this, will you? Share it with Tomas, too, for letting us know where she was.'

Maria pushed away my outstretched hand. I felt a sudden stab of panic. Why was she angry? Wasn't she going to let us leave? What more did they want?

'Keep your money.' Maria tutted. 'We're not beggars. We did it for *her*, not you. Because she's kind.' She bent to Hannah, who was sagging against my side and starting to shiver. 'You say hi to your great-gran, Hannah. Say hi from us. She's a lovely lady.'

I turned Hannah firmly by the shoulders and marched her ahead of me, physically propelling her out through the far end of the arched tunnel and into the embrace of the falling light.

Once we were clear and about to start climbing the steep bank back to the road, I turned and looked back. Maria was still silhouetted there, watching us. Behind her, Sally and her trolley, barely visible in the darkness, were angled towards me.

'Thank you,' I called. I raised a hand. 'Thank you so much.'

Neither of them moved.

47

Hannah slumped in the car, her face buried in her hands, sobbing. 'I'm not going home.' Her voice was an anguished wail. 'I can't. Don't make me.'

I clipped her seatbelt closed, jumped into the driving seat, and locked the doors. 'Don't move. Please.' I pulled out my phone to call Gran. 'Gran's been frantic. We all have.'

As I started to tell Gran that Hannah was safe and in the car with me, Hannah exploded again. 'I'm NOT going home. Don't you understand?' She was almost screaming.

Gran, clearly hearing the shrieking, said, 'Let me talk to her!'

I held the phone to Hannah's ear to make her listen. I didn't catch what Gran said, but Hannah started crying again, her rage softening. 'Alright,' she said. 'Alright. Stop it!' She folded herself forward, her arms around her stomach as if it hurt her. Her hair fell in dirty clumps on her neck. I longed to get her home, to soak her in a hot bath and scour off the filth that still clung to her from being under the bridge. I wanted my little girl back. I wanted to tuck her up in her own bed and watch over her.

Gran sounded exhausted but resolute. 'Bring her to me. She's agreed to that. Whatever's happened, seems like she needs a bit of space, lovely. A bit of distance. Okay?'

I hesitated. 'She needs to go home.'

Hannah cried out at once, 'No! I won't!'

Gran's breath was heavy in my phone. 'Just bring her here for now. You stay too. She needs to rest.'

I frowned. There wasn't room for all of us at Gran's. Sara had taken the spare room. I looked at Hannah, huddled against the door, her head bowed, then sighed, started the engine and drove her to Gran's.

She was waiting there on the doorstep and opened her arms to Hannah as soon as she came up the steps.

Her voice was a gentle murmur, her hands patting Hannah's back. 'Come here, lovely. You poor thing. Let's get you upstairs now. Cup of warm milk, maybe?'

Hannah followed her up the stairs, docile as a kitten, while Gran fussed and fretted around her. 'Let's get these clothes off you, shall we? Have a little wash before I tuck you up? No? No problem, lovely. Come on, then.'

Within a matter of minutes, Hannah was stripped to her underwear and tucked up on the sofa-bed in Gran's tiny box room, her breath ragged with crying but her eyes already closing.

'She'll be fine.' Gran shooed me out of the doorway and downstairs. 'She needs a good night's sleep.'

On the bottom step, my knees buckled, and I stumbled forward, reaching for the wall to steady myself.

Gran, behind me, stopped. 'You're done in. Come and sit down. She's safe now.'

I made it to the lounge and sat, my body rigid, physically trembling. Gran lowered herself into her chair. She looked suddenly very frail, as if she'd drawn on borrowed strength and exhausted her reserves.

'Any idea?' she asked.

I shook my head.

'Where was she?'

'Under the bridge. They've got a sort of camp down there. Maria and Tomas and a few others. They had her in there.'

Gran looked puzzled. 'But why? Why'd she gone to them?'

I remembered what Maria had said. 'She was wandering, apparently. Sobbing. They got her up off the tracks, out of harm's way. That's what Maria said, anyway.'

Gran put her hand to her chest, blinking hard.

'Gran?' I leaned forward. 'Are you okay? Can I get you something?'

She didn't answer, just closed her eyes.

For a moment, I didn't know what to do. I didn't want to leave Hannah, but there wasn't room for me there. I wouldn't get much sleep on the short settee, or on the floor. Also, although I felt exhausted, I was still pumped full of adrenalin, my legs tense and jittering.

I pulled out my phone and checked it. Nothing from Will. It wasn't like him to leave his phone switched off for so long. That was the only explanation I could accept. He surely wouldn't ignore a cry for help. It seemed an age since I'd texted and tried to call him. Anger bubbled. How could he leave me to deal with this on my own? I was still trembling with fear, panic, the horror of searching for a missing daughter. *Our missing daughter.* Where was he? I swallowed hard, my hands shaking. What was he doing?

I jumped up, kissed Gran lightly on the cheek as she dozed, and set out to the car.

48

It was nearly nine o'clock by the time I turned through the wrought-iron gates and headed up the long drive to Greystones. The grand Georgian façade made a louring rectangle against the dark sky. Beside the main building, a modern extension, with iron rafters and gleaming glass panels, shone with light.

I nosed my way into a parking space towards the top of the drive and got out. My feet crunched across the gravel as I headed down towards the building, checking the parked cars as I went. A light breeze blew across the grounds, carrying snatches of dispersing noise from the annex: chatter and laughter and the rhythmical strains of a live band.

I narrowed my eyes to take stock of the party in full swing on the other side of the bright glass. The people within were gathered together in clusters, drinking and talking. The men were stiff in formal suits. The women were elaborately dressed in tight dresses with low necks and unnaturally high heels. A wedding, perhaps, or a monied engagement party.

I stopped dead, my eyes drawn back to the cars I was passing. Wasn't that...? I took a step closer, checking the licence plate, then, as if I didn't quite trust my memory, crept along it to the passenger door, bent my face to the window and peered inside. I blinked. I recognised the dark mound of that back support, attached to the driver's seat, the rim of the sunglasses case poking out from the pocket in the far door. It was Will's, alright.

I stood for a moment, pressed against the cold metal and glass, shaken. I'd imagined he might be there. Of course I had. That's why I'd driven over in the darkness, on gut instinct. But I'd also hoped to be wrong. Now I knew something, at least. Something I hadn't wanted to know. I shivered and huddled inside my coat.

I knew Moira's husband, Rob, had been right about spotting Will the previous weekend.

I knew that if anyone here was a liar, it was Will.

I forced myself to turn away and head past the cars towards the plush front entrance, taking the steps with as much confidence as I could muster. I entered the echoing main lobby and headed past the reception desks, nodding briskly to the staff there.

A bank of lifts to the left suddenly pinged and, a moment later, the doors slid open and a gaggle of young women, smartly dressed, exuding expensive spicy perfume, surged out together, heading towards the annex and the party there.

Grateful for the distraction, I pushed quickly past them, keeping my eyes forward. I breathed in short, hard gulps. In my mind, I tried to picture the layout of the ground floor as I remembered it. There was a cavernous main dining room on the first level where we'd attended a formal dinner years ago. He wouldn't be there. If he had a choice in the matter, I had a hunch where he'd be.

I found my way out of the lobby and into a narrow corridor that ran behind it. I was looking for the rustic Italian bistro I'd seen on the website. That was where we'd always eaten in the past, when we'd driven out here for a meal, enjoying its low lighting and heavy oak furniture.

There it was. The décor was exactly as I remembered. I stopped just before the main entrance, peering into the dimly lit interior visible through the glass. The same pendulous lights hung low over a row of intimate booths with faux leather seating. The same long wooden bar stretched down the far side.

Memories snared me. Happy memories of the two of us, so in love, so at ease together, gazing into each other's eyes across a platter of calamari and a bottle of wine.

I faltered. What was I thinking? He wouldn't deceive me, not Will. How could I doubt him? There must be some innocent explanation, some misunderstanding. That was all. He'd be so hurt if he knew I'd driven there because I didn't trust him. It was madness. It was all this upset with Hannah. I just wasn't myself.

I was about to turn back, ashamed, when my eyes locked on to something. I paused and looked again. My whole body flushed.

Will was sitting in the second booth along, just half of his body visible to me as I stood, peering in. Dirty dishes, the remnants of a meal, were pushed to the edge of the table. Only two long-stemmed wine glasses remained on the table between them, half-filled with red wine.

Will was leaning forward, his lips in a tight, nervous smile, his eyes fixed on the young woman sitting across from him. His gaze was hesitant, as if he weren't yet sure of himself, of his ground, but filled with tenderness. As I watched, he placed his hand, palm upwards, on the table, fingers lightly curled, inviting hers. When she placed her hand in his, hesitantly, his fingers tightened around hers at once, and his smile broadened.

I steadied myself against the window frame, still hidden from their view. I needn't have bothered. His eyes never left her face. He seemed lost in her, incredulous, gazing on her with the intensity he'd once shown me, a long time ago.

She shifted in her seat, and he released her hand at once, his eyes still bright with pleasure, with love, but also careful, as if he were wary of going too far, of overstepping the mark before she was ready. I thought of the way he'd pulled back from me all those years ago, the first time he'd kissed me. How apologetic he'd been.

How charming and caring I'd thought him.

She manoeuvred her long legs to the end of the banquette and eased herself out from the table. He watched her, enraptured as she stood there. The low pinkish light from the hanging lamp caught her face as she turned slightly.

That face. Young and lovely, framed by poker-straight hair falling in a long bob. The grey-green eyes emphasised by kohl.

It was a face I knew all too well. My so-called long-lost niece, Sara.

49

I found Gran sitting in her chair in the lounge, wearing a robe and slippers, waiting up for me. She looked drawn.

I asked at once, 'How's Hannah?'

'Fast asleep.' Gran hesitated. She could tell, of course, that I'd been crying. 'Are you okay?'

I nodded. 'Just tired.' I didn't want to lie to Gran, but I couldn't tell her what I'd just seen. Not yet. My head was in too much of a mess. 'I'll just pop up and check on Hannah, then I'll crash on the couch, if that's okay—? I'm done in.'

'Of course, lovely. Shall I get you some blankets?'

'I can do that.' I knelt down beside her and gave her a hug. 'You get to bed, Gran. I'll be fine.'

She took my face in her hands and gave me a long look. 'Try to get some sleep. She's safe now, that's all that matters. We'll worry about the rest tomorrow.'

'Thanks, Gran.' My lip wobbled and I had to bite it hard to stop myself from crying again. 'Love you.'

'Love you too, petal.' Her voice was breathy. 'It'll be alright, you'll see.'

Once Gran had gone to bed, I sat in the darkness beside

Hannah in the tiny box room, listening to the slow, steady rhythm of her breathing, looking over her pale face. Images crowded into my head: Hannah, lying still and silent under the bridge, covered by filthy coats; the pain in her face when she fought me, saying she wouldn't go home, she couldn't.

What had happened to her? Where had she been? I was frightened even to imagine it. What if someone had hurt her, molested her? I'd kill them. I really would. I squeezed my hands into fists as I screamed silently into the darkness.

And Will. How could he? The very evening I most needed him. When Hannah needed him desperately too. He'd lied to me. I knew that now. I'd been right to be suspicious. I thought of how much I'd always trusted him in the past. Was this the first time? Had he cheated on me before and I'd never even realised?

I felt sick at heart. I'd loved him. I still did. I'd trusted him.

I thought of the frantic, begging messages I'd sent him and switched my own phone to silent until the morning. Let him stew. See how it felt.

Later, I pulled off my clothes and crawled under a scratchy blanket, trying to get comfortable on the couch. It was impossible to sleep.

All I could think about was Will and Sara, lost in each other.

SARA

50

It was a fancy restaurant. Sara had to give him that. He could have got away with paying a lot less. But then he had money – Granny had said so.

He was the success in the family, the one who'd made everyone so proud. If only they knew.

She studied her face in the mirror. The ladies' toilets were dimly lit and the face looking back at her was lovely, if a little blurred by all that wine. She ran cold water over her wrists to sober herself up a bit, then dried them off and unzipped her bag, setting out her lipstick, mascara and powder on the counter in front of her. Her weapons of war.

She had the feeling she mightn't get much sleep tonight. Her head was buzzing. *What a total car crash.* Now what was she going to do?

She pulled the cap from the lipstick, screwed it higher and pursed her lips as she coated them. Will had seemed so nervous at first, he'd hardly been able to look her in the eye. And he was old. Definitely over forty. But he had style. She did like him. He was cool.

She'd sensed something was up by the tension in his voice when he'd called to suggest dinner.

'A chance to get to know each other properly,' he'd said.

Then, when she'd agreed, the sting in the tail: 'Let's keep it our secret for now, shall we?'

He'd seemed so very different from the first time they met, at the barbecue, when he was Mr Family Man. And she'd noticed how careful he'd been: no evidence. No texts or WhatsApp messages, nothing in writing. Just that one short phone call, presumably from his office line. *Number withheld.* He'd had it all planned. He'd even arranged to pick her up in his expensive car a few blocks away from Granny's house. Making quite sure poor Granny didn't see.

Dear old Uncle Will. Well, she'd never think of him as that again, would she? Not now.

She leaned forward, peering at her reflection as she applied more mascara, then considered the effect. She blinked. What about Paula? Please God, imagine what she'd say. Sara hadn't bargained on blowing their marriage apart like this. She bit down on her lip. And what about Hannah? She was a decent kid. She didn't deserve it either.

Too late to worry about that now. It was done. No going back.

She reached for the powder and dusted it lightly over her cheeks, her chin, her neck.

Anyway, it wasn't her fault. It was their marriage.

But now what? What the hell happens now?

She closed her eyes and swayed.

She'd always liked to think she was street-smart. She liked to think that if there was a storm brewing, she was the one who smelled it in the air, who saw it first, gathering on the horizon, long before everyone else. She liked to think she knew how to protect herself, how and when to take cover.

Not this time.

This had come from nowhere and knocked her right off her feet. This had sent her whole world spinning out of control. She couldn't see how it could ever come right again.

PAULA

51

I didn't get much sleep.

In the small hours, I gave up, went through to the kitchen and made myself a strong black coffee.

When I switched my phone back on, it showed several missed calls from Will, all of them from the house. That gave me some idea what time he'd finally gone home. There were no replies to my frantic text messages or voicemails.

I switched my phone off again. I wasn't ready to deal with him yet. He might try Gran's number too, eventually.

I crept upstairs to use the bathroom. Sara's bedroom door had been ajar when I went in to see Hannah last night. Now it was firmly closed. I hesitated on the landing, listening. I hadn't heard her come back. She must have crept straight through the hall and up the stairs. I wondered if she'd seen me, asleep on the couch. If she'd had the decency to feel any shame.

Later, I sat alone in the kitchen for a long time, lost and afraid, measuring the slowly strengthening light of dawn.

It was almost eight when Gran and Hannah came down together, Gran's arm around Hannah's thin shoulders. The shocked concern in Gran's eyes when she saw me told me exactly how rough I looked.

'Hannah.' I jumped up and folded my arms round her, held her close. 'Can you eat some breakfast?'

Hannah sat, hunched, at the kitchen table, hair in disarray, while I made her a slice of toast. Gran, bustling around me, put the kettle on and started to microwave herself a bowl of porridge.

When I set the buttered toast in front of Hannah, her eyes slid reluctantly to my face. Shock registered as she looked me over more closely, presumably concluding from the state I was in that she was in even more trouble that she'd feared. I didn't disabuse her, not yet. Let her think my sleepless night had been because of her. She certainly hadn't helped.

I pulled out a chair and sat heavily. I closed my eyes and tuned into the familiar sounds of Gran's kitchen, noises that stretched back to my childhood: the soft clink of china mugs, the breathy gurgle of the boiling kettle, the suck of the fridge door; Gran's laboured breathing as she moved around me, then came, finally, to set a mug of fresh tea in front of me.

She sat, a heavy puff escaping from her lips. 'She's very sorry, aren't you, Hannah?' Gran, the peace maker. 'She didn't realise how much upset she'd cause. She just didn't think, did you, petal?'

Hannah picked at her toast, her face tilted down towards her lap, hiding from me.

'You were supposed to be at Lizzie's.' My voice was tight. Hannah tensed. 'How did you end up outside, on your own? I was frantic.' Something inside me gave way and my voice became suddenly desperate at the thought of what might have happened. 'You could have been killed, Hannah. How could you? Where did you go?'

Hannah burst into tears, her face hidden in her hands, shoulders tight.

Gran frowned at me. 'Alright, Paula. We don't know, do we? We don't know what happened. Give her a chance.'

I reached out and pulled Hannah to me, holding her as tightly as I could, rocking her. Suddenly, I was crying too, my tears soaking into her hair. 'I was so scared. I thought I'd never see you again. Oh, Hannah, I love you so much.'

Hannah awkwardly opened her arms and grasped me too, sobbing.

We cried together until we were both too tired to carry on, then sat stiffly for a little longer, our arms wrapped round each other. What if she'd died? I imagined her stumbling onto the railway track in the darkness, the metal sleepers humming and sparking with an oncoming train.

And Will, how could you betray me? What a mess, all of it. More than I could bear.

Eventually, we eased apart. Hannah's face was wet and blotchy. I reached into my pocket for a tissue and wiped it, held it to her nose while she blew, then found another to mop up my own.

'What a pair!' Gran tried to lighten the mood. 'Come on, Hannah. Try to eat something.'

She left Hannah sitting mournfully over her toast and beckoned me through into the lounge, shutting the connecting door behind her.

'She's in such a state.' Her eyes scanned my face. 'Look, I know you want answers. I do too. But give her time, will you? Leave her with me for a few hours. We'll just do some baking or something. I won't ask about last night, I promise. Just give her a chance to calm down.'

I put my arms around Gran and hugged her. 'I love you.'

'I love you too. Now, go home and change your clothes. You look terrible.'

She was right. Neither Hannah nor I was in a fit state for a difficult conversation. I didn't trust myself not to cry on her again. I also didn't want to be there when Sara came downstairs. To see me making a scene was the last thing Hannah needed.

I drove home and was just putting the key in the lock when my phone pinged with a message. I rummaged in my bag for my phone. It must be Will, surely, finally responding to my texts from last night.

It wasn't Will. It was an alert from the DNA company to tell me they'd just emailed me the results of the tests, the answer to my question of whether Sara and I really were a DNA match. Now I'd find out for certain if she really was who she claimed to be, or a fraud.

I ran into the kitchen to grab my laptop and logged on, still in my coat.

I opened up the email and ran through the data, staring at the screen, blinking through wet eyelashes.

I had to read it through several times before it finally sank in.

52

The garage buzzed with Saturday morning customers.

Several cars were parked on the forecourt, waiting for collection or for test drives. A lad from the sales team stood, plainly bored, alongside a second-hand Volvo while a young couple clambered inside to check the interior.

I was heading towards the workshops at the back to look for Alan when the hard-faced boss appeared from the showroom.

He was wearing the same cheap suit, the belt straining to contain a flabby stomach. 'Can I help you?' He managed to make it sound like a reprimand.

'Morning.' I forced myself to smile. 'I'm Alan's sister. I was just...' I slowed and gestured towards the mechanics' area.

'I know.' He didn't attempt to smile back. 'I know who you are.'

'Right.' I stopped, wondering why he seemed so hostile. 'I won't be long. I just wanted to—'

'Didn't he tell you?'

I hesitated, trying to understand. I didn't like the way he was glaring at me, thuggish but also self-satisfied.

'Tell me what?'

'I fired him. Ten days ago.'

My stomach tightened. *Oh, Alan, not again.* 'Why?'

He tipped his head to one side, looking at me coolly. 'Misconduct.'

I blinked. 'What do you mean?' He'd been doing so well.

'Too cocky by half, your brother. You tell him from me. He needs to watch it.' He pointed a fat thumb at his own chest. 'I'm the boss around here.'

I hesitated, frowning, tying to make sense of what he was saying.

'Kept butting in and giving advice where it wasn't welcome. Undermining me. In front of customers too. He wants to watch his mouth.'

I shook my head slowly. 'I bet he was right.'

'Pardon?'

'Whatever it was he said about cars, engines, whatever it was, I bet he was the one who was right. Not you. You just didn't like being shown up.' I imagined this loutish man turning on Alan, cutting him down to size and giving him the boot. Alan couldn't afford to lose another job, he was barely keeping himself afloat as it was. 'There's nothing about cars my brother doesn't know. Nothing. He's been taking them apart and putting them back together all his life. What were you paying him for all that experience? Buttons, I bet. You were lucky to have him.'

He puffed out his cheeks, his face reddening. 'Excuse me, you—'

'Oh, please. Don't start on me. Alan is worth ten of you, you jumped-up bully.' I took a step nearer. I was close enough now to see the sheen of sweat on his forehead, at his temples, to smell his cheap aftershave. He lifted a hand as if he were ready to fend me off in self-defence. 'Look at those nails. Not a trace of dirt on them. When were you last on your back, under a chassis?'

He gave a sudden leer and said softly, so only I could hear, 'When were you last on your back, love? That your problem, is it? Old man not up to it?'

'What did you say?' Anger bubbled up from nowhere. I took another step and put my face in his, menacing. I didn't know what I was doing. I'd never hit anyone in my life. I was just a woman who'd had enough, who had nothing left to lose.

His eyes widened, suddenly alarmed as he read the fury in my eyes.

I repeated, '*What* did you just say to me?'

'Alright there, boss?'

The young salesman came striding over. Behind him, the couple, climbing out of the car, gaped.

The boss gave me a final glare, then turned abruptly and headed back into the showroom, his back stiff with tension.

The young guy nodded to me and said quietly, 'Sorry. Don't quote me, but he can be a bit of a... well, fill in the blank yourself.' He grinned. 'I'd offer you a free coffee and a sales tour, but I don't think it'd go down too well.'

'I'm Alan's—'

'—sister. I remember.' He turned and we started to walk together across the tarmac, back towards my car. 'I liked Alan. He taught me a lot. And he didn't put a foot wrong – you mustn't think that. It was just himself.' He inclined his head back towards the showroom. The boss was standing inside the floor-to-ceiling glass, glaring out at us, watching me leave. 'Like I said, bit of a so-and-so. Won't be corrected. Even if he's wrong. In fact, especially when he's wrong.' He hesitated as we said goodbye. 'I'm Geoff, anyway. Say hi to Alan, will you? He's a good guy.'

53

Alan's apartment was on the ground floor of a shabby house conversion. The tenants in the two flats above him — another one-bedroom apartment on the first floor and a poky studio apartment in the roof — came and went so often I'd lost track of who was there. They were usually research students or trainee nurses who were new to the area and hadn't yet saved enough to move to a better neighbourhood.

Alan kept his own rent low by acting as the building's unofficial caretaker and handyman, mending broken taps and unplugging sinks and, when the youngsters finally got enough cash together to move on, borrowing a van and acting as a removal man too.

Today, the house looked as depressing as ever. The path was peppered with litter and the row of bins overflowed. I had to hammer on the door for several minutes before I finally heard heavy footsteps inside.

Alan opened the door a crack and peered out at me through bloodshot eyes. He was unshaven and wearing a grubby tracksuit.

'Alan?'

He shrugged and turned to shuffle back inside. I pushed my way in, disturbing a layer of flyers and unopened mail on the inside mat. The air was stale and dank. I followed him into his apartment, off the communal hall, into the tiny kitchen. Dirty dishes and mugs covered the counter surfaces, abandoned cups of milky tea greying with mould.

Alan searched in a cupboard for a clean glass, poured himself a shot of cheap whisky and downed it with a shudder.

I said, 'Bit early, isn't it?'

'Hair of the dog.'

I reached out and prised the whisky bottle from him. I needed him as sober as possible.

'Aw, come on,' he said. It was only a token protest. He looked too done in to fight me.

'Why didn't you tell me?'

He lolled back against the sink and kept his eyes on the floor, avoiding my gaze. 'Tell you what?'

'I just went to see you. At the garage.'

'Oh.' His face fell. He looked like a sheepish little boy who'd been caught out. 'I was going to.'

I strode across to him and put my arms around his strong body, buried my face in his shoulder and hung on. His skin, his breath, stank of stale spirits, but I didn't care. He hesitated for a moment, uncertain. We weren't usually given to outbursts of affection. Finally, he lifted his arms and put them awkwardly around me to give a cautious hug back.

A few moments later, he stepped back and started to busy himself with making me a cup of coffee. He then led me into his messy lounge, lifting old papers and crumpled clothing from an armchair so I had somewhere to sit.

'Geoff says hi, by the way.' I remembered the scene at the garage. I felt suddenly embarrassed. What had I been thinking? He was a thug, that boss. Trouble.

Alan nodded.

'He's a piece of work, isn't he?'

He looked surprised. 'Geoff?'

'Your boss.' I thought of his sweaty face and sausage fingers. 'Has he ever actually fixed a car?'

Alan shrugged. 'He doesn't need to. That's what he's got mechanics for.'

I looked at the mess on the floor: discarded bottles of cheap spirits, torn papers, dirty socks.

'Well, you should have told me.' I toed an empty bottle. 'That's not the answer, for a start.'

His arms hung limply at his sides. 'I knew you'd say that.'

'You know I'm right.' I sighed. 'There'll be other jobs. And I can help you out if you're broke, tide you over.'

His jaw set. 'I'll manage.'

'How, exactly?' I knew how hard-up he must be. He was always on the verge of paying off his debts but never quite seemed to manage it, however hard he worked. Now, after ten days without an income and too much money going on booze, however cheap, he'd be sinking backwards again. 'Did he at least pay you off properly?'

He winced. 'Not for that last week. He was looking for an excuse, I could tell. I put him right about something in front of a customer.' He hung his head. 'Maybe I should've kept my mouth shut. It just came out. And the customer needed to know the facts. Anyway, he didn't say much at the time, but I could see he was livid. He let me work another week after that and then, just before payday, bang! He made a big fuss about something else I'd said, something and nothing, nitpicking, you know, just for the sake of it, and fired me.'

I shook my head. 'He can't do that. You earned it. It's your money.'

He gave me a hard look. 'Right. So, what am I going to do, sue him? Get real.'

I sipped my coffee and shut up. Maybe he was right. His boss looked the vindictive type. Maybe it wasn't worth the battle. I just hated to see Alan treated badly. He never was very good at standing up for himself, at fighting back.

'Anyway.' He shook himself slightly and looked across at me, changing the subject. 'What did you want to see me about? Everything okay?'

'Not really.' It was hard to know where to start. I reached for my phone. 'Alan, there's something I need to tell you. About Sara.'

He frowned. Clearly, that wasn't what he had been expecting. 'What?'

'There's no easy way to say this.'

His eyes narrowed. 'Go on, then. Spit it out.'

I steadied myself and just said it, 'It isn't her. She isn't really Sara.'

He shook his head at once and moved forward to the edge of his seat as if he didn't want to stay to hear any more.

'Just listen.' I lifted a hand to stop him. 'I've got proof.'

'Proof?'

'I did a DNA test.'

'You did what? What did you do that for?'

'I just wanted to be sure. Don't get worked up. She agreed.' I hesitated, remembering the difficult conversation we'd had. 'I wouldn't have done it otherwise.'

'But how?' He stared at me, hostile and confused. 'I don't get it.'

'It's easy enough. I just bought a kit online. Took a swab from my cheek and one from hers, and sent them off to see if we match. That's all there is to it.'

He blinked hard. 'And that proves she's not Sara?'

I took a deep breath. 'We're not related. This young woman and I. We're not a match. She's not who she says she is.'

He stared at me for a long moment, and the significance of what I was saying seemed to penetrate. His shoulders slumped and he lowered his head to his hands. The room was silent for a moment. The strains of a rhythmical beat, the dregs of music, leached down from one of the flats above.

Finally, he lifted his head. 'It's wrong. That's all. They've made a mistake. Got the samples mixed up, or something.'

'It's a lab, Alan. They don't make mistakes like that.' I found the email on my phone and tried to show him. 'See for yourself. I just got the results, this morning. It's all there in black and white.' I hesitated. 'I'm sorry. Really. I know how much you wanted it to be her. I get that. But what could I do? I couldn't not tell you.'

He said sharply, 'You could have not done it in the first place. Why did you, anyway? Why didn't you just leave it all alone?' He took my phone from me and flicked through, scanning the data and the conclusion at the end. 'It's wrong,' he said again, and handed it back. 'They've made a mistake. I don't care what it says. I know it's her.' He looked me in the eye. 'She even looks like Jackie. The shape of her nose. Her eyes. You can't deny that, right?'

I hesitated. 'Lots of people have grey-green eyes. That's not proof of anything but the—'

He tutted. 'There's more to it than that. You weren't there when we had dinner together. We talked all evening. You should have heard the stuff she came out with about Jackie. Little things. Things she said and did. She knew her, Paula. The way she liked to stew that stinky green tea in her mug after dinner and keep mushing it with her spoon. The way she insisted she didn't have a sweet tooth but always kept a secret stash of jelly babies tucked away in her bag, as if no one ever knew.' He batted the air, dismissing me. 'You were a kid back then. Maybe you don't remember.'

He looked lost in memory for a moment. I thought about the way his eyes used to shine when he saw Jackie, the fact he'd never quite dared to believe he was good enough for her and the way he fell apart when she left and took their daughter and his happiness with her.

I started, quietly, 'Maybe she knew Jackie and Sara. Maybe that's how she found out what had happened and saw an opportunity—'

'No!' His vehemence startled me. He handed my phone back to me. 'I don't believe it, Paula. Stop it. And don't go upsetting Gran either. Leave it alone.'

Gran. I put my phone away and went back to drinking my coffee, waiting for him to calm down. It wasn't like him to be angry. I wondered how much more to say. Whether to tell him that, whoever she was, whether she was really Sara or not, she was trying to steal my husband. And she was also a thief. Stealing from Gran and selling stuff on and hadn't denied it.

'You should go.' He paused, and looked at me.

I wondered what he saw, if he could tell I hadn't had much sleep, that my hands were shaking. I could almost see the cogs turning as he thought about the fact I was there with him, sitting in his lounge on a Saturday morning. 'Where's Hannah, anyway? She and Will gone off somewhere?'

I bit my lip. That was the other part of the puzzle. How could I tell him that the young woman he was so determined to put on a pedestal, so certain was his long-lost daughter, was having a clandestine affair with her so-called uncle? With my beloved husband.

A traitor as well as a thief.

My bitterness must have shown in my face. He seemed to sense it. 'What, Paula? What is it?'

I shook my head, annoyed with him for refusing to believe what I'd just proved to him. How much clearer could it be?

'Nothing. She's with Gran, that's all. Will was out last night. Late.'

I got to my feet and took my cup through to the poky kitchen, filled the sink with hot, soapy water and started to gather together the filthy cups, plates and dishes, making a dent in the chaos before I went home.

54

My temples throbbed as I approached the house. Will hadn't been there when I dashed in earlier. I'd guessed, from the state of the bedroom, that he'd got up early and gone out for a run. I'd kept my phone switched off since then, but I knew I couldn't avoid him forever. I just didn't know what to do, what to say to him. I was still in shock.

As I let myself in, the pulse of the security alarm came as a relief. The house was empty.

I walked through to the kitchen. The day was overcast and the surfaces, usually so gleaming, seemed dull. I stood for a while, dazed with tiredness, and leaned heavily against the counter.

I remembered the first time I saw this house, before Hannah was even born. We'd already seen several in the area, but I knew as soon as I walked in that this was the one. I didn't know why. I just knew. This was our family home, where we'd raise our two or three children and be happy. Already I had been imagining how we'd live in it – the dinners, the birthday parties, the barbecues on the patio. Yes, it needed work, but that didn't seem to matter at the time. We could afford it, thanks to Will.

As we were shown from room to room by the zealous estate agent, I'd kept trying to catch Will's eye. I needed to know if he felt the same. He'd looked so serious, so unimpressed, as he asked all about the state of the windowsills and the age of the floorboards.

It was only later, when the estate agent drove off and we walked, hand in hand, down the street, that I dared to ask him, my voice breathy with trying not to let my excitement show, 'What did you think? Did you like it?'

He gazed down at me. 'It needs work.' He gave me his slow, steady smile. 'But yes, I liked it. I really did.'

I looked now at the stretches of shining metallic trim, at all the expensive appliances – the new coffee grinder to the mixer with its polished chrome bowl – and at the pristine stretches of counter, spotless and still. For the first time, I saw it all not as a blessing, a gift to be cherished, but as something sinister: a kitchen that was sterile and dead and myself, the slave in it, not a woman who was cherished, as I'd always felt until now, but one who had been first bought off and then betrayed.

I heaved myself upstairs, peeled off my clothes and stood under the shower, scouring myself with water as hot as I could stand until I lost myself in the steam.

Afterwards, I dressed slowly, then sat on the edge of the bed, looking out of the window at the trees, desolate.

I was still sitting there, unable to move, when the gate squeaked. Footsteps sounded on the path.

My mind took in the rattle of the key in the lock and the sound of the door opening.

Will's voice rang out, 'Hello!' The click of the closing front door, his soft tread crossing the hall. A kitchen cabinet opened and banged closed. He'd been to the shops, maybe, stocking up on the heavy, bulky items I found harder to carry.

I bent forwards, my arms tight round my stomach, and tried to breathe.

He called up from the hall, 'You upstairs?'

Always, if I were in the house when he came home, I stopped what I was doing and went to greet him. At the very least, if I was arm-deep in laundry or cooking or cleaning, I hollered to tell him where I was, asked him to come and find me, to tell me about his day.

Today, I didn't answer. I couldn't. I just sat, heart thumping, listening to the creak of the banister under the weight of his hand as he took the stairs. He appeared in the doorway, then stopped abruptly as he caught sight of me, sitting there, hunched forward, gazing right back at him.

'You alright?' His tone was cautious, reading me. He looked around. 'Where's Hannah?'

He didn't even know. Why hadn't he switched his phone back on and checked for messages? Was he so lost in love that he hadn't bothered to look?

I thought about the panic of last night, the frantic dash to the park, through the streets, to the railway to rescue our girl, our baby, to bring her home safely. My throat was so tight, I could barely breathe.

He said stupidly, 'Is everything okay?'

'Didn't you get my messages?'

He frowned. 'My battery's out.' He took his phone out of his pocket and showed me the black screen as if it were evidence. 'Must've left my charger in the office.' He paused. 'Why? Is it Hannah?'

I blurted out, 'She went missing.'

'Missing.' Colour drained from his face in an instant. 'What do you mean?'

I hesitated a moment, letting him suffer, before saying, 'She's at Gran's now. I found her. She was down by the railway, under the bridge.'

He gaped at me, as if I were speaking a foreign language and he was struggling to understand. 'Hannah?'

'Yes!' I snapped.

'But what...?' He faltered, still at a loss. 'Why was she—'

I interrupted, my anger rising. 'I called you. I kept trying—' I broke off. What was the point? He'd lied to me. He'd abandoned us and taken his lover for a romantic dinner. I muttered, 'Forget it. I found her, in the end.'

He crossed the room. The bed creaked and sagged as he sat beside me and reached for my hand. His large, skilful doctor's hands, meant to soothe, to heal. As familiar as my own.

I remembered the way they'd reached for hers and pulled my fingers away.

'Tell me.' He frowned. 'What's going on?'

It was a struggle to form the words and when they did emerge, they seemed strange to me, choked but also distant, as if someone else was speaking, as if they were floating in the air without meaning.

'I know.' I swallowed. 'I know about you and Sara.'

Even then, even as I said the words, I still didn't entirely believe it. My eyes were on his face, watching.

If only he'd looked puzzled or confused; if he'd shaken his head, baffled, or maybe laughed. I imagined him pulling back from me, stung, saying, 'What are you talking about? Me and Sara? That's absurd. Paula, don't be ridiculous. I'd never do that to you. Listen. I can explain everything.'

Instead, he flushed, and his eyes closed for a moment in a heavy blink. When they opened again, he looked away from me, fixed on some empty place on the far side of the bed. He wore the look of a man who was exhausted and finally knew the game was up.

A man who'd been well and truly caught.

Will, my hero, the man who had always seemed to me the epitome of adult cool, sounded lost. 'Paula, please. I don't know what to say. I'm sorry. Really, really sorry. I've been meaning to, well, we need to talk. Look, I know, well, I don't know, I can only imagine, I mean...'

He trailed off into silence. What did he expect me to do? Find the words he couldn't and help him out with this? Reach out, squeeze his hand and tell him everything would be okay? Say that he'd made a stupid mistake, but we could fix this, I could handle it, I still loved him?

Was that even true?

I pulled myself to my feet and pushed past him.

He jumped up too and tried to block my way. His face was drawn. 'How did you—'

'How did I find out?' I shook my head in disgust. 'Is that what matters, Will? How you got caught?'

'No!' There was a desperation in his face, something I'd never seen before. 'I wanted to tell you, Paula. I did. I kept meaning to. I was just, you know...'

'Frightened?' I stared at him, wondering if I'd ever really known him before. 'Frightened of what I'd say? What did you expect? That I'd pat you on the head and say never mind, no hard feelings?'

He stood and stared at me, wordless, his eyes brimming.

I turned and headed downstairs and, on my way out to the car, did something I knew he hated: slammed the door behind me so hard the glass shook.

55

Gran's house smelled of freshly baked cookies.

Usually, I loved that. Today, the cloying sweetness made my empty stomach turn.

There they were, cooling on a rack on the kitchen table. Bowls and spoons were washed and set to dry beside the sink.

'Gran?' I wanted her, very badly. I went through to the lounge and found her sitting there in her recliner, her feet up, eyes closed. I lowered my voice: 'Gran?'

For a moment, my heart stopped. I took a step closer, listening, and caught with relief the sound of her low breathing. I looked around. No sign of Hannah.

I headed upstairs. Hannah was in the spare bedroom, the one Sara was using – Sara, or whatever her real name was. She was hunched forward over Sara's laptop, eyes intent on the screen.

'Hannah?'

She jumped and spun round. 'Mum!'

'What are you doing?'

'Nothing.' She slammed the lid of the laptop closed without powering it down, her face guilty.

'Has Sara told you it's okay to use her computer?'

She shook her head. 'You won't tell her, will you? I just, I just needed to—'

I sat beside her and opened up the laptop again. The screen flickered and flashed as it came rushing back to life: a pixelated landscape of sparkling blue lakes and tree-clad mountains with blocky computer-generated animals and fairies darting across the foreground.

'*Magiclands*, right?'

She nodded.

I wasn't sure what to say. She needed to, what? Sneak into someone else's room and play games on their laptop, after all the trouble she'd already caused? I was bewildered. I thought I knew my daughter. Now I was starting to wonder if I really knew anyone in my family.

My eye was caught by words, flickering in a box at the top right-hand corner of the screen. An invisible hand was typing a message: '*Sorry, babe. Don't get mad at me. You know I love you.*'

I stared, then pointed. 'Is that to you?'

She nodded, then made a poor attempt to press the laptop shut again, to hide the conversation from my sight.

I held it open and peered closer. The username was meaningless to me: LIONBOY101. 'Who's he?'

She flinched, shrinking away from me. 'Just a friend.'

I hit the textbox and tried to scroll higher to see what else they'd been saying, but it didn't seem to move.

'Don't!' She pushed my hand away from the screen with force, then burst suddenly into tears and wailed: 'Mum, stop it, can't you? Just don't!'

I set down the laptop, then opened my arms and drew her into a hug. She resisted for a second, then her body collapsed and gave way. She pressed herself into me and let me rock her and stroke her hair as she sobbed into my chest.

'Oh, Hannah. What's happened? Please tell me. Be really brave and tell me. Can you? What's been going on?'

It took her a long time to calm down enough to talk. When her sobs finally subsided, I held a tissue while she blew her nose noisily, then sat with my arm tightly around her, the two of us pressed side by side on the bed, facing the wall.

'Who is this guy? Do you even know him?'

Her tear-stained face was miserable. 'Sort of. He's friends with one of my friends. I don't message strangers. I only talk to people we know. I'm not stupid.'

Oh, Hannah. She sounded as if she thought herself so worldly-wise, when she was really still so naïve, as innocent as an eight-year-old should be.

I took a deep breath and tried to stay calm. 'We've talked about that, haven't we? About keeping safe online.'

'Yes!' She sounded exasperated. 'I know! We've done it in school as well. Everyone does.'

I tried to think. 'So, is this a boy at school?'

She frowned. 'Maybe. I think so, yes.'

'But you don't know his name?'

'Of course not. We don't use real names online. No one does. For safety.'

I swallowed hard. 'So, what's he been messaging you about?'

She blinked, suddenly coy. 'He really likes me.'

'What do you mean, likes you?'

'*Likes* me. As in girlfriend and boyfriend.'

I thought back to the message I'd seen on the screen: *You know I love you.* It didn't sound to me like an eight-year-old boy. But what kind of sick adult would send a message like that to a child? I didn't want to alarm Hannah and have her clam up, but it was hard not to react. She'd started talking, now and then, about the other girls at school gossiping about boyfriends, about flirting, about which boy was in love with which girl. It was ridiculous. They were eight years old, for heaven's sake. They should be racing around the playground, boys and girls together, kicking a ball or playing chase, not fretting about romance.

She tipped her face up to mine. 'It's serious, Mummy. I think he wants to marry me.'

'Hannah, you're a bit young to get married.'

She rolled her eyes. 'I know. Not now, obviously. When we're grown up.'

I was having trouble fitting all this together, still trying to tread carefully in case I lost her. 'But... you don't know who he is?'

She hung her head. 'Not exactly.'

'What does that mean?'

She paused and pulled away from me. 'I'm not telling you.'

'Oh, sweetheart.' I swallowed hard. 'Clearly, something's happened that's upset you – upset you a lot, isn't that right?'

She gave a brittle nod, her jaw clenched.

'Please try to talk to me about it. I really want to help.'

She breathed heavily. Her small chest heaved. 'You'll be mad.'

I considered this. 'I'll try really hard not to be, okay?'

'Really hard?' Her eyes slid to my face to check my expression. They were wary.

'Really hard.' I touched her cheek. 'I'm worried, Hannah. I was so frightened last night. I thought something had happened to you. I didn't know where you were. See?' My voice trembled and I stopped and forced myself to take a deep breath. 'I love you so much. You know that, don't you?'

'You might not if I tell you.'

I smiled, despite everything, at the absurdity of that. 'Oh, Hannah. I will. I might be sad sometimes or disappointed, but I will always, always love you. Even if you did something really terrible, like killed someone. That's the worst thing I can imagine. I'd still love you. I'd still visit you in prison.'

She frowned. 'I haven't killed anyone. It's not that.'

'Good. I'm glad.' I pulled her close again. 'So, tell me. What happened?'

She bowed her head and stared miserably at the patch of carpet at our feet, so familiar with its pink and green swirls. I'd traced them with my eyes a million times over the years.

'He knows me. He says so. He just won't tell me who he is.' Her mood lightened as she talked about it. She looked almost proud.

'Why won't he tell you?'

'It's part of the game, see? He said as soon as he heard I'd joined *Magiclands,* he found out my screen name so we could chat. PixieGirl22, remember?'

'I remember.'

'So he started messaging me. That's the game. Kind of "guess who I am?" sort of thing. And it's true, he does really know me. He knows stuff about me.'

'What sort of stuff?'

'Oh, just stuff. What I look like and my favourite subject and stuff.'

'Okay.' My insides twisted. 'And you messaged him back?'

She shrugged. 'Yep.'

'So, then what happened?'

She stiffened slightly. 'He asked me to meet him. You know, for a date.'

'Hannah!'

'You said you wouldn't be mad!'

I let out a hard breath. 'I'm not mad, I'm just...' I couldn't begin to explain how sick I felt at the thought of anyone, whatever age he was, trying to take my eight-year-old out a date as if she were an adult. I steadied myself. 'I'm sorry. I'm not mad. Go on. He asked you on a date.'

Then it hit me.

'That was last night, wasn't it? That's where you went?'

She nodded slowly.

56

I had a sudden image of a predatory man, someone foul with decaying teeth and a paunch, actually meeting up with my sweet, beautiful young daughter. Possibly hurting her. My heart stopped.

'What did he do, Hannah? You must tell me. Please.'

She frowned at me, not understanding why I seemed so anxious for her. 'He didn't show up. I sat there for ages, waiting, all on my own. It was awful. People kept staring at me. I even had to buy my own cup of tea.'

I stared at her, relief flooding through me that he hadn't actually been with her. 'You don't drink tea!'

'I know.' She shrugged. 'I just thought I should.' She hesitated. 'It's alright, I used my pocket money. And I left a tip.'

I squeezed her to me, imagining her slight figure hunched over a cup of tea she didn't want, pretending to be grown up. I saw her laboriously counting out the change when she was asked to pay and deliberating about how much more to leave the waiter. Her pocket money was so precious to her. She only got a pound a week.

I swallowed hard. 'Why didn't you tell me?'

'You wouldn't have let me go,' she said simply.

She pulled free again and I carried on, 'Where was this, anyway?'

'In a café.' She shrugged, as if to say, *What does it matter?*

'So you sat there with a cup of tea and he didn't come?'

She nodded.

'Then what?'

She flushed, remembering. 'The waiter said I had to leave. They started to close up. So I did.'

'Why didn't you just come home?'

'I thought you'd find out I wasn't at Lizzie's, like I said I was. She'd said she'd cover for me. She had it all planned out. It was her idea to fix up a play date and then, on the day, she just told her mum I'd gone home ill and that it was off and so her mum thought I was at home and you thought I was at Lizzie's. And it worked, sort of.'

I found it hard to keep the bitterness out of my voice. I might have known Lizzie would be involved. 'Why was Lizzie so eager to help?'

'She's my friend.' She looked exasperated. 'She wanted me to meet him, find out who he was. She's been super nice.'

I imagined the two of them huddling together at break times, plotting and planning. I hadn't forgotten what it was like to be their age. It was great to have a secret. And having Lizzie's attention like that must have felt to Hannah like a dream come true. I could see how it might have run away from her, this crazy plan. She wouldn't want to let Lizzie down by chickening out. But also, she hadn't had the forethought to think ahead to the end of this supposed date and how she'd extricate herself from the lies.

'You could have hurt yourself, you know, on the railway.'

She didn't answer.

I softened my tone. 'It must have been pretty scary down there, all on your own, in the dark.'

She nodded, hiding her face.

'Why did you choose there?'

She hesitated. 'I didn't want anyone to see me. I felt so stupid.' She lifted wide eyes to me, and her lip trembled. 'What am I going to do? What am I going to tell Lizzie on Monday? She'll tell Susie what happened – that he didn't even come and left me sitting there. They'll laugh at me.'

I hesitated. What her friends might think was pretty low on my list of things to worry about. This was serious. Whoever this man was, given the message I had just seen, it didn't look as if he'd given up.

I said, 'We'll think of something. Don't worry.'

She looked panicked. 'But what if we can't? What if they tell everyone?'

I pulled her close and hugged her again. Her ribcage, pressed against mine, felt so fragile. Her heart was beating fast. My eyes fell on the computer on the floor at our feet. I needed more information about this stranger.

I took a deep breath, trying not to frighten her, and said evenly, 'So, what's he said to you today? Did he have a reason for not turning up?'

'Kind of.' She bit down on her lower lip. 'He said he's really sorry.'

'Right. But he didn't explain what happened?'

'No.' She struggled to admit it. Clearly, there was part of her still clinging to the idea of all this attention, still excited about having a boyfriend. 'But he did say sorry, and he wants to try again.'

'What?'

She frowned. 'Stop it, Mummy! You scare me when you get mad.'

I was about to say: *I'm not half as scary as your Daddy's going to be when he hears about someone preying on his little girl*. Then I remembered: Will and Sara, and the way he hadn't even tried to deny it.

Thinking about it, the bottom fell out of my world all over again. I wiped my eyes. 'Did Sara know about this?'

She looked evasive. 'About what?'

'About any of it. The messages, the fact he wants to meet up with you.'

She considered. 'The messages, maybe. A bit. I told her it was someone I knew, though. So, she wasn't worried.'

'Did she know you were going to go out and meet him?'

She shook her head vigorously. 'No one knew that. Just me and Lizzie.'

I considered. The game was downloaded on to Sara's laptop, as well as mine. If she'd helped Hannah choose a user-name and set up an account, surely she'd have the security details to log in to read Hannah's messages?

I wasn't sure I could bear it, but I might have to ask for her help.

I made Hannah and Gran sandwiches for lunch. I couldn't eat. My thoughts swayed from one crisis to the other. *Will and Sara. Someone trying to groom our beautiful daughter*. It all seemed so impossible, so unreal. I couldn't burden Gran with it all. I just couldn't.

Afterwards, Gran settled back in her chair to doze, and I bundled Hannah off to art.

Usually, she dashed into the studio with such enthusiasm, eager to grab an apron and set up her table. Today, she hung by my side, looking forlorn. When she finally headed in, her shoulders drooped.

57

'Feeling better?' His voice was cheerful. 'We missed you on Monday.'

Hugo was waiting for me in the entrance hall again. My stomach twisted at the sight of him: the broad muscular shoulders and floppy fringe. I thought of last weekend and the way we'd headed off for coffee.

Things had seemed so different then, so innocent. It was just a flirtation, not a serious threat to my marriage, that's what I'd told myself at the time. I frowned to myself. How naïve I'd been. I'd had no idea what Will was doing behind my back.

Hugo pushed himself to his feet and fell into step at my side as I reached the exit. 'All ready for Tuesday?'

I shrugged. 'Just about.' The job interview was the last thing on my mind at that moment. I was more worried about Hannah and my car crash of a marriage.

He hurried a few steps ahead, then turned to face me and block my way, forcing me to a stop. 'Are you okay?' His eyes were creased with concern. 'I don't want to intrude but if you—'

'I'm fine.' I turned to face him. 'Look, thank you for talking to everyone and for the notes and everything. They've been a real help. But, well, I'm sorry, but I just don't think this is a good idea.'

He blinked.

'I'm sorry.' I had the sense I'd caught him off guard. 'It's nothing personal. I've just got a lot going on right now.'

When I peered back over my shoulder a few steps on, he was still standing, looking after me, an odd expression on his face.

I wasn't sure where to go. Not home. I didn't want to be anywhere near Will. I carried on down the road and found myself heading for the park by the river. I buttoned up my coat against the breeze and started to walk in a brisk circuit on the path, trying to calm myself and think.

The first hint of autumn was in the air. The dense, heady smell of leaf mulch rose from the undergrowth and, where the breeze picked up, early fallen leaves spiralled across the mud.

The swings in the children's playground creaked back and forth, the shrieks of young children flying into the air as I passed. Hannah still loved the swings, the climbing frame and, most of all, the spinning dish that made me dizzy just pushing it. She was growing up fast, but she was still a child. How could someone target her the way they had? It was obscene. I pursed my lips. She wasn't going to be going online for a while, not unless I was sitting right there next to her. This was all my fault. *I should never have let her try that stupid game in the first place.*

I pushed my hands in my pockets and strode on. And Will? What was I going to do? We'd need to sell the house, that much was clear. I'd really need a job now, not just as a way of keeping busy but to pay my way. I had a bit of money of my own saved up and the house was in both our names, but any other savings belonged to Will.

I shook my head. I needed to see a lawyer and get proper advice. Whatever happened, one thing was certain: Hannah was staying with me. I'd do whatever it took to earn a living. I wasn't losing her too, not without a fight.

I couldn't imagine Will being mean about giving us maintenance money but, until a matter of days ago, I couldn't have imagined him being unfaithful to me either. I wiped my eyes with the back of my hand as I walked, trying to stare fixedly forward as an elderly man walking his dog passed me.

I was just groping for a tissue when my phone rang. I pulled it out to check it. If it was Will, I didn't want to speak to him, not yet. But it wasn't a number I recognised.

'Hello?'

'Mrs Bates?' A woman's voice, not one I knew. The clipped tones of a middle-class professional. 'My name's Martha. I'm calling from Drayton's Antiques. Is this a bad time?'

I cleared my throat and sniffed. I didn't need this right now, but I said automatically, 'No, go ahead.'

'I believe you bought two silver-plated goblets from us just recently. From my business partner, Greg?' She paused, then carried on. 'I just wanted to let you know that we've had a third in, just now. Same seller. I'd said there was a lot of interest. I'm pretty sure it's from the same set, as it's got the same decorative markings. But this one's dented, I'm afraid, on—'

'—on the base,' I said. 'A small triangular dent, maybe a centimetre long.'

'Yes.' She sounded surprised. 'That's right. You know it then?'

'Hold it for me, would you?' I turned and headed back towards the gates. 'I'll be with you very soon.'

58

I hurried to the antiques shop as fast as I could, heart thumping. First, I wanted to buy the goblet back, for Gran's sake. She had such a kind, loving heart, I couldn't bear to see her targeted like this, by someone living in her own house.

After that, maybe it was time to go to the police about it. I owed Sara nothing, after all. She wasn't a member of our family. In fact, she was trying to break it apart, by stealing my husband.

I slowed as I reached the heavy door of the antique shop, still thinking. I tried to imagine an interview with the police. I needed to report an online predator targeting my little girl, and an imposter niece who was also a thief. They'd think I was a fantasist. The fact Will and Sara were having an affair complicated things too. They might see me not as a caring granddaughter trying to protect her elderly gran, but as a vengeful wife, out to cause trouble. I'd have to be very sure of my facts.

I pushed open the door and the old-fashioned bell jangled. My mind was working hard. I needed more concrete proof that it was Sara. Otherwise, she might say I was only accusing her out of spite because of Will. She might claim I'd set her up. The police might even believe her.

A young woman, still in her twenties, came bustling through from the back as soon as I strode in. Her hair, tied back in a high ponytail, swung as she moved. She was wearing crisp tan slacks and a high-necked, light blue jumper. Quality clothing.

'Martha?' I approached the counter. 'You called me about the silver goblet?'

'Mrs Bates?' She reached out and gave me a firm handshake, a broad smile. 'Thanks for dropping by. Greg told me you'd been in. It's here.'

She rummaged under the counter and set it on the top. It was Gran's alright. I was sure of it. I knew that chip. I ran a fingertip lightly over it. It had been there as long as I remembered. It had always bothered me, the feeling this one had been wounded and never healed.

'Are you okay?' Martha looked worried, her eyes on my face.

I took a deep breath. 'Fine. Yes, I'd definitely like to take it, please. I think you're right – it's part of the same set.'

She wrapped it up in tissue paper, keeping her eyes averted now as if she sensed the tension in the air.

I said, 'Greg said you were the one who actually bought the goblets, from a walk-in. This one too?'

She nodded. 'That's right. Not long before I called you, actually. It took me a while to track Greg down and get your number, but I called you as soon as I could. He said you were keen on building a set. I did ask if there might be more coming, but I didn't get much of an answer, to be honest. Just a mumble.'

She counted my money and stowed it away in the cash drawer, then set the wrapped cup on the counter between us. 'I'll certainly get in touch if there is another one. If you're still in the market?'

'Could I ask you something?' I hesitated, not sure how to put this. 'Could you describe the person who's been bringing them in? As much detail as possible, if you can. It might be important.'

She was clearly observant. Her description was thorough – rough age, height, build and a pretty detailed run-down of what they were wearing too. Clothing I knew all too well. I brought out my phone and scrolled through the photographs stored in it, then found what I was looking for and tipped my phone to show her the screen.

She nodded at once. 'Yes, that's the one. Definitely.' She looked from the screen then back to me, frowning. 'So, it's someone you know?'

I just nodded grimly, then picked up the goblet and hurried to leave.

59

I took Hannah to a café on the high street after her art class. Usually, this would be a big treat, but we were both subdued. Although I hadn't eaten all day, I struggled to get even a few mouthfuls down.

Hannah seemed to have sunk into herself. She nibbled on a ham and cheese toastie, normally her favourite, without enthusiasm. Her eyes were heavy-lidded. I could hardly bear to look at her. She suddenly seemed so vulnerable. I kept imagining her sitting on her own in that café, trying to look grown up, waiting to meet a complete stranger. All I wanted was to protect her. Instead, she was about to be plunged into another crisis.

She'd be devastated when she found out that Will and I were splitting up.

When she finally set down the remains of her toastie and pushed the plate away, I reached for her hand and squeezed it. 'I love you, sweetheart. You know that, don't you?'

She nodded, but her face was miserable. 'I love you, Mummy.'

She paused, looking around the café. It was busy with shoppers, teenagers and parents with young children. We'd have to leave soon, but I wasn't sure I could face taking her back home. The question was where else we could go. Back to Gran's, maybe?

'Mummy?' Hannah spoke carefully, her forehead tight. 'Why are we having dinner here and not at home?'

'I just thought it'd be a treat,' I lied. 'Cheer us both up.'

She kept her eyes downcast. I wasn't fooling her for a moment.

'Are we hiding from him?'

For a moment, I thought she'd somehow understood, that she knew I was reluctant to go home because Will was there, waiting for us.

I tried to keep my voice steady. 'What do you mean? Hiding from who?'

'Lionboy.'

I let out a breath. 'No, my lovely. You mustn't think that.'

She blinked hard. 'Am I still in big trouble?'

'Of course not!' I reached over and gave her a clumsy hug across the table. 'You're not in trouble. I'm not mad, I told you. I'm just very worried about keeping you safe. And I really, really wish you'd told me what was going on.'

'I have!' She looked stricken.

'I know, I mean, earlier.' I took a deep breath. 'We need to have a big talk about all this, Hannah. I know it felt like a game, but what he did was very wrong. We need to find out who he is and stop him. Make sure he doesn't do this to anyone else.'

She hunched her shoulders, sullen.

'And I'm sorry, but, until it's all sorted out, I don't want you going online again.'

She looked up at once, glaring. 'But, Mum—'

'Promise me. This is serious, Hannah. I may have to—'

We were interrupted by the sound of my phone ringing. I fished it out of my bag. Will's name flashed up on the screen. I hesitated, trying to decide whether to answer.

Hannah, peering forward, said, 'Daddy!' She looked from the screen to me, puzzled, clearly wondering why I wasn't already taking the call. 'It's Daddy,' she said again.

I pressed the green button and opened with a pre-emptive: 'I'm with Hannah.'

'Where are you?' He didn't sound like himself, his voice pinched with tension.

'Out.' I could feel Hannah's eyes on me. I twisted to stare sideways out of the window at the people scurrying past, heads down, arms laden with shopping bags.

I didn't want to talk to him. I didn't want to talk to him ever again.

I forced myself to say, 'Not a good time, actually.' I was tempted to end the call there and then, but I didn't want to upset Hannah. She was distressed enough as it was.

'Just listen, will you? Please. It's really important.' His voice was breathy.

I glanced across at Hannah. She was watching me closely, her face anxious. 'Okay. Make it quick.'

'You're right. I should have come clean before now. I'm sorry.'

I wasn't in the mood for this. 'If that's all—'

'Listen!' He sounded distraught. 'Please, Paula.' His voice broke, then he paused and seemed to recover himself. 'I've invited the family round for a drink. Your gran and Alan.' He hesitated as if he weren't sure about saying her name. 'Sara and I have got something to say.'

My cheeks flamed. 'If you think—'

'You don't have to do anything. I'm doing it. Just turn up, okay? And Hannah should be there too.'

I let my eyes slide briefly back to Hannah's pinched face. 'I'm not sure that's—'

'Both of you. Please. Let's just get this over with.' He hesitated. 'I'm not sure I can do it more than once.'

Get this over with? My shoulders sagged. I felt suddenly defeated and very exhausted. The life I thought so stable was suddenly spinning out of control.

'Okay.'

'Okay, then.' He sounded resolute. 'See you at six.'

I ended the call and sat for a moment, staring out at the street and the blur of passers-by.

Hannah said, 'Are you okay, Mummy? What is it?'

I blinked hard. 'Daddy was just saying he's got something to tell everyone later.'

'What?'

'I'm not sure. Let's see.' I swallowed, trying to hold back tears. *Let him do his own dirty work.* 'Gran and Uncle Alan are coming round.'

'And Sara?' The eagerness in her face made my stomach turn.

'Yes.' I looked at my watch. It wasn't quite five yet. 'Let's go and have a play in the park first, shall we?' I remembered the creak of the swings and the shrieks of small children. It seemed terribly innocent. *She'll always remember this*, I thought. *From this evening, her life will be divided into two parts, the time before and the time after.*

'Are you crying, Mummy?' Hannah's voice was a worried whisper.

I wiped my face as I got up. 'Of course not, sweetheart. Come on, let's go and have a good swing before we head home.'

60

It was already quarter past six by the time Hannah and I arrived at the house.

I'd deliberately kept Hannah in the park as long as possible. It was selfish of me, perhaps, but I didn't want to risk being alone with Will before the others came. I also didn't want to find myself rushing around the kitchen, as I always did, getting everything ready. Let Will do it for once. Or Sara. This was their party.

By the time we arrived, Alan's car was parked in the street outside our house. I guessed he would have come via Gran's house and given her a lift over too.

I stood on the doorstep for a moment with my keys in my hand, stalling. My insides were leaden. I didn't want to go in. I didn't want to hear what they had to say. I didn't want it to be real. I didn't want everything in my life to change.

I twisted to look at Hannah, tired now, busy scuffing up clouds of dirt at the edge of the path with the toes of her train-ers. I took a deep breath and put the key in the lock.

Alan was sitting in an armchair, halfway through the bottle of beer in his hand. He looked as if he'd showered and shaved since I had seen him that morning, but his eyes were dull. I wondered how many drinks he'd already had.

Hannah ran straight over to Gran who was enthroned on the settee. My heart ached at the sight of her. She was, as always, smartly dressed. Her earrings were inlaid with blue enamel, picking up the colour of her dress and cardigan, and her face was floury with face powder. A glass of iced water sat on the table at her side.

'Hello, lovelies!' She put her arm around Hannah and kissed the top of her head as she cuddled up into her side. 'How was art?'

'Good!' Hannah caught sight of the bowl of crisps on the table and lunged forward to take a handful. I didn't even bother to object. I felt like a visitor in my own house. I sat down beside them on the sofa.

Hannah said, 'Where's Sara? Is she coming?'

Gran smiled. 'She's here. In the kitchen, I think, with Will.'

I wondered how much Gran knew. I was glad she was there. She made me feel safer. I wanted her to hear for herself what Will had done and, as I always had since I was a child, I felt reassured by my faith that she'd know the right thing to say, to do. She'd help me through this.

Will appeared in the doorway. He was taut with nervous tension. His hair was tousled as if he'd been running his hands through it. Or maybe someone else had. 'Paula! Can I get you a drink?'

'No, thanks.' I could barely look at him. My cheeks flamed.

Hannah said cautiously, 'Hi, Daddy.'

Will held out his hand and suddenly Sara was there at his side, holding tightly to him, their fingers interlaced. She too looked nervous. They shared a steady look as if they were bolstering each other's courage, giving each other support. My insides turned to ice.

'Thank you for coming, for being here. I'm sorry. You must

be wondering...' Will looked around nervously at us all. Sara seemed to press closer to his side. 'There's no easy way to say this.' Will's voice had become wooden, as if he'd been rehearsing the words inside his head for so long, they'd lost all meaning. 'So, I'd better just come out with it.'

He paused.

The silence weighed on us all as we waited. I reached a hand to Hannah and laid it on her leg. He wouldn't take her from me, whatever happened. I wouldn't let him. I wasn't like Alan. I'd fight.

'Don't blame Sara, please. This is all my fault, not hers. She's an innocent victim, just as much as you all are.'

Alan said, 'Victim of what?'

Will didn't seem to register that he'd spoken. 'And I'm sorry. So sorry. I know that's easy to say, but, well, I know this is going to be a shock. I've let you all down. I realise that. And what I'm going to tell you will cause a lot of hurt. Hurt to the people I love very much.'

His eyes slid from Alan to me. I looked away.

Sara said softly, 'Just say it. They need to know.'

Will closed his eyes for a moment. His breathing was heavy. 'I suppose I'd better start at the beginning.' His knuckles blanched where he gripped Sara's hand. 'With Sara. Gran, I know she came here saying she was your great-granddaughter. Well, I'm afraid that's not true.'

61

'I *knew* it!'

Something inside me seemed to explode. All the rage, the anguish I'd been struggling to contain burst free. 'I *told* Alan and he wouldn't believe me.' I turned to Gran. 'I did a DNA test, Gran. For Sara and me. It came back negative. We're not a match. We're not related. She's been a fraud this whole time.'

Will looked pained. 'Don't, Paula. Please.'

I pointed a shaking finger at him. I couldn't stop myself. 'We all believed it because we wanted it to be true. Gran most of all – didn't you, Gran? You wanted it to be her. We all did.'

Gran's face was grey. She sat very still.

'Paula,' Will carried on. 'Let me explain.'

I didn't want to hear it. I was in full flow. 'That's not all. She's a thief too.'

Next to me, Gran gave a low tut. I sensed she was scolding me, not Sara.

Will slowly shook his head at me in disbelief. 'That's an awful—'

'It's true! Isn't it, Sara?' I turned my eyes to her. Her face was white. 'I saw you taking money out of Gran's bank account.

It was her card you were using, wasn't it? Her account. And you went to a café and handed it over to that thuggish man. What were you buying? Drugs?'

Sara stared at me, transfixed.

Gran said sharply, 'Stop it, Paula. Right now.'

'Gran, I'm trying to look out for you! That's all. I saw her with my own eyes, withdrawing a big stash of notes. Hundreds of pounds, probably. When did you last check—'

'Two hundred and forty pounds, actually.' Two angry red patches appeared on Gran's neatly powdered cheeks. 'Please stop this, Paula. Stop treating me like a fool. I may be old, but I haven't lost my marbles, not yet.'

'But, Gran, she—'

Gran was breathing hard. 'How do you know what she did with it, anyway? Did you follow her? You spied on her? Really, Paula. You may mean well, but it's none of your business.'

I stared at Gran, stung. Her lips were pursed. For a moment, I felt like a little girl again, struggling not to cry. I took a deep breath. 'But she's been stealing from the house, Gran. I told you about the silver goblet. The first one. She's taken three now, passing them on to Alan to sell for her.'

Sara let out a cry. 'That's not fair!'

I said, 'Don't you dare deny it. I've got evidence. I tracked them down and bought them back. And I know you got your so-called "dad" to do your dirty work for you and sell them on. You knew he'd do anything you asked, didn't you?'

Sara turned to Alan and said quietly, 'Well, go on. Tell her, won't you?'

Alan's eyes were on his hands, pressed down hard on the tops of his thighs.

'I don't blame you, Alan.' I tried to reassure him. 'I know you—'

'It was me.' His mumble was barely audible.

'I know you were the one who—'

'It was all me.' Alan finally raised his eyes. They were bloodshot. 'I'm broke. Losing my job and everything. I'm running on empty.'

I gaped. For a moment, I couldn't speak. Finally, I stuttered, 'But you should've told me—'

He gave a short, hard laugh. 'What? Ask my little sister for more pocket money?' He wiped the back of his hand across his face. 'I just wanted some cash in my wallet so I could take my girl, my daughter, out for a pizza and a glass of wine without being frightened I couldn't pay the bill at the end of the meal. Is that so bad? I'm her dad, Paula. I didn't want her to be ashamed of me, that's all.'

There was a long silence.

Alan's face glowed scarlet. 'I'm sorry, Gran. I never meant to...' – he struggled to get the words out – 'well, you always said they'd be ours someday, didn't you? All that stuff. I just thought of it as a sort of cash advance, you know, and as soon as I was on my feet again, back in work, I was going to buy them back.'

I looked at Gran. She had an odd look on her face, one I couldn't quite read. Hurt, perhaps. Or loving disappointment.

I ploughed on, 'She was involved, though, wasn't she?' I turned my attention back to Sara. 'Why didn't you deny it, if it wasn't you? I gave you the chance. I asked you straight out.'

She hesitated, her eyes on Alan. 'I saw they were disappearing, one by one. Then I clocked that, each time, it was after he'd been over. But, I just thought...' She shrugged helplessly. 'Well, how could I tell you that? I couldn't grass on him. He was my dad.'

Will said pointedly to me, 'Seems like you got it wrong, Paula.'

My mouth opened and closed. I still didn't quite believe it.

He went on, 'So you owe Sara an apology, don't you?'

His hand was tight on hers. The two of them were standing so closely together, I could hardly bear it.

'And what about you?' I burst out. 'Strange sort of uncle you are, wining and dining her in a posh restaurant. Lying to me. And you think *I*'m the one who ought to be apologising?'

Will swallowed. 'How did you know about that?'

'I saw you. Both of you. Cosying up in a booth in the restaurant at Greystones. Some medical conference, Will? You should be ashamed.'

He looked physically winded, as if I'd punched him in the stomach. 'I am.'

'And that's it, is it? That's the big announcement? Sorry, darling, this strange young woman has turned up, a fraud, pretending to be someone she's not, and now I'm in love with her?'

Will stood there, wide-eyed, just staring at me.

'Well, go on. Say it. Isn't that what you wanted, to get it over with?'

Sara tilted her face to his and they exchanged a glance.

His voice was strangled. 'It isn't what you think.'

'What is it, then?' I steadied myself, Hannah's small, hard body pressed warm against mine.

'She's my daughter.'

62

The room was still.

For a moment, time seemed suspended. Gran let out a long, soft puff of air.

I said, 'Your *daughter?*'

Will looked utterly desperate. 'I'm sorry. Alan, I'm so sorry. What can I do to make it up to you? It was a long, long time ago. I was an idiot, a hopeless, besotted idiot. Jackie and I just... well, I'd always adored her. It nearly killed me when you two got together. You were so in love. I'd been so sure there was something there, something between her and me. I kept hoping, early on, when you were first dating, that you'd break up and I'd be in with a chance. But you never did.'

'You had sex with her?' I stared at Will in disgust. 'With *Jackie?*'

'Just once. We were kids.'

'With your friend's wife?'

He winced. 'Don't look at me like that, Paula. I can't bear it.'

'When?' Alan's voice was husky. He was staring at Will as if he'd never seen him before.

Will faltered. 'Don't, Alan. You don't want to know.'

Alan said, 'Yes, actually. I do.'

'Yes, go on. Tell us.' I glared. 'Don't spare us now.'

Will shuddered. 'It was a Saturday night. Late. We'd all been out together, a gang of us, and got drunk and, afterwards, I came back to crash at your place. You were out for the count, Alan. She came into me, in the lounge, and said you were snoring or something, said she couldn't sleep. And I don't know, we got talking and she put some music on, and we started to dance and...' He trailed off. 'We both felt wretched afterwards. Both of us. We realised how badly we'd betrayed you, Alan, and we agreed that was it. Never again. We kept to it too. I went back to Uni and buried myself in work and tried to forget about her.'

Sara lifted his hand and touched it to her lips. Her eyes were full of tenderness. I stared at them standing there together, side by side.

Father and daughter.

'Then Jackie wrote to me. I don't even know how she'd got my address. From my mum, maybe. She said she was pregnant, and she thought it might be mine from that night. I didn't know what to think. I mean, she was married to you. I could see there was a chance it was mine, but more likely it was yours, right?'

Alan spoke through gritted teeth, 'So you decided to keep it quiet.'

Will shrugged. 'I wrote back and asked her what she wanted me to do. I was ready to step up to the plate if she really wanted me involved. I was a student back then, I didn't have any money, but I'd have done what I could. Whatever she wanted, you know? But I never heard from her again. That's the truth.'

'So that was it?' Alan said.

Will nodded. 'Some time later, I heard you two had had a baby girl. I assumed Jackie had made a mistake and written to me in a panic, then regretted it. It made more sense that the baby was yours all along. You were married, right, and for me it was just that one time.' He hesitated. 'Maybe she decided it was better that way, better for everyone to think Sara was yours. And that was it. Until Sara turned up, out of nowhere.' He was silent for a moment, thinking. 'And then we had the barbecue.'

I shook my head. 'The barbecue? What difference did that make?'

He flushed. 'That's when I realised. I was standing up, cooking, and she was sitting down, talking to Gran.'

'So?'

'So she's got a double crown. See?' He lifted a hand and tipped Sara's head towards us to show the way her hair erupted from her scalp in two separate clusters. 'Same as my mum. And my gran. It's genetic. I just thought, maybe...'

I pulled a face. 'Is that your proof? A double crown?'

'No. That just got me thinking.' Will looked sheepish. 'I did a DNA test too. Sara didn't even know about it. After the barbecue, when we tidied up, I took the drinking straw she'd used and sent it off with a sample of my own saliva for a paternity test. It came back as a match.'

I paused, thinking. 'That doesn't add up, though.' I turned to Sara. 'You just said you protected Alan when I asked you about the goblets because he was your dad. But you must have known he wasn't.'

Will cut in. 'She didn't, though. I couldn't tell her, I just couldn't. That's why I went off to Greystones that first Friday, just to get away on my own somewhere, to have some head space and a few drinks on my own and work out what to do.'

I thought about all the nights in the last two weeks that Will had stayed up late, sitting alone in his study. It hadn't been work, then. It was anguished time alone in the darkness, while his wife and daughter slept and he tried to face up to what had happened.

'The second time, last Friday, I asked her to come out for

dinner with me. I said I wanted to get to know her properly. I needed some time to talk to her, somewhere private, where no one would see us. Somewhere we could both have a quiet drink and relax. I knew what a shock it would be.'

I turned to Sara. 'Is that true?'

She nodded, her eyes on mine. 'He knew Alan had taken me out for dinner the weekend before. He said it was your idea that the two of us had a meal together and hung out a bit. A sort of welcome-to-the-family from my uncle, no big deal.'

Will said, 'I knew I had to tell her the truth. I nearly bottled out. She kept asking me at dinner all about the past, what I remembered about her mum when she was young. And you, of course.' He turned to Alan, who was staring fixedly at the carpet. 'You were her dad, as far as she was concerned. How could I tell her I'd been your mate, that I'd danced at your wedding – and then, explain what I'd done?'

I looked from Will's face to Sara's. Maybe there was a slight resemblance. The shape of their faces, their chins. Maybe. Maybe not. 'But why lie to *me*?'

Will hung his head. 'I'm sorry. I've been so frightened. I don't want to lose you, Paula. I love you. I didn't know what you'd say.'

I thought back to seeing the two of them together. Will had looked so besotted, Sara so happy. Was it possible that what I'd seen was really an adoring father gazing at his daughter?

I said flatly, 'I don't believe you.'

Will turned back to me. 'You've got to! I told her halfway through the meal. Just blurted it out. It was a shock, I saw that, but she was so forgiving.' He squeezed Sara's hand. 'I'm grateful. And it was such a relief to get it off my chest. I was going crazy, brooding about it.'

I glanced across at Alan. My poor brother. He looked as if someone had stuck a knife into his heart and twisted it.

Something slotted suddenly into place in my mind. 'Is that

the real reason why Jackie left Alan?' I said. 'Is that why she wouldn't let him stay in touch and be a proper father to Sara?'

Will looked ashamed. 'I think so. I guess maybe she knew. It sounds as if she tried her best to carry on as normal for those first few years, but I think she struggled. I've spent the last two weeks trying to imagine it. I guess it must have eaten into her. It wasn't just Alan she was deceiving, after all. Your mum adored Sara, didn't she? Her first grandchild. And Gran too. I think the weight of all that, the burden of keeping it a secret, must have got to her in the end. The fear of what would happen if it got out.'

'All these years.' Alan looked stricken. 'All these years and you never said a word.'

'How could I?' Will hung his head. 'I convinced myself she was your baby. Why wouldn't I? I stayed away a long time, but my parents never stopped trying to persuade me to come home to practise round here.' He swallowed hard. 'They were getting old. They missed me. And when I did come back, finally, I found out Jackie had left you and what a mess it had all been. Would it have helped if I'd told you then what had happened between us, when I wasn't even sure if that had anything to do with it? And, anyway, I met Paula and fell in love with her and that changed everything.'

'Right.' I knew I sounded bitter, but I could hardly bring myself to think about it. I'd been so innocent when we met. I'd trusted him completely. I remembered the way I'd confided in him about Alan. I thought about the fact my parents had loved Will for coming to the rescue and helping Alan, getting him out into the world again when he was so hurt and depressed. We'd thought Will such a hero.

And, all the time, he'd been at the heart of the secret that had blown our family apart.

'You lied to me too, Will,' I said. 'Our whole relationship, our marriage, was built on a lie. Do you really think I'd have married you if I'd known what you'd done? If I'd had any idea of the way you betrayed my brother? The *hurt*, Will. And not just for him – my poor mum and Gran as well. You knew how much they loved that little girl, how they pined for her. And now you're saying it was all your fault?'

Will looked haunted. His eyes filled and he pulled his hand from Sara's to wipe them off with his palms.

Hannah piped up. 'So Sara's not my cousin, then? She's my sister?'

I turned to look at her. She was the only person in the room who didn't seem to understand how devastating this was for the family. She had an interested gleam in her eyes as if this were good news. Perhaps to her it felt as if it was.

I said in a low voice, 'Half-sister.'

Something moved. A blur of motion across the room. Heavy strides. I looked around in time to see Alan barrel into Will, his fist raised, ready to strike.

Sara screamed and jumped back as Alan's knuckles struck Will full in the face, sending him staggering.

Will fell back into the wall, a hand clutching his nose, his other arm limply fending Alan off. Blood spattered in an arc of droplets across the carpet, leaving an indelible, dotted trail.

'Alan! Stop!' I jumped up and ran to him, grabbing his arm to stop him from taking a second swing.

He made no effort to pursue him any further. Trembling from head to toe, he stared down at Will, who now sat slumped against the wall, his legs splayed, his eyes glazed, his hand pressed to his face.

Swiftly, Sara crouched at his side, tipping his head back and mopping at the bleeding with a crumpled tissue.

'No!' Hannah's voice, behind me, was a scream.

'It's alright, Hannah. Calm down.' I took a deep breath. Alan let me steer him slowly backs to his chair. His limbs were stiff as he fell back onto the seat. 'Daddy's okay.'

Hannah shouted, 'No, it's Gran! Look!'

I spun round.

Gran was listing to one side, her mouth drooping. Her breathing was short and fast.

'Gran? Gran!'

Her eyes were vague, as if she were already faraway, out of reach. If she could hear me, there was no sign of it.

Will, staggering to his feet, came lumbering across, the blood-soaked tissue still pressed to his nose. He took one look, then pulled his phone from his pocket and tossed it to me, easing Gran sideways onto the sofa with the other hand. 'Call an ambulance. Now!'

63

The rest of that night was a blur. Dead, lost hours sitting on cheap chairs in sterile corridors, looking up sightlessly at stark, buzzing ceiling lights. Waiting. The soft squeak of nurses' shoes as they passed, brisk and efficient. Bitter coffee in plastic cups. The fumes of hospital disinfectant, undercut with the sour tang of urine.

Alan, pale-faced beside me, made a straight line of his body, legs fully stretched out in front of him, head tilted back beyond the chair to rest against the wall. He seemed to close in on himself as the hours passed, his cheeks sunken, his eyes closed, mouth slack as he breathed. I wondered what he was feeling: about Gran, but also about Jackie and the daughter he'd spent so many years mourning, only to discover she had never been his.

At some grey hour of the night, one o'clock in the morning perhaps, or two, a nurse, older and stouter than the rest, came out for a word. She perched beside me on the edge of one of the wretched chairs and I elbowed Alan awake to listen too. Her eyes were sad and sympathetic. They made me want to clutch her arm and cry. Instead, I sat, still and stiff, and tried to absorb what she said about Gran being stable.

She listened patiently as I blurted out all the questions in my head about whether they were sure it had been a stroke and, if so, how much damage had it caused and would Gran make a full recovery, what could we expect and, please, when could I go in and see her?

She gently shook her head. The doctor would do her rounds first thing after breakfast, she said. We were welcome to stay and talk to her afterwards or, if we wanted to go home and get some rest, they'd be sure to call us.

When she left, I told Alan I'd get us both another coffee from the machine. I headed towards the main doors to the ward. I punched the big green button to release the lock and made my escape.

The air changed, becoming cooler and fresher, as soon as I stepped into the atrium.

The vast hospital was built on half a dozen floors, with banks of lifts at either end, wide and deep enough to accommodate unconscious patients lying on wheeled trolleys.

The open, central area I had just entered was topped by a high dome. Now, it dropped thin slivers of light from the city night sky down onto the concourse below, which was ghostly with closed cafés and flower shops, a newsagent's and a pharmacy, pockets of deserted chairs arranged in groups here and there on industrial carpeting.

Walkways, empty and silent now, stretched across at mid-level and connected this wing to the opposite one. I knew there must be hundreds of people inside the building, patients, nurses and other night workers, yet it seemed hushed.

I started to walk along the corridor, past the entrance to the next ward. My feet sounded too loudly on the shiny flooring. I felt as if I were the only moving, living person out there, trapped in a nightmarish no-man's land.

Just beyond the next ward entrance, a door was set back into the corridor. Children's crayoned pictures were stuck around the alcove. Bright yellow suns in blue skies shone down on ribbons of green grass. Stick mums and dads stood in a line, holding pencil hands with stick children, all beaming with thick red smiles. I took a step closer to see, thinking about Hannah and the drawings that had always adorned our fridge door.

A laminated sign, screwed to the wood, read *Prayer Room*. Underneath, a cardboard sign had been tacked: *All Welcome*. I pushed the door. It swung open.

It was for all faiths and none, that was clear. The room was wood panelled and properly carpeted, an instant relief from the glare of paint and vinyl everywhere else. There was a mild scent of lemons. Air-freshener, perhaps. A long, varnished table stood at one end, in front of half a dozen rows of padded chairs. It bore a cream silk cloth with a vase of fresh flowers. Behind it, a metal arrow pointed the way to Mecca. A shelf at the back of the room offered a row of leaflets about people to contact for support and a selection of printed prayers: 'For the sick' and 'In times of trouble'.

I didn't intend to pray. I was just grateful for the chance to sit quietly for a moment or two, away from the shiny anonymity of the ward, alone and out of sight. I slid into a chair at the back and gazed at the flowers and the abstract, wheeling pattern on the wall behind it.

My eyes filled with tears at once. Without meaning to, I found myself asking for help. For strength. I didn't know who I was asking or what I expected. I felt very much alone. There was no one to listen. But the words poured into my mind just the same.

Please look after her. Please. I know she's old, but we need her. We love her. I love her.

The flowers blurred and I put my face in my hands and sobbed. I wanted to bargain with someone, to plead.

What do you need? I'll do anything. Just a bit more time. A few more years.

I'd tried to imagine in the past what might happen to Gran when she was really old and struggling on her own. It had been hard to envisage. She'd always been so feisty and independent. But she was slowly aging – I'd seen that. I'd always expected she might come and live with us and wondered if we'd drive each other crazy, sharing a kitchen and rattling round the same house together all the time. I never thought it might end like this.

So much had happened to the family in a matter of hours. I was still reeling. Heaven knew what Gran had gone through, hearing that the great-granddaughter she'd welcomed back with such joy wasn't her grandson's child after all. All those years she'd waited in the hope of seeing her again, all those times she'd heaved herself out of her chair to answer an unexpected ring at the door, hurrying in the forlorn hope that she was standing there, the prodigal daughter, home at last.

And now what? Did it break her heart that Sara was Will's daughter after all?

I thought about Will's stricken face as he stumbled to explain, so frightened of sharing the truth. Poor Alan. He must be broken.

I shook my head.

Will wasn't having an affair. I'd been wrong about that. He hadn't deceived me, not in the way I'd believed.

In fact, given the mess he was in, maybe he'd tried his best to be honest. After all, if he hadn't been determined to find out the truth, if he hadn't done the DNA test, if he hadn't decided he had to tell Sara who he was, it was possible no one would have found out. The only other person who'd suspected he was Sara's father was Jackie, and she'd taken the secret to her grave.

My head ached. I hunched forward and wiped my wet face, rubbed my temples. The air was so still in there. It really was a sanctuary. I was lucky to have found it. I took a deep, shuddering breath and tried to sit longer in the quietness.

Something else bubbled up inside me. Shame. I'd been so

full of hurt and rage, I'd hardly given Will a chance to explain. I'd jumped to all sorts of conclusions about Sara and been quick to make some terrible allegations.

I remembered her face when she'd heard me accuse her of stealing from Gran. She'd looked stricken, not indignant or angry. Stricken not for herself, but for Alan. After all, when she'd suspected him of taking the goblets, she'd kept it quiet, trying to protect the man she'd then thought was her father.

I hung my head. What gave me the right to set myself up in judgement? I'd got it all so wrong. Was it fair to blame Will now for something he did when he was a young man, all those years ago?

I blinked hard and tried to remember Jackie. So much time had passed. I knew her more from photographs now than from memory; I sensed as much as really remembered her in her white, fairy-tale dress, floating down the aisle to join Alan. She'd seemed so adult to me, at the time. So certain.

But then I was just a child. Maybe she hadn't been sure. Maybe she'd been afraid, even then, that she was marrying the wrong man but thought it was too late to turn back.

I thought about Hannah and the life that lay ahead of her. Whatever mistakes she made, I'd always stand by her, always love her. I knew that. Whatever she did.

I don't know how long I sat there, crying now and then, then blowing my nose and sitting quietly, trying to think, to make sense of the chaos inside my head, only to start sobbing all over again.

Always I kept coming back to the same plea: *If you can just look after Gran, I'll be kind. I'll be generous. I'll forgive Will and welcome Sara into our home, if that's what he wants. But please, don't take Gran. Not yet. I need her. I love her too much.*

64

Slowly, the black and white clock in the waiting area ticked through the night.

At six thirty, new nurses came in, fresh and starched, ready for the day shift. Their voices sounded down the ward, calling good morning in loud, brisk tones to patients who must still be half-asleep. Trolley wheels rattled as a thick-waisted orderly, wearing a plastic apron, started to take round breakfast. Another nurse rattled pills into paper cups as she worked down a list of morning medication.

Alan stretched, yawned and scratched at his stubbly chin. His clothes were crumpled and his eyes sunken. The idea of starting a new day on so little sleep seemed impossible.

He twisted to look me over. 'You look wrecked.'

I raised my eyebrows. 'You don't look so great yourself.'

He shrugged and headed off in search of somewhere to wash.

The doctor finally came out to see us at about eight, carrying a neat clipboard. She looked younger than me, her dark hair tied back in a ponytail, her white coat starched. Her freshness made me feel all the more decrepit.

She drew up a chair in the otherwise empty waiting area and spoke to us in earnest, low tones, her eyes on our faces. I wondered if she'd been trained to do this: how to have difficult conversations with relatives.

'We believe your mum—'

I interrupted at once, 'Gran. She's our grandma.'

She nodded and started again. 'Sorry, yes, of course. We believe your grandma has suffered a haemorrhagic stroke.' She looked from one blank face to the other. 'That's a bleed in the brain. When a blood vessel suddenly bursts.'

'Is she going to be alright?' It was a stupid question, but it was all I wanted to know.

She blinked hard. 'She's doing very well,' she said carefully. 'We've been doing a series of assessments and there are lots of good signs.' She looked down at the clipboard. 'She's recovered most motor function. Moving her arms and legs. She's coherent, able to verbalise thoughts and respond to simple commands.'

'But?'

She frowned at me.

I said, 'There's a "but" coming, isn't there?'

She put her head on one side. 'Well.' She paused. 'We are seeing some minor facial paralysis and aphasia.'

Alan said, 'What's that?'

'Her language seems affected. That could just relate to the facial paralysis, though. Most of all, she needs to rest. That's the best way of helping the body recover. The next twenty-four hours could be crucial. If she were to have a secondary stroke, for example—'

'Is that likely?' I couldn't keep the alarm out of my voice.

'Not likely, but possible. The more rest she gets, the better. We'll also run some more tests today, including another MRI scan. That should give us a clearer idea of what's going on.'

I swallowed hard, thinking of the gran I knew, pottering

round her kitchen and making me endless cups of tea. 'Will she get back to normal?'

For the first time, the doctor's eyes flickered down and focused firmly on her papers. 'Too early to say. Her age may be a factor. But there's every reason to stay positive.' She got abruptly to her feet and pushed back her chair. 'Hopefully, I can tell you more at the end of the day, when we have the scan results in.'

I said, 'Any idea when she can go home?'

She gave me a tight smile. 'She needs to stay in for a little while so we can keep her under observation and get a clearer picture of the impact of the stroke.'

I jumped up too, trying to stop her from leaving. 'Can I see her?'

The doctor looked at her watch as if she were considering Gran's medical schedule. 'I should think that would be alright. Once the nurses have finished their morning rounds. Check with the staff nurse first. And keep it short, please. She mustn't tire.'

Alan and I agreed to do shifts. He'd head home for a few hours' sleep and come back in the afternoon to relieve me. He nodded and turned to leave.

Something in his shambling walk cut me to the quick.

I jumped up, ran after him and turned him round for a hug. He hesitated, then his thick, muscular arms closed around me. I pushed my face into his sweater and breathed in his stale smell.

He said, 'It's going to be okay. You'll see.'

I couldn't answer him. I was trying too hard not to cry. I wasn't sure if he meant Gran or Sara or Hannah. Everything crowded in, dark and forbidding.

He patted me on the back with his big mechanic's hands, disentangled himself from my arms and rapped the tip of my nose, the way he'd used to tease me when we were children, all that time ago.

After he had gone, I set about trying to pull myself together before I saw Gran, washing as best I could in the basins and buying myself a fresh cup of coffee and a croissant at the café in the atrium. I didn't want to worry her.

By the time the nurse came looking for me and nodded for me to follow her, I was ready.

65

It took me a moment to recognise Gran.

She was lying near the windows, in an alcove of four cubicles separated by curtains on tracks, all apparently occupied. The head of her bed was slightly raised. She lay back, propped up on pillows.

Her face was pale and naked without her usual layer of make-up. Her eyes were closed. Her hair was straggly, the strands reaching in wisps across the pillow. One side of her mouth still twisted down, as if an invisible hook were tugging it. My heart gave a sharp contraction in my chest.

The nurse placed a chair by Gran's bed for me and left us alone.

I sat in silence for a while, gazing at the contours of her face as they blurred. I loved her so much. She'd always been there for me, always solid and sensible and kind. She always seemed to know what I was thinking and feeling, ever since I was a child; when and why I might be sad, or anxious, sometimes before I realised myself. We used to call it her sixth sense or her 'witchy power', but I knew now, looking down at her lined face, slack in sleep, thinking about everything she'd done for me for so many decades, that she was simply wise.

Kinder and wiser than anyone else I knew.

She gave a sudden twitch and I reached out and took her cool hand, lying limp on the sheets, between mine. She opened her eyes and peered at me. It took her a moment to focus.

'Hello, lovely.' Her grin was lop-sided. Her voice was thick and muffled. It was clearly an effort for her lips to form the sounds, but she spoke slowly enough for me to make them out. 'What a to-do!'

I leaned in closer and kissed her cheek. 'How are you feeling?'

'Been better.' She gave a shrug. 'Sorry to be a nuisance.'

I shook my head. 'You're not a nuisance, Gran. Don't say that. You just need to rest and get properly better.'

Gran's eyes narrowed. She paused and seemed to gather strength for the next sentence. 'I want to go home.'

'I know.' I patted her hand. 'I'll keep asking the doctors. They want to keep an eye on you for now, Gran. Make sure everything's okay.'

She rolled her eyes.

I went on, 'You're going to be fine. The doctor sounded very positive.'

Gran closed her eyes for a moment, and I thought she was drifting back to sleep. Then she snapped them open again and steadied herself to speak again. 'You were wrong about Sara. Good girl.'

I felt my cheeks flush. 'I know.' I patted her hand. 'I'm sorry.'

'Didn't I always tell you—'

'—to give people the benefit of the doubt?' I jumped in to save her the effort of finishing. 'Innocent until proven guilty? I know. I never learn, do I?'

I tried to give an apologetic grin and saw an answering

gleam in her eyes. I wanted to put her mind at rest, but I also knew it wasn't over yet. I still wasn't completely satisfied. I'd been wrong about Sara being an imposter – she really had thought she was Alan's daughter, right until that evening at Greystones, when Will had finally found the courage to explain the truth. And I was wrong about her being the one who stole the goblets.

But that wasn't quite everything. There was still the question of the money she took out of Gran's bank account and gave to that dodgy-looking guy in the café. Two-hundred-and-something pounds, Gran had said. I frowned to myself. If Gran had already known about that, why hadn't she told me? And why hadn't she seemed worried?

Gran let out a long sigh. Her breath smelled stale, of chemicals and emptiness.

I sat quietly for a while, tracing the map of raised veins along the back of her hand with the tip of my finger. After a while, I said, 'Alan was here too. He's just gone home to get some sleep. He'll be back later.' I paused. 'Everyone sends their love.'

A thought struck her, and her forehead creased with worry. 'Where's Hannah?'

'With Will. Don't worry. She's fine. Sara's with them too, apparently, round at our place.' I hesitated, trying to think of something positive to say to cheer her up. 'I think Hannah's really pleased. I mean, about the fact she's suddenly got a half-sister.'

Gran clawed at my fingers, trying to clasp them. Her eyes, as always, seemed to read my mind. I leaned in closer as she started to speak. 'Don't you worry yourself about things that happened long ago. Before you even knew him. Forgive him.'

I grimaced. It wasn't quite that simple.

She said, 'He's a good man. A good husband.'

'I know, Gran.' My eyes slipped down to our clasped hands.

'Well?'

I shook my head. 'Let's not talk about this now. You need to rest.'

Her grip on my hand tightened. 'Might not be here tomorrow.'

'Gran! Don't say that!'

She pulled a cheeky face and smiled her new, lopsided smile. My heart ached. It was something Gran always said: *Might not be here tomorrow.*

This was the first time it had ever felt real.

She nodded towards the locker beside her bed and the plastic jug of water there. I got up and poured her a fresh glass, then held her head so she could sip some and gently wiped her lips. She nodded a thank you.

'So,' she said, 'Will. What's so terrible?'

I bit down on my lip and took a breath. 'That he could have done that. Betrayed his best friend. My brother.' I hesitated. 'And he knew, all this time. He knew it was possible, just possible, that Alan's daughter might be his. And he never told me any of it. That just, well... it changes everything. I thought I really knew him. Now I feel I don't, not really.'

Gran said, 'All this time, he told himself it was a mistake, that she was Alan's girl, after all. That's how he lived with it. Everything was fine, wasn't it? Until she turned up.'

I shook my head. 'It was fine because it was built on lies. And anyway, it wasn't fine for Alan, was it? He was broken-hearted.'

'That wasn't only Will's fault, was it? That was Jackie. She didn't have to leave.' Gran nodded to herself. 'We all make mistakes, Paula. Nobody's perfect. Not even you.'

Hugo. I felt myself flush. I'd enjoyed his attention. I'd been flattered, I knew that. No one had made me chat to him, flirt with him, go for coffee with him. I bit my lip. I hadn't crossed the line. Not exactly. But – those muscles, that cheeky grin – I hardly knew the man, but I had been tempted.

Gran, watching me, said quietly, 'It was all a long time ago, Paula. Before he even knew you.'

I swallowed. It still hurt. I wasn't sure I could forgive him, not quite yet. 'He kept a secret from me, a big secret, all these years.'

Gran said slowly, 'Lots of marriages have secrets. Sometimes, they just have to.' She sighed. Her voice dropped to a whisper, and I had to lean in close to catch what she said next. 'I had a secret from your grandad. A big one. Something about me he never knew.' She gave a little shrug as if to say: *Don't ask.*

'Gran!'

She gave a slight shake of her head, then closed her eyes and, at once, her breathing thickened. I wasn't sure if she'd genuinely fallen asleep or was pretending. It felt as if it were her way of closing the subject and dismissing me.

I sat there beside her for a little while longer, but her eyelids didn't flicker and, eventually, I stroked the hair from her forehead, planted a kiss there and tiptoed away.

RUTH

66

It was a rambling old house set at the end of a rough track: a tunnel through two lines of overhanging trees which made me think bitterly of married couples emerging from church.

My father, who'd driven me from home for four hours without a word, parked in the deserted drive. The silence, once he switched off the engine, was oppressive. No traffic, no voices, just distant birdsong and the sudden lowing of cows from across the fields. He lifted my small suitcase out of the back, and I followed him up the steps, full of foreboding.

The woman who answered the door nodded at me and gestured for me to come inside. She wore a plain brown dress with a lace collar and sturdy lace-up shoes. Our feet clattered on the tiled floor. A large crucifix dominated the hall.

My father set down my case and turned to say a brief, dry goodbye, then he was gone. I put my hand on my stomach. It was just the two of us then, baby and me. My insides fluttered in panic.

The woman looked stern. 'It's not a summer camp,' she said. 'You've sinned. You know it and God knows it. This is where you pay the price.'

I didn't answer. I wanted to be home again, with life back to normal. I shook with cold and fear.

The woman led me up an imposing staircase to one of the dormitories. It was a sparse room with six beds that were neatly made with rough blankets, and six small lockers. Dresses hung along a communal rail at the back. She pointed me to a bed.

'This is yours,' she said. 'See you behave yourself and do what you're told. You'll have time here to think about what you've done, about the shame you've brought on your poor parents. Make sure you use it wisely.'

Downstairs, a group of young women, some hard-faced, many with protruding, rounded stomachs, sat around a scrubbed table, smoking and chatting in low voices. They looked up when I joined them. My face must have given me away.

'You'll get through, love,' one of them said cheerfully. 'You'll see.'

Perhaps they didn't mean to be unkind, those meaty-faced women who ran the home, day to day, stout and strong with the arms of washerwomen and the tongues of fishwives. Perhaps they really believed they needed to teach us all a lesson – we foolish, fallen girls – and that suffering would set us back on the path of righteousness.

I did get through. As my stomach swelled, I grew used to washing alongside the others at a row of basins each morning, looking forward to my lukewarm, pre-booked weekly bath. I polished banisters and swept stairs, scrubbed tiles and chopped vegetables, just the same as the others. I didn't want any more trouble: I'd had enough already.

In the afternoons, when we were free, I read or took walks in the countryside, venturing into town once in a while with the others, to the shops. I became hardened to the jeers and sucking noises that followed us through the streets. These were strangers, at least; people we all knew we'd never see again, after we left.

My body contorted and stretched into a strange new shape. My baby stirred and kicked at night, and I stroked my taut skin and crooned to it in a low voice, wary of being heard.

I gave birth at the local hospital. They didn't bother much with us girls from the mother and baby home, I'd been warned about that. The doctors fussed first over the local girls, the decent ones who were married to boys they'd also delivered in this same unit, once upon a time.

I remember cream-coloured ceiling tiles and stirrups and screaming so loudly the young nurse told me to shush or Matron would be after me. She held my hand as the baby came and squealed when I crunched her fingers hard in my fist.

Afterwards, I called to her as she mopped up. 'Where's my baby?' My voice was an animal's wail. 'Can't I hold my baby, please? Just once. For the love of God!'

My breasts were veined and dripping with wasted milk.

'Don't you go shouting out about God!' She looked round, afraid to talk to me, and whispered, 'Shush! Be quiet and lie still, can't you? You'll upset the others.'

Later, when the shift change approached and Matron had left for the day, she crept back, a bundle in her arms. My eyes were so sore with crying, I could hardly see.

'Just a minute, mind. Don't go getting me into trouble.' She placed the blanket in my empty arms. I parted the folds and gazed down at the scrunched-up, red face, eyes tightly closed, skin wrinkled. Wet tufts of dark hair were plastered to her mottled forehead.

'A girl?'

The nurse nodded. 'Nothing wrong with her. Nothing at all.' She spoke as if she'd expected my beautiful, perfect baby to have devil's horns and a forked tail.

I put my face close to hers and breathed in her fresh, milky smell. 'Hello, beautiful,' I whispered. 'I'm Ruth. I'm your mummy.'

I explored every inch of her, learning every birthmark, every freckle, pulling off the white woollen mittens and booties to kiss the soft, flaky skin of her fingers and toes.

As soon as I started to cry, the nurse reached down and plucked the child away from me before I could resist. 'Don't make things worse for yourself. I told you. You're not supposed to see them. You only get upset.'

You're not supposed to see them. She hadn't just meant me, I thought. She'd meant all the unmarried mothers giving birth there without husbands to fuss over them, without family to visit, bringing babies into the world; only to see them snatched away at once to be placed in the eager arms of strangers, ready to adopt.

She hurried away. It was only after she'd gone that I found a tiny, stray bootie caught up in the folds of the sheet. I pressed it to my wet face, trying to find my daughter's smell there, then quickly hid it away to keep.

67

When my father finally drove me home, my mother was waiting in the hall to meet me. She looked smaller than I remembered. Shrunken. So did the house.

She kissed me on the cheek as if I were a visitor and asked me if I'd like a cup of tea, then disappeared into the kitchen.

The house had a woody, musty odour I'd never noticed it before. It had never smelled of anything to me – it was just home.

My father set off up the stairs with my suitcase. I unfastened my coat and hung it on its peg. The face in the hall mirror looked older than I remembered. Gaunt with dull eyes.

'Your father's made inquiries about secretarial college,' my mother called brightly from the kitchen. She came out carrying a tea tray, laid with an embroidered cloth, china cups and saucers and a plate of buttered scones. She crossed the hall, heading for the lounge. 'Bring the teapot, would you, dear?'

I sat with her in a daze, looking around the lounge as if I were seeing it for the first time. The fading wallpaper, the mantel clock, the twee porcelain figurines arranged on either side. At the far end, the family silverware, laboriously polished once a month, arranged along the sideboard: the teapot and sugar bowl with its tiny tongs, the condiments set of three-lidded pots lined up on their own narrow silver tray, and the six silver goblets, always positioned in the same symmetrical pattern. I'd inherit them, one day, I supposed. I'd be the one expected to dust and polish and keep the family name untarnished.

'There's a course starting after Easter,' she said. 'Shorthand typing and bookkeeping. Apparently, their young ladies are in great demand afterwards. Some of them find work in big corporations.'

I thought about my baby's tiny, flailing fingers and the scrunched-up face, red and fresh and beautiful.

My mother pulled a lace-edged handkerchief from her pocket and leaned forward to press it into my hand. 'We've finished with that business, Ruth. You understand? You must put it behind you.'

I wiped my eyes. My daughter wasn't finished, she was just beginning. How could I ever put her behind me and forget?

She watched me closely, her forehead creased. 'Your father and I have discussed it. It's best if none of us speaks of it again.'

And so it was. In the year that followed, I learned to type and to keep accounts and to fashion myself into a lie. On the outside, I was an innocent young girl, carefree, perhaps a little naïve. If I seemed pale and rather thin, we put it down to an illness which had left me delicate but from which I was fast recovering.

By the time I graduated, Douglas was already calling round, eager to court me. He must have been flattered when my parents welcomed him so eagerly. After all, his family wasn't a particularly prominent or wealthy one, and he was only a bank clerk.

When we married, people put my strained smile down to nerves and I got away with it, passing myself off as a virgin bride, trussed up in white, promising to love, honour and obey the new husband who must never find out the truth about how sinful I really was.

PAULA

68

They were all there in the kitchen, sitting together around the table, *my* kitchen table, sheepish looks on their faces: Will, Sara and Hannah.

Will jumped up guiltily. I paused in the doorway, taking stock. I had the sense that, whatever they'd just been discussing, they'd broken off abruptly at the sound of my key in the lock. I raised my eyebrows at Will.

'We were just saying' – he could hardly look me in the eye – 'we were just saying, Hannah and I, that maybe Sara could stay here a night or two. I mean, only if that's okay with you, of course. In the spare room. Just until Gran's home.'

Sara pitched in from behind him. 'No, it's okay. I'll be fine on my own. Really.'

'Of course.' My voice was flat with exhaustion. 'She's welcome. She's your daughter.'

Will rocked awkwardly on his heels. 'Thanks. I mean, I know...' He trailed off, then extended a hand to Hannah. 'You want to come and play a game with Daddy, sweetheart? How about a board game?'

Hannah shook her head, her eyes on me.

Will hesitated. 'Well, I'm here. If there's anything I can do.' He turned and fled the kitchen, getting out of our way.

I filled the kettle, then pulled open the fridge door and stood there for a moment, staring inside. It blessed me with a rush of chilled air on my face and the comfort of all those ordered contents: jars neatly stacked inside the door, above the milk and cartons of juice. Lettuce and tomatoes, onions, carrots and apples all in their places in the salad drawer. Cheeses and meats arranged above on separate shelves. I closed the door again without taking anything out. It helped, somehow, to know it was all still there.

'Hug?' Hannah got up from the kitchen table and put her arms around me. 'How's Gran?'

I let out a sigh. 'She's not very well, sweetheart. They want to keep an eye on her.'

Hannah looked worried. 'When's she going home?'

I reached down and kissed the top of her head. 'Not just yet. Maybe soon. They're doing some tests. They need to keep her in hospital for now.' I tightened my arms round her. 'She's very old, Hannah. You know that, don't you?'

Hannah followed me as I crossed to a chair and, when I sat down, she climbed at once onto my lap and pressed her face into my neck. I closed my arms round her and, big as she now was, rocked her back and forth, slowly and steadily.

As the kettle boiled, Sara got up and went to make me a cup of tea. It was strange to see her moving round my kitchen. It would take me time to get used to the idea of having a step-daughter, one not so much younger than myself. But, right then, all I wanted to do was hold my daughter close, inhale her fresh, soapy smell and feel the solid, reassuring weight of her in my arms.

Sara sat down opposite me. 'Hannah and I have been doing some talking,' she said. 'About last Friday.'

'Right.' I hesitated, wondering what she meant. Did she

mean they'd talked about Greystones, and everything that had happened between Sara and Will?

Sara looked down into the mesh of her fingers. She looked younger suddenly, and more vulnerable. I squeezed Hannah tighter. I'd been so busy nursing my suspicions that I hadn't stopped to imagine what Sara must be feeling. I hadn't made an effort to imagine everything she'd been through: her mother's death; then the hopeful search for her father, followed so swiftly by the shock of discovering he had never been the man she thought. I wondered how she'd felt, seeing how close our family was, realising what she'd missed, growing up apart from us all.

Hannah twisted in my arms and planted a wet kiss on my neck, then climbed down from my lap and settled on the chair beside me.

I turned back to Sara, took a deep breath and softened my voice. 'You had a talk about Friday?'

Sara nodded and raised her eyes cautiously to mine. 'We went onto *Magiclands* and did some detective work together. Didn't we, Hannah?'

I stiffened. 'You did *what?*' I turned on Hannah. 'I told you not to go online! That's naughty, Hannah.'

'It was me.' Sara lifted a placatory hand. 'I'm sorry. It was my idea.'

I switched my anger to Sara at once. *How could she be so stupid?* 'Don't you understand, he's still out there! He's still trying to—'

Sara interrupted me, 'I know. Just listen, though. Please.'

I sat in silence, fuming, while she went on.

'We had a good look back through Hannah's messages and figured out a few things. Like what times LIONBOY101 was online. And who else was online then. And who wasn't.'

I blinked, not really following what she was trying to say. 'What do you mean?'

Sara looked at Hannah as if checking it was okay to carry on. 'Whenever Lionboy popped up and started sending her messages, guess what?'

'What?'

'Lizzie had just logged out.' She raised her eyebrows at me. 'Every single time.'

I shook my head. 'So...?'

Hannah blurted out, 'It was her, Mummy! Lizzie! She was Lionboy all along.'

I stared. 'She pretended to be someone else?'

Sara shrugged. 'She must have set up a second account. That's all. It's not difficult. So when they were all playing and she knew Hannah was online too, she'd log out as herself and log in as Lionboy.'

'But why?'

Hannah said hotly, 'To trick me, of course. To be mean. She and Susie must have made up the whole thing. She pretended to be a boy, someone interested in being my friend. She made out he *liked* me and wanted to meet up, then she pushed me into going. I hate her!'

Her lip trembled and I reached out and threaded my arm around her again, squeezed her tight. 'Are you sure?'

'I called her bluff,' Sara explained. 'We sent her a message online saying we knew exactly what she'd done and that we'd just reported her to the police for fraud and grooming offences, so she'd better make sure her parents had a good lawyer.' Sara exchanged another look with Hannah. 'She rang here in a real state about two minutes later, didn't she? Crying her eyes out and saying how sorry she was. Full confession. She just meant it as a joke, apparently. Ha bloody ha.'

'Lizzie?' My mind was still racing, trying to catch up. Could that really be what happened? So there was no predatory older man, trying to groom my lovely girl? There was no lurking paedophile? All this heartache had been the work of a silly, sly schoolgirl.

Something deep in my stomach pinched, then fell away. I was angry, certainly. But, most of all, washed with relief.

'It's alright, Mummy.' Hannah, watching my face, reached up and stroked my cheek with the tip of her finger. 'Don't cry.'

'I'm just so happy you're safe, sweetheart.' I took her hand and kissed it. 'Very happy.' I thought of Hannah, wandering down by the railway tracks, blinded by tears. 'A joke?' I took a deep breath and looked across at Sara. 'She could have been killed.'

'I know.'

I hesitated. 'Have you really reported her?'

'Of course not.' Sara allowed herself a thin smile. 'But she doesn't know that. Let her stew for a bit.'

Hannah said, 'Don't worry, Mummy. I'm not ever being friends with her, ever again.'

I stroked her hair. 'Good. You're worth more than someone like Lizzie, sweetheart. Much more. There are so many other girls who'll want to be friends with you, I mean, real friends. What about Lorna? Do you think she'd like to come for a play date?'

Hannah grinned. 'Sara's got a plan, Mummy.' She nodded at Sara. 'Tell her!'

Sara looked hesitant, as if she weren't quite sure how I'd react. 'I just thought, now that we know we're sisters, maybe I could walk her to school sometimes and hang out in the play-ground before class starts.' She paused. 'Maybe even pick her up after school now and then.'

'We'd love that, Sara.' I nodded.

I didn't know if I'd get the art school job next week. Maybe, in some ways, it would be better if I didn't. I was already resolved to keep away from the place for a while, at least until

Karen was modelling again and there was little chance of bumping into Hugo. I didn't wish him ill. I just knew now, more than ever, that I wasn't interested. My life was here, with my husband and daughter. Now, with my stepdaughter too.

But I was ready to get some sort of job. And it didn't mean we had to stop trying for another child. It just meant it was time to take life off hold.

I said softly, 'You know, I'm going to be looking for regular childcare if I go back to work. Paid, obviously. Maybe, if you do enrol on a teaching course round here, we could sort something out?'

Sara hesitated, then smiled.

'That would be *so* cool, Mummy!' Hannah's excited face was a picture. 'But wait till you hear the next bit.' She turned from me back to Sara. 'Go on, tell her about the other thing!'

'Well, I just thought maybe we could start a movie night for Hannah, maybe once a month. Invite a few girls round for pizza and popcorn on a Friday evening. I'd do everything. Maybe even make it a sleepover.' She looked at me anxiously, trying to see how I was taking this. 'Only if you think, I mean, I don't want—'

Hannah's face was shining. I saw how much it meant to her that she suddenly had a cool big sister to show off to her friends. 'And *not* Lizzie or Susie,' she said with relish. 'Even if they *beg*.'

I kissed Hannah on the top of the head and smiled. 'That sounds amazing,' I said. 'Thanks, Sara. Sounds like a brilliant plan.'

'Yay! Best Mummy *ever*!' Hannah jumped up and ran across to Sara. 'Told you she'd be cool with it.' She grabbed Sara's hand and half dragged her to her feet and towards the kitchen door. 'Let's go and check out some movies together, yeah? Something really amazing. Can we?'

I sat very still, listening to the sounds of their feet and the trail of Hannah's excited chatter out into the hall, then up the stairs. My shoulders sagged. I felt suddenly terribly tired, as if the burden of all this, of the sudden revelations, the past deceptions, the worry about Gran, was too heavy to bear.

69

After a little while, Will appeared in the doorway. He looked nervous, weighed down by guilt.

'Okay?'

I nodded. 'Okay.'

He pushed his hands into his pockets and leaned against the frame, stretching those long, strong legs. 'She told you about Lizzie?'

'She did.' Before all this, I would have expected to feel furious, to leap into vengeful action at once. Now, I simply didn't have the energy. 'Sara did well.'

'She did.' He paused, frowning slightly as he looked at me, as if he were wary of a trap. 'What's the news then, about Gran?'

'They're not sure. They told me what sort of stroke it was.' I hesitated, trying to remember.

'Haemorrhagic?'

I nodded. 'That's it. They want to run more tests. They seem worried she might have another one.'

'They're just being careful.'

I took a deep breath. 'What if she did? I mean, would it...?' I couldn't finish.

He paused. 'We just have to wait and see.' He pushed himself off the edge of the door and came into the kitchen. 'Did you see her?'

'Briefly.'

'And?'

I hesitated. I thought about Gran's pale face on the pillow. I clenched my jaw to stop it from shaking and closed my eyes.

He strode over and knelt down beside me, wrapped his thick, warm arms around me and pulled me close. He smelled of soap and talc and fresh sweat. Of husband. 'I'm sorry, Paula. Really,' he mumbled into my hair. 'I feel it's all my fault. If I hadn't, I mean, if...' He broke off. 'What can I do?'

I gave him a hug, then disengaged and pulled myself upright. 'Look after the girls, would you? Don't let Hannah stay up too late. There are sausages in the fridge. You could do chips, maybe, or pasta.'

'I'll sort it, don't worry.' He looked beseeching. 'Aren't you going to eat anything?'

I shook my head. I felt too sick.

He took a deep breath. 'I've been thinking. About Alan. I know there isn't anything I can do that would set things right. Nothing's going to be enough. But, well, maybe I could offer to set him up with his own garage business? I've got savings. He could have them.' He paused. 'What do you think? Do you think he'd say yes?'

'I don't know.' I shrugged. 'Maybe.'

Will looked encouraged. 'He'd need someone reliable on board. Someone to handle customers and maybe help with the paperwork. But he's such a brilliant mechanic. He'd make a success of it, I'm sure he would.'

I thought about Geoff, the young salesman who'd intervened at the garage and rescued me from the boss. He'd seemed smart, and he clearly thought well of Alan too. 'I'll talk to him about it.'

'Later. Of course.' Will managed a tight smile. 'Are you going back to the hospital?'

I nodded. 'I need a shower first and maybe a nap, then I'll head over to Gran's. I said I'd take a few things in for her – you know, overnight stuff.' I pushed myself to my feet and passed him, heading for the door.

'Paula?'

I turned. He was still there, on the floor by my chair, down on one knee as if he were about to propose all over again. What a long time ago that seemed.

'About us.' He looked stricken. 'I mean... you know how sorry I am, don't you?'

I couldn't quite answer. I didn't know what to say. I thought about Gran. *We all make mistakes*, she'd said. *And it was a long time ago.*

I said flatly, 'You should have told me.'

He just stared. His eyes were desperately sad, and his skin looked sallow with tiredness. It struck me in a rush how many years had already passed since we met, how little we knew about how many years together still lay ahead.

'Paula.' He hesitated. 'We will be alright, won't we?'

I sighed. 'I think so. Give me time.'

70

Gran's road was solid with parked cars. I had to drive a little further down, past the house, to find a space. My feet dragged with tiredness as I walked back along the pavement.

I'd spent a few hours lying alone on the bed at home, my eyes fixed on the shafts of afternoon light creeping across the ceiling, my body rigid with tension.

I'd been too anxious to sleep. Now all I wanted was to get back to the hospital to see Gran for evening visiting time, to sit close to her and hold her hand in mine. I wanted to look after her, the way she'd always looked after all of us.

The road blurred and I stopped to wipe my eyes. Ahead, the sky over the rooftops was patterned with cloud, tinged with the last remnants of yellowish, clotting light as dusk gathered.

At the bottom of Gran's path, I paused for a moment, looking at the house. Gran had lived there ever since I could remember. Grandad too, once. Now the curtains stood open, despite the oncoming darkness, and the rooms within were lifeless.

I was so mired in sadness that I didn't notice at first what was underfoot. I creaked the gate open and set off down the path and almost stepped on the long-stemmed, loose flowers strewn here and there on the faded tiles. They looked as if they'd been tossed there, ripped in anger from a bouquet and scattered. They had a dejected, full-blown look, as if they were long since past their best, discarded or scavenged: A white rose with browning petals, a sunflower with a broken stalk, a pink carnation. I frowned and bent closer to look.

They weren't thrown randomly, as I'd first thought. They formed some sort of pattern. What was it? I narrowed my eyes and tilted my head, trying to make it out. They were in the shape of a rough heart.

'Is she alright?'

The sudden voice made me jump. I turned quickly. Maria was standing at the gate, a solid dark shape made bulky by too many layers of donated clothes, piled one on top of another and topped off with her grubby, oversized coat.

'How is she? Your gran.' She repeated herself as if she were used to being ignored by people, used to being insistent to get a response. I remembered how hostile I'd been when I found her sitting at Gran's kitchen table, chatting. I'd give anything to see that now.

My shoulders sagged. 'She's in hospital. They say she had a stroke. They're not sure...' I faltered.

Maria gave a knowing nod, her eyes on mine. 'We heard an ambulance came. That's why we're here. To show respect.'

When she said 'we', she gestured back over her shoulder. I looked past her. She was standing alone on the pavement, and, for a moment, I thought she was delusional, referring to imaginary friends standing beside her or ghosts only she could see.

Then, further off, under the trees on the far side of the road, a shadow shifted. And another. And another. I peered hard. Still black statues silently faced the house, ranged here and there beside tree trunks and bushes, just beyond the cones of light falling from the streetlamps. I took a few steps towards the gate where Maria was standing and stared past her into the copse.

As I looked, the outlines of more figures emerged and became faintly visible in the gloom.

Wasn't that Tomas there, near the front? Tall, with those bowed, muscular arms? And a stooped, older man near him, shorter and frailer. Over to the left, a thin female silhouette had her head covered by a yellow headscarf which shone eerily in the half-light. And Sally, broad and Amazonian, was there on the right. A hand rested on her laden supermarket trolley as if it were a chariot. And yet more shadow people, quietly keeping watch.

I whispered, 'They all know Gran?'

Maria raised her eyebrows as if it were a stupid question.

'Tell her hello, would you?' Her breath came in sour puffs. 'And tell her we'll always keep an eye out. Whatever happens. She needn't worry.'

I didn't understand. 'Keep an eye out for what?'

She smiled, showing brown, crooked teeth. 'Just tell her. She'll know.'

RUTH

71

We'll always keep an eye out.

I smiled inside when Paula gave me Maria's message.

Paula didn't understand and I didn't explain. It's the duty of the old to protect the young. That's what we do. We shield them from as many of the hurts and harms of the world that we can, even our own pain in it.

Just now, before she left, Paula sat close by the edge of my bed, her hands so warm and soft around mine, pressing life into my tired old fingers. Her face, still young, still full of future. I couldn't speak. My crooked mouth struggled to obey me and, besides, I needed to save my strength. Instead, we gazed on each other, sharing the silence.

Her jaw was tight as she bent over me to kiss me goodbye. I know that look. She'll cry in the car before she drives away. She doesn't have faith that I'll beat this.

I know I will. I'm made powerful by love. No mother gives up on her child.

I only dared to start searching for her after my Douglas died. I had so little to go on – only the name of that dreadful place where my father drove me to wait out my pregnancy and give birth. I knew I needed someone else's help.

That's why, when Tony turned up on the doorstep, selling those oven gloves and dishcloths and whatnot, I seized my chance. As soon as he told me he'd trained in the police force, I knew it was worth a shot. He was glad of a bit of private detective work.

I couldn't risk him visiting the house a second time to tell me what he'd found: Paula or Alan might have caught him in the kitchen and made a fuss. So, once I realised I wasn't well enough to get out to meet him myself, I asked Sara to do it for me. She took the cash from my bank account to pay him, then handed it over in that café, somewhere I thought no one, not even Paula, would know. In return, he gave her the scraps of information he'd managed to find.

It wasn't Tony's fault there was so little. He did his best. He's registered my name now with the government, on their adoption register. So, I can be sure that if – I prefer to think *when* – she finally does decide to look for me, she can find me there.

She must be in her seventies now. I imagine her as retired and having time to reflect on her life, looking at her own children and grandchildren and wondering whose eyes they've inherited, whose character. Maybe that will spur her on to look for me. I pray so.

Tony traced the mother and baby home where I'd stayed before she was born. It's an old people's home now, apparently. But he'd no sooner found it than the trail turned cold: their documents were destroyed in the 1970s, when a fire gutted their records office. There were no computer backups in those days, just a paper trail which burnt to nothing. *Ashes to ashes.*

I lie here now, listening to the clatters and bangs in the ward, the low groans from the woman in the next bed, poor soul, the calm voices of the nurses, bustling to and fro.

Paula thinks she knows me, but she doesn't, not completely. She asked me once if the tiny, yellowing bootie on the mantelpiece, half-hidden by a picture frame, had been Sara's. I just smiled and changed the subject. She never realised that my pain, when Sara was taken from us, was really a fresh outpouring of grief for the loss of my own baby girl.

That's why I befriended so many strangers – the desperate, the sad and the lost. That's why I invited them into my home and fed them and listened as they told me their stories. I imagined that if my girl fell on hard times and needed kindness, some other woman, not so different from me, might offer tea and biscuits and a sympathetic ear, just as I did.

And it was always possible that one day, one of those strangers, in their travels and troubles, might have heard something of her. I asked them to look out for her, once I got to know them. Maria knew. Tomas knew. And so many others, over the years. They'd listen for news of her, out there on the road, somewhere in this vast, chaotic world. They'd keep an eye out.

I never stopped thinking of her, you see. I never stopped loving her. And I'll never stop searching for her. What mother would?

She was the reason I always prised myself from my chair and hurried to answer the door, however late the knock. Just in case, one day, she might be the one standing there. My own child, grown now into a woman, come to seek me out.

Not a stranger but my angel, home at last.

A LETTER FROM JILL

I want to say a huge thank-you for choosing to read *Long Lost Girl*. If you enjoyed it and want to keep up to date with all my latest releases, just sign up at the following link. Your email address will never be shared and you can unsubscribe at any time.

www.bookouture.com/jill-childs

What did you think of Ruth, the loving grandma in the novel, and the way she was treated when she fell pregnant as a teenager?

It's astonishing to me how radically society has changed in just a few generations. I sense it when my eight-year-old girls ask me about my own childhood and look incredulous when I explain that no, we didn't have smart phones or even mobile phones in 'the olden days', or laptops or computer games or the internet or even DVDs. They shake their heads at me pityingly, clearly convinced I was born in the Stone Age.

But go back another few decades before that, to the years following the Second World War when Ruth was growing up, and it was radically different again. Plenty of children were still listening to a wireless radio, not a television; relied on coal fires because there was no central heating; while many families struggled to afford decent food, clothes and shoes for their children.

Of course, the big differences between then and now aren't

only about modern technology and steadily growing affluence. They're also about shifts in our ideas of personal rights. There've been years of debate about the way society should treat unmarried, pregnant teenagers. It's a controversial topic, even today.

My own young girls are so passionate about their rights that I think they'd struggle to understand that, as late as the 1950s and 1960s, many unmarried teenage mothers were as harshly treated as Ruth is in the novel and denied a say in what happened to them.

I can't imagine the trauma of having a baby taken away at birth, without the young mother's genuine consent. I suspect that for many, as for Ruth, it was a loss which haunted them for the rest of their lives.

It was out of these thoughts about the chasms between different generations and an awareness of real stories similar to Ruth's, that *Long Lost Girl* was born.

I hope you loved *Long Lost Girl*. If you did, I would be very grateful if you could write a review. I'd love to hear what you think, and it makes such a difference in helping new readers discover my books for the first time.

I love hearing from my readers. You can get in touch on my Facebook page or on Twitter. Thank you!

All best wishes to you and yours,

Jill

facebook.com/jill.childs.71

twitter.com/author_jill

ACKNOWLEDGEMENTS

Thank you, as always, to my wonderful editor Kathryn Taussig and all the team at Bookouture.

Thank you to my brilliant agent, Judith Murdoch, the best in the business.

Thank you to all my family for your love and support – especially to Alice and Emily for bringing such joy. And to Nick, for everything.

Emily, this one's for you.